BEARIGO
INTERNATIONAL

www.bearigo.com

: "I am… Angelina - Book I"

Authors: Elesangela Bearigo and Daniel Smart

ISBN: 978-1-7385226-2-0 (Ebook)

ISBN: 978-1-7385226-0-6 (Paperback)

ISBN: 978-1-7385226-1-3 (Hardcover)

Disclaimer:

This book, "I am… Angelina - Book 1" is a work of fiction based on real-life events as recalled by the author, Elisangela Bearigo. The narrative is a blend of actual experiences and fictional elements, created for the purpose of storytelling. The names and locations mentioned in this book have been altered to protect the privacy and identities of individuals involved.

While every effort has been made to accurately portray the events, the author acknowledges that memory can be subjective, and some details may be interpreted differently by others who experienced the same events. The author apologizes for any potential misconceptions that may arise and emphasizes that this work is a product of personal recollection, shaped by time and perspective.

Readers are encouraged to approach the content with an understanding that certain aspects have been dramatized or altered for narrative purposes. The intention of "I am… Angelina - Book 1" is to entertain and engage readers with a compelling story, and any resemblance to real persons, living or dead, or actual events is purely coincidental.

First printing edition 2024.
Bearigo International LLP
71-75 Shelton Street
Covent Garden
London
WC2H 9JQ
UNITED KINGDOM
www.bearigo.com

INTRODUCTION

My ancestors are my guiding light, their legacy burning bright within me. I pay homage to every single one, from the African elders whose blood runs through my veins to the distant souls who paved the way for our spiritual liberation. Each breath I take is a tribute to their strength, their resilience, and their unwavering faith in our shared heritage. I am forever grateful for the gift they have bestowed upon us, and I will honour them until my last breath.

My heart is filled with unwavering love and respect for my family, from my cherished children to my devoted parents, loyal dogs, and adoring partner. But above all, I hold a special place in my heart for my beloved grandfather who left this world when I was just thirteen years old. The memory of being the last person to see him alive and discovering his lifeless body still haunts me to this day. I will forever regret not taking the chance to tell him how much he meant to me, and how he was my hero in every way possible. Belarmino Jose Tiago Junior, you are forever ingrained in my soul and I will love you until eternity's end.

My name is Elisangela Bearigo, and I've lived for forty-seven long, hard years. My story is a mixture of reality and carefully crafted fiction to add some excitement. Come along with me on the incredible journey that is my life, as we delve into the first installment of this wild adventure together within the four-book set.

Chapter I

My name is Angelina and as I close my eyes, the vivid memories of my early years immerse me in a whirlwind of emotions. The farm in São Paulo emerges from the depths of my consciousness, a sprawling landscape that cradled our dreams, struggles, and the fierce spirit that defined our family.

My father, Valente Sanches, was born into crushing poverty and forced to work alongside his uncle at the tender age of six. His own father's financial struggles meant he received meagre rations and a mere corner in his uncle and aunt's home as payment for his labour. But as he grew older and honed his skills through hard labour, a fire burned within him for independence and a place to call his own, driving him forward with determined fury.

At twenty-two years old, my father approached his uncle in a decisive conversation.

Valente my father said "I am ready to manage a farm of my own, I am very good at what I do. I wish to start a family or you uncle, start to pay me or I have to leave." His uncle, with grown sons of his own, saw no need for another pair of paid hands and simply replied with an indifferent response "Okay, you can leave."

And so, my father set out on his path towards building a new life for himself and our future family.

Years later, my fathers met my mother and we settled on a sprawling farm as work hands. Our small family consisted of myself, my sister Rebecca, and our wise grandfather. The land was owned by a wealthy Italian immigrant family and their vast property stretched out before us, a sea of green and gold. The fertile earth was nourished by a river that ran through the middle of the land, providing endless possibilities for crop growth. At the heart of the farm stood the grandiose Italian-style farmhouse.

But we live all together, despite our close living quarters, we called a small, humble house on the land our home. A faded blue hue covered the exterior walls, with wooden windows and doors that showed their age through visible gaps and cracks. When the heavy rains came, the roof leaked so fiercely that we had to scurry to plug up buckets and containers to catch the drips. And during sand storms, a common occurrence in Brazil, the fine grains would creep into every nook and cranny of our home, creating a gritty layer over everything.

The house consisted of four rooms, the kitchen, living room, and two sleeping rooms. The bathroom was outside for a shower with a bowl and a cup. The toilet was also outside in a wooden hut with one hole in the ground to shit.

The house had no electricity and no light at night, no television, no fridge. Everyone went to bed at 6.30 pm when it got dark. Dinner was usually by candlelight.

My earliest memory, a traumatic one burned into my mind. At the tender age of three, I am being bathed in a tub, adorned with playful fish toys on the handles. But playtime quickly turns into torture as I refuse to wash my hair, knowing the stinging pain of cheap soap in my delicate eyes. My mother's patience runs thin as she insists for the third time, her voice growing more stern and harsh. In a fit of rage, she grabs me and holds my head under the water, forcing me to drink it as punishment for my disobedience. Gasping for air, I feel myself choking on the salty liquid while tears mix with the water streaming down my face. It is a lesson I will never forget, etched deep into my psyche at such a young age.

My mother Laura's story is one of sorrow and tragedy. Her ancestry is traced back to a powerful line of African magicians, with my grandmother being the chosen one - blessed with the gift of magic.

But this gift proved to be both a blessing and a curse.

But when it was time for her grandmother to inherit this power, she couldn't handle it. She refused her abilities and never used the power, cursing like this herself.

But the real tragedy came when my grandmother met an untimely end in a strange accident at the age of nineteen. While reaching for an orange from a tree, she was impaled by a sharp spike that became infected with Tetanus. In just days, she was gone.

My mother and her twin sister were left orphaned at the young age of four, passed around from relative to relative until they eventually ended up in an orphanage. Although my mother never inherited the gift herself, her painful past still haunts her every day, a constant reminder of what could have been if not for the destructive nature of magic in the wrong hands.

My mother's uncle returned from his time in the army and made a legal request to adopt both of the twins. This man was highly respected and honourable, but also feared by many due to his imposing stature and strict demeanour.

He had given up so much for these two children, sacrificing himself as a man. But despite his dedication, he struggled to show his affection or emotional love for them, leaving my mother feeling distant and frustrated.

This frustration has trickled down to her own relationships and even towards me, making her incredibly strict and hard on those around her.

I am sure I used to try her patience, I used to ask her an endless barrage of inane questions. "Why does the sun follow me when I walk?" I would ask, taunting her with my childish curiosity. "Why do I have a shadow?" I'd never tire of asking, even though her response was always the same exasperated sigh. "Why do I have to eat, sleep, and poo?" My relentless inquiry drove her to the brink of insanity. And when I dared to question why the sun never meets the moon, her answer became a scream: "It just is, okay?!"

The first rays of sunlight barely peeped through the darkness as my mother wearily rose from her bed daily, knowing the never-ending tasks that awaited her. She would go outside to tend to the animals - horses, pigs, and dogs - who depended on her for survival. With muscles straining and sweat trickling down her face, she would lower the heavy bucket into the well, retrieving water for both the animals and our family's needs.

Breakfast and lunch preparations followed, and then I tagged along with her and my older sister Rebecca on the long walk to wait for the school bus (school starts at noon in Brazil). The 1.5 km walk under the scorching Brazilian sun was too much for my small legs, so my mother would carry me, her strength dwindling by the day. But there was no rest for her yet - the house needed cleaning, sweeping, and laundry done by hand.

As the days wore on and temperatures rose, more trips to the well were necessary to keep the animals hydrated. Though I was warned against it, I couldn't resist exploring the fields and grass around our home. But lurking dangers like scorpions and snakes kept us on high alert during our long days alone. My mother's exhaustion was palpable, but she continued to work tirelessly for us without complaint or respite.

My mother was often left alone with us, as the men in our family worked tirelessly on other farms and sometimes even in other states to provide for our family. They rotated their duties between planting and maintaining the farm, and their constant travel meant that they ware away from home for days or even weeks at a time. This left my mother as the sole caretaker of the household, responsible for everything from tending to the animals to preparing meals and keeping the house in order. Sometimes, when the men are working in distant areas, she could be left alone for months at a time. Despite this daunting responsibility, my mother handled it all with strength, a true pillar of our family.

I remember this year as night falls, the women of the farm community huddled together in terror, knowing that their husbands and sons are off working in other states. Because there is something else to fear - a deranged wanderer was roaming from farm to farm, his twisted mind consumed with thoughts of rape and murder. When he stumbled upon a vulnerable group of women and children, he unleashed his twisted desires upon them without mercy, leaving behind a trail of broken bodies and shattered innocence. The mere mention of his man strikes fear into the hearts of every woman in the nearby farms.

During this time the women of our farm community banded together, determined to protect their families at all costs. They huddled together in the main farmhouse, clutching 12 gauge shotguns tightly in their trembling hands, ready to defend against any intruders. There were five mothers here with their children, while their husbands were away. My mother's words still echo in my mind: 'Stay quiet, stay hidden, act as if no one is home'. We lived in a constant state of terror for months, never knowing when the enemy would strike again. But finally, after what felt like an eternity, he was caught and our community could breathe a sigh of relief - for now.

As the seasons shifted, so did the atmosphere. The familiar warm breeze turned into a sticky, suffocating humidity that seemed to hang in the air like a thick blanket. And with the change in weather came a devastating pandemic that swept through the children of the area. Though I had been vaccinated, I was not immune to its grasp. The disease that struck me was measles, and it hit me harder than any other child in the area. I clung to life as my body burned with a fever exceeding forty degrees, covered in a rash that relentlessly itched and spread from my feet to my tongue. The rain poured down outside, relentless and unyielding, seeping through holes in the roof and making our muddy floor even more treacherous. My mother fought to keep me cool with wet towels as she prayed for help. But help was six kilometres away, and our only means of transportation was a donkey - impossible to use in this weather. Through it all, my sister Rebecca stayed by my side, offering comfort and words of encouragement. I remember her saying tearfully, "I'm so sorry to see you like this...but I'm here."

But somehow, through natural herbal remedies and sheer luck, I managed to survive. It was an exhausting battle, but eventually, the fever broke and the rash faded. And though I would never forget the pain and fear of those days lying on a makeshift bed, I also couldn't forget the love and support of my family who stood by me until the storm passed.

After my near-death experience, I felt a shift in the air around me. It was as if I was constantly surrounded by an unseen presence, and I no longer felt alone. This newfound sensation became normal to me, and I often found myself engaged in one-sided conversations with this invisible force, much to the confusion of my sister and mother.

My mother would ask, "Who are you talking to?" And when I would explain who it was and what we were discussing, she would become terrified.

She knew I was communicating with someone from our farm, our house, or even a deceased family member. In desperation, my mother started praying for me, calling upon my guardian angel for protection through the burning of a 7-day candle. But to our surprise, the candle would burn and melt within minutes, leaving my mother even more fearful and anxious.

This incident only fuelled the rumours in our community that I was a 'Demonic Child', causing my mother to seek advice from other women who shared her beliefs.

The weight of my newfound reputation hung heavily on my shoulders, fuelling a rebellious fire within me. I refused to blindly follow orders and let the spirit gate open wide, unleashing a torrent of lies and horrifying tales from my twisted imagination. My family was appalled and for these acts, my mother punished me daily with cruel spankings that left welts and bruises on my body.

As a child, I despised her and dreaded each day as it brought another beating with belts and flip-flops. One day, in a fit of rage, my mother commanded me to retrieve the strongest branch from a nearby tree. And when I returned with it, she rained down blows upon me until I sobbed uncontrollably, leaving deep marks on my arms and legs.

But my grandfather intervened, his voice laced with desperation as he begged me to stop crying so that my mother wouldn't kill me. He warned me to never let her see me break, for she thrived on watching me suffer. "You must die standing up," he said firmly, "but do not fall to your knees."

The beatings continued relentlessly, each one more vicious than the last until the belt sliced through my skin, staining it with blood. Through tears and pain, my mother taunted me to cry out in agony. But through gritted teeth, I bravely proclaimed her defiance - "No! Kill me now or I will come back to destroy you!" This was a dark turning point in our relationship as mother and daughter - one that would shape our fate for years to come.

My life was a relentless torment, with the constant presence of voices haunting me even when I was alone. I could feel a spirit lingering around me, its energy heavy and suffocating. The more I heard the voices, the angrier and sadder I became. It was clear to me that I did not belong in this place, in this existence. Every day was a struggle and I longed for it to end.

At just five years old, I made my first attempt at taking my own life. Defying my mother's warnings, I ventured into the river with its powerful waves and strong currents. I swam to an area that was strictly off-limits, driven by a deep unhappiness and desperation. In the midst of being pulled under by the merciless current, a piece of wood larger than myself appeared out of nowhere. It slipped beneath my body and lifted me to the surface, carrying me towards the bank of the river. As I gasped for air and clung to that unexpected savoir, I was struck by a profound sense of isolation and despair.

Returning to the house, tears streaming down my face, I felt like a failure - consumed by guilt and a heavy heart. Mixed emotions swirled inside me - relief at still being alive but also questioning why I hadn't perished in that river. Why was I even here if all I felt was pain?

Chapter II

When I turned six years old, we moved two kilometres to a new bigger farm, where my father was now working. The new house stood proudly on the farm, a symbol of progress and modernity. It was a spacious home with three bedrooms, complete with electricity and an electric shower. The kitchen gleamed with brand-new appliances, and for the first time ever, there was a comfy sofa in the lounge. No longer did I have to use a hole in the ground for a toilet - we now had one inside the house. My father even splurged on a shiny new fridge.

As we moved into our new home, my father surprised us by purchasing a black and white television. The walls of the house were painted a cheerful shade of yellow, making it stand out among the green fields and trees. I couldn't help but feel stunned by this luxurious new house.

But the main farmhouse was even more impressive. It boasted a modern design and even had its own swimming pool. The vast orchard of fruit trees added to its charm, all owned by the same Italian family but this was the older brother's farm. Despite the upgrades, the river still flowed through the land, giving it a sense of continuity and tradition.

The farm itself was now more functional and organised. The livestock were kept closer to the house, making it easier to tend to them. We also started new vegetable gardens and planted more fruit trees, adding to the abundance of nature around us.

And with my grandfather retired from work, he was now able to spend all his time at home. It was wonderful to have him around, and I cherished every moment spent together in our beautiful new house on the farm.

As we settled into our new farm, my relationship with my mother had only gotten worse, and her beatings had become more frequent and severe. I often found myself daydreaming of a life where I could explore my love for animals without fear of being punished.

One of my fondest childhood memories was spending time with my sister Rebecca. We would often wait for the farm owner to leave for the city on the weekends, then sneak off to where the horses were kept. We would steal a horse for the day and ride bareback through the fields. It was in those moments that I felt truly free like nothing could hold me back.

In the quiet countryside, where we lived before, the farm owners, a close-knit Italian family, loved to celebrate. These festivities were not limited to just one occasion - they included good harvests, birthdays, weddings, Christmas parties, and any other reason to come together and rejoice. The celebrations would start in the early hours of the day and continue late into the night with a bonfire casting flickering light and warmth over the revellers. Children from all other farms would gather at these joyous gatherings, their laughter and chatter filling the air.

As the night went on, there would be music and dancing, led by one of the Italian owners who could expertly play the accordion. Everyone would gather around, clapping and singing along to the lively tunes. The smell of freshly cooked Italian food filled the air, and children's faces were painted with joy as they eagerly awaited their turn to dig into the delicious spread.

I remember one particular Christmas party where our family was invited to join in on the festivities. It was my first time experiencing such a grand celebration, and I couldn't contain my excitement. My sister Rebecca and I spent hours getting ready, putting on our best dresses, and braiding flowers into our hair.

The party was a feast for the eyes, with colourful decorations adorning every corner of the farm. Twinkling lights hung from trees, while festive banners were strung up between buildings. Children ran around in their best holiday outfits, their faces glowing with excitement.

The warm and inviting scent of Italian food fills the air, making mouths water and stomachs grumble in anticipation. Lavender and pine scents mingle with the aroma of freshly baked bread and hearty stews.

As we arrived at the party, we were greeted with open arms by the Italian family. They had welcomed us like we were a part of their own family. We joined in on all the activities - playing games and dancing until our feet couldn't take it anymore.

Finally, we ate the delicious food, the taste of homemade pasta, cooked to perfection and covered in rich sauces and herbs, it was unforgettable. Traditional Italian desserts like panettone and cannoli melt in your mouth, leaving a sweet and satisfying aftertaste.

But what I remember most vividly from that night was when an older Italian woman pulled me aside and said something to me in her native tongue. She handed me a small piece of paper with a drawing on it before giving me a warm hug.

Later, I showed my father the drawing - it was a picture of a little girl riding a horse with words written underneath that translated to "Follow your dreams."

Those words have stayed with me ever. From then on, whenever life got tough or my mother's beatings became too much to bear, I would look at that drawing and remind myself to keep following my dreams.

Summer break had finally arrived, and so did my daily chore of collecting eggs from the chicken coop. As usual, I was wearing my favourite Thundercats t-shirt and using it as a makeshift basket. But things took a hilarious turn when I had to urgently use the bathroom.

My mother was busy cooking and cleaning in our "outdoor" kitchen, separated from the backyard by a low wall and gate to keep the dogs out. I begged her to let me pass through the still-wet kitchen floor, but she exclaimed with urgency, "Stop, stop, don't move!" Turns out a sneaky green Cipo snake was climbing up the wall right next to me. And as my mother went to grab something to kill it, I couldn't hold it anymore and ended up peeing myself from fear. Thankfully, my heroic mother defeated the snake with a piece of wood from the flaming oven. Let's just say that was one unforgettable day on the farm.

My mother is a spunky 4'11" with sleek black hair, warm brown eyes, and a cute button nose. She may be on the curvier side for her age of 32, but don't underestimate her - she can chase away snakes like nobody's business and give me a mean whooping if I misbehave.

On a beautiful summer day, my sister and I join a group of girls for an afternoon of play. As always, I have a grand idea, one that seems harmless at first but ends up turning into a comedic tragedy.

In the distance, we spot a large truck making a delivery to a nearby field. It is filled with ground limestone, ready to be used on the soil before planting. The girls gather around as the truck empties its contents, forming a tall white mountain of powder. My imagination kicks in and I declare it to be a desert island. The girls quickly jump into playing 'Paradise Island', with the soft red soil serving as the sea. We spend the entire day pretending to fish and swim in their makeshift paradise.

As the sun starts to set and it's time to go home, everyone is covered head to toe in dirt, a real sight from their adventures in the limestone powder. My sister and I quickly shower and clean up, trying to rid ourselves of the white residue.

But later that evening, there's a knock on the door. It is the mother of two of the girls and she also is the farm owner's wife, her name was Maria. Maria is furious and says to my mother "My daughter came home completely filthy and now her hair is falling out in tufts!". My mother was surprised and replied, "What? That's impossible. My daughter is clean and her hair is completely fine.". Maria gets more animated and her voice raises "Don't lie to me! I saw your daughter with my own eyes and she was covered in that white powder. Now my daughter is losing her hair and it's all your daughter's fault. I know it was her idea!". For once my mother saw the funny side and was slightly amused. She pulled at my hair and it too came away in her hand. My mother said, "Oh, I was wondering why Angelina came home looking like a white ghost". My mother pacified the angry woman, with promises to deal with me.

My mother decides to punish me by cutting my long locks short like a boy's haircut. In that moment, amidst all the chaos and drama, I can't help but laugh at how my innocent idea turned into such a disaster. But in the end, I don't give a shit about my new short hair.

My friendship with the girls who lived in the main farmhouse, all around my age, opened up new experiences for me. One of these was watching a colour television for the very first time. We huddled close together on the couch, giddy with excitement as the screen flickered to life and a program called 'Fantastic' began playing.

This particular episode focused on fashion, showcasing beautiful women walking down catwalks in glamorous outfits. It was a whole new world to me, vastly different from the simple farm life I was used to.

My eyes couldn't tear away from the screen as these stunning models confidently strutted their stuff, some wearing Brazilian-style bikinis that left little to the imagination, some even had bare breasts. I couldn't believe the confidence and poise they exuded, even while wearing high heels and barely-there panties.

Feeling inspired, I suggested we play our own version of 'Catwalk' on the farmland. But first, we had to change into proper model attire. We discarded our shorts and rolled them into a ball, deciding they weren't fashionable enough. In just our t-shirts and panties, we giggled and pulled our underwear up our backsides to mimic g-strings, just like we saw on TV.

Pleased with our transformation, I declared us ready to be real models and off we went, strutting through fields and pastures as if they were high-end runways. To avoid any distractions, I stashed away the shorts somewhere along the way. As evening fell and it was time to head back home, we realised that my brilliant idea had resulted in us losing track of where exactly those shorts were hidden amongst acres of farmland.

In a moment of panic, I remember thinking how all the land looked the same, making it impossible to find our missing clothing. To this day, those shorts have never been found. We returned home in just our underwear.

Within the hour, there was a knock at the door. My mother is getting used to these visits and is prepared for anything. It was Maria, she looked even angrier than on her last visit. My mother greets her with a smile but deep down she knows something is wrong.

Maria started the conversation by saying "Angelina is out of control, a bad influence, and teaching immoral behaviour to my daughters." She explained what had happened to my mother. Maria was equally angry about the shorts and said "Angelina also seems to have a lack of responsibility. She lost not one but two pairs of expensive shorts that belonged to my daughters and didn't even bother to apologise or offer to replace them". She then went on about how my mother should control me. Not trusting my mother to do so, Maria decides the punishment and says "Angelina's behaviour is not acceptable and I will not allow my daughters to be influenced by it. Your daughter is banned from seeing my daughters and coming to the house for at least one month".

Following this ban, I started to get as close to them as possible. If I heard them playing in their fruit garden, I would go to the boundary of our land. I would climb the nearest tree and start to scream and shake the tree like a monkey. I was desperate to get their attention and to play with them again.

My parents had observed this bizarre behaviour and decided that I needed discipline and direction. For this, my father suggested he take me to learn Kung Fu at the public, training facility in the city.

On the first day, I was overcome with shyness as I stepped into the unfamiliar place. Children were scattered about, some practicing painting, others dancing, and a few sewing. This was a government-funded program designed to keep kids off the streets and away from gangs.

My dad had insisted on coming with me, his excitement for this new adventure evident in his eager stride. As we entered the room, he spotted another man around his age and turned to me with a wide grin. "Do you think they'll let me join in on the fighting later?" he asked, his eyes gleaming mischievously.

I couldn't help but laugh, knowing my dad's love for any physical challenge.

We made our way to the Tatami mat- the walls were adorned with an array of weapons - nunchacks, swords, sticks, and ropes. The teacher, a mature man in his forties, stood at the head of the class with his son beside him. Despite being the same age as me, the young boy already boasted a formidable red belt around his waist.

As I looked around at my fellow students, a mix of feelings rushed through me - fear of not fitting in, excitement for what could be learned, and shame for my initial hesitation. But as I watched them begin sparring, their movements swift and fluid like a well-choreographed dance, my heart raced with exhilaration and I knew that this was where I belonged. Even though I was surrounded by boys and there were no girls to be seen, I was determined to prove myself and become a skilled fighter like those before me.

My father was ecstatic that I shared his passion for martial arts; it had always been one of his dreams to be a fighter. He took pride in supporting me, even if it meant buying a kimono, shoes, and sports underwear for my training. I dedicated myself to training six days a week after school. It was a four-hour long session, starting from 7 pm after I got out of school, and my father would pick me up at 11 pm every night. The training centre was located 6km away from my school, but the distance didn't faze me - I was full of energy and ready to push myself to become the best female fighter I could be.

I vividly recall my first proper day taking part in the Kung Fu class, a mix of nervousness and embarrassment coursing through me. I watched the other students with awe, their movements fluid and precise, while I struggled to even imitate them. But by the end of it, I surprised myself by engaging in conversations with my classmates and feeling more at ease in this unfamiliar environment. I couldn't wait to come back the next day.

However, when I reached home, exhaustion hit me like a ton of bricks. Despite my fatigue, I still had to complete the assigned homework. My mother, strict as always, wouldn't allow me to shower or eat until I finished my work. She warned, "Angelina, if you shower now and eat, you'll fall asleep right away. Finish your work first." That night, after pushing myself too hard during class and then completing my homework, I developed a high fever. My body was overwhelmed and fatigued from all the physical activity.

The following day, I could barely move due to my fever. Attending school was out of the question. My mother's stern voice echoed in my head, "If you don't go to school today, you won't be able to continue learning Kung Fu." And indeed, I also had to skip my Kung Fu lesson that day. But despite not yet having a coloured belt or the skills of my male classmates, I remained determined and eager to improve. Deep down, I knew that with dedication and hard work, I could become just as skilled as them.

All Kung Fu has a style but not all Kung Fu is the same. Kung Fu is an art, a lifestyle, and a science. Fighting styles differ because you can take the movements from animals or any other archetype. Once you are a master of a style, you can develop it into a new form, a form that is personal to you like your fingerprint. Bruce Lee, an incredible fighter, his fighting base originated from the same source as I was being trained and this was Shaolin Temple in China. He was the inventor of Wing Chun, he was a master.

My personal style of martial arts was truly unique and unlike anything I had ever seen in my travels around the world - though to be fair, I have not been to China yet. My movements were inspired by various animals, requiring me to embody their spirit and energy as I practiced. My style was based on eight animals, including a praying mantis, each representing a force of the universe.

I honed my skills to emulate a flying stork, gracefully moving and utilising powerful, wide-winged strikes. As a woman, I had two advantages - flexibility and agility - which I used to my advantage in combat. Some of the other animals that influenced my movements were the eagle, leopard, tiger, monkey, crane, snake, and heron. While all of them were important to my style, the snake and praying mantis held a special place in my heart. The tiger and leopard were used primarily for attacking while the birds were more defensive. However, the snake was my first choice because it allowed me to both defend and attack with its low-to-the-ground movements.

The praying mantis style was also one of my favourites, but not as practical in actual Kung Fu fighting. Still, I integrated some of its techniques into my own personal style - I often imagined many times using my finger positions to blind or strike an opponent's throat. Of course, during our training, we were not allowed to cause any serious harm to each other.

Years of brutal training have flown by, sculpting me into a lean and powerful woman at just twelve years old. Standing tall at 1m 68cm, my physique is honed and ready for battle. I am confident to the point of arrogance, looking down on others with disdain. Trained to be a living weapon in the art of Kung Fu, our code forbids us from using our skills outside of controlled matches - we could easily maim or even kill someone.

But my intense rage often gets the best of me, and I find myself picking fights with boys twice my size at school. In an attempt to channel my aggression, I joined the volleyball team and quickly rose through the ranks as my height and strength gave me an advantage. However, as I represent the city at the training facility, there is also a city team of boys who bully me relentlessly, calling me names like 'Bamboo' and even groping girls during practice. My pent-up fury explodes into physical confrontations with these boys, leaving them bruised and bloodied as I fight tooth and nail to defend myself and my teammates.

Their parents were fuming with anger, furious that their boys had been caught fighting. They wasted no time in reporting me to my master at the Tatame dojo, accusing me of being an uncontrollable dangerous fighter. And when the next training session rolled around that evening, my master's disapproving gaze was enough to send shivers down my spine. "This girl wants to fight? Then fight her. All of you," he bellowed to the group, his tone dripping with disdain. My heart sank as I recognised luck was not on my side - only six fighters were present today, and only two of them were truly skilled.

Carlos, one of my training partners, refused to face me. I knew if no one would fight I would have to fight the master and this was not a good idea. Panic set in as I threw a punch at my so-called friend and launched into a frenzied barrage of kicks and jabs against anyone who dared stand in my way. But with each blow, I landed, more pain seared through my body - a split eyebrow, a black eye, bruised hips from powerful kicks. It was no longer just a training session but a brutal battle, and before long the master's voice boomed over the chaos, "Stop!" he commanded us before someone got seriously injured.

With the lesson firmly ingrained in my mind, I focused all my energy on training. My days became filled with long hours of practice, pushing my body to its limits. I sought out new breathing techniques and learned the art of meditation, sharpening my mental fortitude. As my dedication grew, so did my endurance; I took to running laps around the lake in the heart of the city, determined to build up my stamina. In a bold move to eliminate any distractions, I cut off my long locks and opted for a short, sleek hairstyle that allowed me to fully concentrate on combat. Gone were the days of boys tugging at my hair during sparring matches.

After three relentless months of exhaustive training, the highly anticipated state tournament finally arrives. Fighters from all corners of Brazil flock to compete, creating a fierce battlefield where only the strongest will survive. The competition is so intense that it spans six long months, with brutal fights taking place every single day. With my father in the stands, I step into the ring for each match, feeling his intense gaze burning into me. He screamed humiliating taunts like "Rip his eye out!" and "Show no mercy, boy!" - he constantly emphasised that he saw me not as a girl, but as his little boy. As the final round approaches, nerves eat away at my stomach until my father has to rush off and bring back pills for my diarrhoea - a testament to my overwhelming fear and anxiety. Despite coming so close to my goal, the looming possibility of failure consumes me. Standing across from me in the ring is a boy with an eerily familiar physique - one who has defeated me countless times before on the mat. But something is different about him this time...he moves impossibly fast, possessing a skill that should not come naturally to someone like him. With a sinking feeling in my gut, I understood that this may be my toughest opponent yet.

The fight was a brutal battle, lasting seven rounds and 45 minutes in total. The adrenaline coursing through my veins kept me going, numbing any pain that attempted to break through. My opponent's style was fierce, using the strength and agility of animals like tigers and horses. But I used my own arsenal of fighting skills, honed from years of practice and determination. I started with the leopard, its closed fist representing my determination to win against his tiger claws. When the praying mantis didn't work in the early rounds, I switched to the snake, embodying its deadly strikes as I imagined myself as a venomous rattlesnake hunting its prey.

My intense training and running stamina gave me an advantage on the ground, where my opponent struggled to keep up with my swift movements and changing tactics. He called for time-outs in desperation, unable to keep up with the relentless pace of the fight and struggling to counter my techniques. I dominated him over seven rounds and came out victorious on the cards. Blood covered my face from the fierce battle, but tears of joy streamed down my cheeks. As I held up the gold trophy in triumph, I laughed at the ironic situation, because the trophy was a figure of a Kung Fu boy, with his hand in the fighting style of the tiger. As the first female champion in my state, I felt a swell of pride and accomplishment like never before.

Fast forward two years, and I proudly earned my black belt in Kung Fu. Then, just one year later, I achieved the rank of first and then second Dan Black Belt.

Chapter III

My school, a massive high school painted in shades of vibrant green and crisp white, loomed over the bustling city. Its grand campus encompassed a sprawling playground area, boasting 100 drinking taps to combat the unbearable heat that plagued the students. From ages 5 to 18, children from all walks of life gathered here to learn, with an astounding total of over 11,000 students filling its halls.

As a student, I had no idea how our teachers kept track of our performance or attendance. This was a public school that catered to the impoverished children of the city, even those who were deemed "criminals". Survival was a daily test for us all.

On one side of the playground stood a small shop, offering snacks and drinks to those who could afford it. As for me, I couldn't even dream of buying anything as simple as a snack. The school building itself was a maze of corridors and classrooms, where I often found myself lost in the chaos.

There was one place that always felt like home: the heart of the school, where a massive kitchen churned out meals for us each day. The aroma of warm soup and freshly-made sandwiches filled the air, all made with soya bread and meat due to its abundance in the local area and lower cost.

The school day felt like an eternity, spanning six hours of monotonous teaching. Each lesson was a mere 45 minutes long, yet it dragged on and on without an end in sight. And when I did not like the teacher, which was often, I simply would not go to their class. This was especially true with my maths teacher, Mr. Henry. His face resembled that of a bulldog, with sharp features and a stern expression. He towered over us like a stick, his long limbs seemingly endless. But what truly repulsed me were his teeth, crooked and yellowed, as if he had never bothered to get them fixed. Every time he smiled, it sent shivers down my spine.

I wasn't the only one who felt this way about Mr. Henry; it seemed the whole class shared my sentiments for him. And I believe he knew it too, as he was often a very rude and dismissive man. To maintain order in his classroom, he resorted to physical punishment, spanking students' hands or even their bottoms with a wooden stick. It was barbaric and unnecessary.

Attending Mr. Henry's class, I had only one alternative - escaping from school with some friends altogether. We would gather our things and skilfully climb over the towering wall that encircled the campus, relishing in the sense of liberation waiting for us on the other side, away from the rules and restrictions of school. Looking back now, it wasn't my best idea.

But at the end of the year, the consequences of my actions caught up with me. It was noted that I had missed so many classes that I was forced to attend extra lessons and take remedial tests, or worse - repeat the entire school year. All because I couldn't stand being in the same room as Mr. Henry for 45 minutes a day.

At the age of 15, I found myself desperately seeking an escape from the boring routine of school. My solution? Climbing the wall every day. I found myself wandering to other campuses and causing trouble for the unsuspecting students. It was a game for me, seeking out mischief wherever I could find it. In my rebellious pursuits, I encountered a variety of people who were also skipping school. One day, I met Alessandra, a girl and our friendship began immediately.

We would often roam around the nearby lake, talking and laughing as we enjoyed our freedom from the confines of school walls. One day, as we strolled along the water's edge, Alessandra turned to me with a mischievous glint in her eye and said, "Angelina, I have a meeting later today. Do you want to join?" Curiosity piqued, I asked her what kind of meeting it was.

With an excited grin, she explained that it was a gathering of members from a local gang called "Robson's Crew." They were known for their break dancing skills and their regular community clean-up events. However, they were facing a challenge - a dance tournament against rival groups in the area. And they needed more dancers to join their team.

As she spoke about the group's passion for graffiti art and their mission to beautify their neighbourhood through their talents, I couldn't help but be intrigued by this unconventional group.

As I joined the group for the first time, it was a completely new experience for me. I felt a sense of camaraderie with the other kids, even though some were older than me. Robson took an interest in me and liked me, he said "Why don't you join?". I agreed. And so we began our training in dancing, thinking that we were doing something good for society. Little did we know, we were just wasting time and unknowingly preparing ourselves for a future behind bars.

It wasn't until later that it was explained to me our group, was actually called the 'Black Panthers' and we had a fierce rivalry with another gang called 'The Yanks'. When we would come across each other on the streets, some of them even lived near my new home in the city (a far cry from my early farm life), tensions would immediately rise. We engaged in provocation and name-calling, quickly escalating into physical altercations.

In one instance, I even spanked a boy and four girls from the opposing group. Things got out of hand and the neighbours all came onto the streets and eventually, the police were called. Everyone was herded up and taken to the police station. The seriousness of the situation was evident when our parents were summoned to the station. In my case, this was my mother. We listened intently to the head policeman's stern lecture about our behaviour, before I was allowed home.

Writhing with internal humiliation, my mother's eyes flash with unbridled rage as she delivers a swift and punishing spanking. Despite knowing it would end this way, I couldn't help but provoke her time and time again. As the judge and punisher in my life, she was the only one who could tame the beast within me. But whenever I encountered people who ignited my inner fury, it stirred and manifested as reckless physical aggression.

I remember the last time I was arrested, so clearly. A group of wealthy, mixed Japanese and Brazilian boys, including my friend Samuel, roamed the streets like kings. I did not appreciate my friendship was going to be a problem. Little did I know, he had captured the attention of a girl named Liandra, who lived only one block away.

As the sun began to set, the school bell rang and I made my way home. The sky was a magnificent blend of orange, brown, and gold, a dramatic contrast against the city skyline. I settled into my room and opened my textbooks, determined to study until late in the evening. With a crucial test scheduled for the next day, I intended to work diligently until midnight. The streetlights flickered outside my window, casting a soft glow over my desk as I poured over equations and notes. The distant sound of cars honking and people chatting added to the bustling energy of the city night.

At 11 pm, Liandra appeared at my door, she shouted "Angelina, I wanna talk to you". At this time of night, to visit me it must be important. I did not know she was possessed and in a fit of jealousy. Liandra was two years older than me. As I stood before her, she hurled insults at me "Angelina, you are bitch. Samuel is mine. You know this?", stunned I replied "I do not know what you are talking about! Samuel is just a friend." She hurled insults and threats at me, calling me a liar.

My nerves were already frayed from the pressure of school, and this vile creature had come to taunt me. I calmly stated "If you come here again, or you talk to me again about this bullshit. I am going to really teach you a lesson". Liandra looked me coldly in the eye and said "This will be the last time I ask you nicely to leave Samuel alone." Then she turned and walked away into the darkness of the night.

But the next day, as I innocently talked to Samuel outside our school gates like every other day, but sensed Liandra's presence. Her piercing gaze burned into me from afar and I knew she was watching me talking to him. That evening, she appeared at my doorstep like a predator stalking its prey.

"Angelina," she sneered as I emerged to greet her, the disgust evident in her tone. I stood my ground, ready for whatever she had in store for me. I said "Really? You're going to continue with this nonsense? I warned you it would be a mistake." With stubborn determination, I faced her head-on.

But Liandra was much taller than me, towering over me like an intimidating figure. She spewed venomous words at me, waiting for me to retaliate. And without warning, I did. I struck out with all my pent-up anger and punched her square in the nose.

She stumbled back, holding her face in shock and pain. But as her strength returned, she tried to flee. "No" I growled, chasing after her and grabbing her by the hair from behind. I spun her around to face me, my grip tightening as we glared at each other.

In a fit of rage, she yanked on my hair and spat in my face. That was the last straw. Without hesitation, I pushed her back and delivered a powerful Sparta kick to her chest. She collided with my neighbour's wall with a sickening thud, gasping for air in immense pain.

As she crumpled to the ground, whimpering and defeated, I stood over her triumphantly. "You dare come to my house again?" I seethed. "Well, you deserve that." And with one final victorious glare at Liandra's motionless form, I turned and walked back into my house.

Not even thirty minutes had passed when a mob consisting of Liandra's entire family, including her mother, brother, relatives, and neighbours, showed up at my doorstep. They were accompanied by a police officer. My mother was in the middle of cooking when the policeman addressed her. "This woman came to the station with her daughter to file a complaint against your daughter for causing harm. She has a broken nose and chest pain. We need you to come to the station and sign some paperwork, as well as possibly provide an explanation." The officer continued, "Your troublesome daughter has a history of aggression and it is becoming a serious issue. Please, for the love of god, try to explain this behaviour."

The stench of the police station hits us like a wall as we enter, the air thick with the smell of stale alcohol and drugs. The waiting area was a chaotic mix of drunk and high individuals, some were passed out on the dirty floor while others screamed and shouted at each other. I follow the officer to an interview room, my heart pounding in my chest as I sit down next to my mother. Across from us sits a stern-looking man in his 60s, dressed in a beige uniform that seems to radiate authority. The lighting is harsh and yellow, casting deep shadows across his face that are etched with years of hard work.

I try not to show it, but I am terrified. Not of the lieutenant sitting across from me, but of my own mother. Her eyes bore into mine, filled with rage and disappointment. I know she's already planning my punishment when we get home.

The lieutenant spoke softly to my mother, "Listen, this girl has come here for the same problem multiple times." He continued, "In just two more years, your daughter will turn seventeen. If she continues down this path, she will end up in jail and never come back out. With her aggression and reckless behaviour, she will likely become a criminal - a drug dealer, a murderer, or a thief. We need to do something here."

My mother reassured him and promised to talk to me at home. But I know what that really means - I am in for one hell of a beating. For the first time, I truly heared what the policeman was saying. I grasp that if I don't make a change now, my life will spiral even further out of control. Yes, I may have a temper and be impulsive at times, but I am not a criminal.

As my mind raced with thoughts and regrets, a flashback hits me like a punch to the gut. This same policeman was there when I was arrested for graffiti - a reminder of my past mistakes and missed opportunities to change.

But now, as I sat in this cold and unforgiving room, I vow to myself that this will be the last time. I will make a change, no matter how difficult it may seem. Because I refuse to become what the policeman predicted - a criminal, a drug dealer, or a murderer. It's time for me to turn my life around and break free from the chains of my past choices.

I strived to be a model student, diligently attending school and working hard. However, on weekends during the summer, all of that responsibility melts away as the lake becomes the epicentre of fun. On this particular Saturday evening, I strolled along the shore with my two closest friends, Adriana and Meire. The sun's warm rays still lingered in the sky and a gentle breeze enveloped us in its embrace. It was a typical scene in our bustling city - groups of boys flirting with girls while sipping on cold beers or revving their engines behind the wheels of sleek cars. This was just how things were done around here - a customary way of life for young adults looking for some excitement and romance on a summer night.

I was well aware of my appearance and the effect it had on others, so I dressed to impress. My form-fitting t-shirt and short shorts left little to the imagination and garnered plenty of attention from a group of three boys. They were cruising around in a sleek and expensive white Cadet convertible, sipping on drinks and blasting music. As they passed us by one of them called out, "Hey girls, why don't you come over here?". Despite their bold invitation, we remained shy and hesitant, causing them to circle around the lake to keep us in their sights. Eventually, they pulled up next to us and the conversation began. One of the boys introduced himself as

Caesar, his eyes seemed to be fixed on me as he asked where I went to school. He stood tall at 6'2" with a muscular build, piercing green eyes, and long black hair. His skin was fair in colour.

After that day, he made it a habit to wait for me outside of school every afternoon. As Caesar and I spent more time together, my eyes were drawn to him. His muscular arms, chiselled jawline, and intense gaze seemed to ignite a spark within me. Every time I saw him, my desire grew stronger, like a flame that couldn't be extinguished. Finally, one day he asked me to come celebrate his first nephew's birthday with him.

I mustered up the courage to ask my mother for permission, and to my surprise, she granted it. As a young woman with limited means, I had very few clothes of my own. So I turned to my sister, Rebecca, for help. She was working now and had a vast wardrobe filled with more clothes and shoes than I could imagine.

My mother laid out the terms of my attendance "Angelina, you can go but with one condition. You have to be home by no later than 11 pm". Excitement bubbled within me as I imagined what the evening would hold.

As the sun began to set, my sister helped me get ready. With her skilled hands, she applied makeup and picked out the perfect outfit for me - a short peach skirt paired with a light pink blouse. To complete the look, I slipped on a pair of black sandals with 9 cm high heels. Simple, elegant, and innocent - I felt like a million dollars in my ensemble.

My luscious, long black hair cascaded down my back in silky waves, styled with care by my talented sister. My nails were perfectly manicured, painted a vibrant shade of red that matched my bold lipstick. The scent of my sister's perfume lingered on my skin, adding a touch of elegance to my overall appearance. I could barely contain my excitement as I waited for Caesar to arrive in his father's luxurious car to pick me up.

Caesar lived in the heart of the bustling city, surrounded by towering skyscrapers and bright lights. The party we were attending was close to his parents' house but held in a lavish function room. As we drove to his parents' house, I couldn't help but admire the opulence and sophistication of Caesar's life. He may not have been a millionaire like some of his friends, but he had a refined and classy lifestyle.

Upon arriving at his parents' house, I couldn't help but feel intimidated. His father was a highly respected and famous lawyer, known by many in the city. He was also a 33-degree mason, adding an air of mystery and intrigue to his persona. Despite his impressive status, he was incredibly kind and welcoming.

His mother, on the other hand, exuded grace and poise with every movement she made. Her slim figure and porcelain white skin gave her the appearance of an English aristocrat. She carried herself with confidence and authority, always maintaining a poised and commanding posture. Despite her intimidating exterior, she was always polite and gracious with me.

Caesar's introduction of me to his family caught me off guard. "Everyone, please meet Angelina, my girlfriend," he announced with a sly smile. My heart skipped a beat and my face flushed with heat. Goosebumps rose on my skin as his hand grazed mine, igniting a fiery desire within me. But as the words left his mouth, I felt a sense of unease wash over me. We hadn't even shared a kiss, yet here he was claiming me in front of everyone like a possession. My mind screamed for a private conversation about this unexpected bombshell, but I remained frozen in shock and discomfort.

It was time to go to the party, Ceasar said "The party is two blocks from here, I think we should walk" - we walked alone and I thought it would be a great opportunity to talk. The scent of his cologne, a mix of musk and sandalwood, lingered in the air whenever he was near, adding to the intoxicating pull he had on me.

As we walked he began to talk, With every word he spoke, a fire ignited inside of me, a low growl of desire building in my chest and echoing in my ears. It was like a symphony of yearning, and I couldn't help but listen. He said "Do you want to be my girlfriend, you are nice, intelligent and I fancy you"

My voice trembles as I question him, "Do you really think your family will accept someone like me? I have no wealth or status to offer." Without hesitation, he assures me that it won't be an issue. A rush of flattery washes over me and I eagerly reply with a breathless "Yes."

As his lips descend upon mine, my stomach tightens with a mix of excitement and nerves. But our kiss quickly turns into a frenzy of misplaced teeth and awkward collisions, like a wrecking ball demolishing any hope of a romantic moment. And yet, despite the disastrous kiss, adrenaline courses through my veins like a sinful elixir and I can't help but revel in the intense sensations. This is what it feels like to indulge in something forbidden.

My mother had never broached the subject of sex with me, so I felt uncomfortable and out of place. The topic hung heavy in the air, unspoken yet present. My thoughts were tangled like a thorny vine, trying to make sense of something that had always been kept hidden from me. It was like standing on the edge of a vast ocean, unsure of how deep it truly went or what lay beneath the surface. The weight of my ignorance cast a shadow over our conversation, making it difficult to find the right words to express my confusion and curiosity.

The party was a pleasant evening, filled with laughter and warm conversations. I had the opportunity to meet his family, who welcomed me with open arms and made me feel like a part of their own. As the night came to an end, he offered to drive me home, and I felt content and accepted in his presence. The streetlights illuminated our path, casting a soft glow on the familiar streets as we drove by. It was a peaceful and comforting ride, filled with the warmth of new connections and the promise of more to come.

The weeks flew by in a blur of newfound love and comfort as I basked in the warmth of having a boyfriend. But, there were moments when Caesar would suddenly become absent, disappearing for days on end without a word. It was a strange behaviour that left me feeling uneasy, but I tried to convince myself that it was normal in relationships. However, deep down, a nagging doubt lingered in my mind.

For one year, every time we met, he would try to touch me in a sickeningly erotic manner. What was once innocent butterflies in my stomach now twisted into a knot of fear and discomfort. I was not ready for this attention, for his vile hands on my body. But I had no one to confide in, no one who could understand the turmoil I was experiencing - was it fear? Guilt? Disgust? In school, the girls chattered about sex but their words held no meaning for me. And as his groping became more aggressive, like an octopus with its writhing tentacles, I found myself relieved when he would disappear. Yet at the same time, I felt increasingly uneasy and violated by his persistent advances.

Self-doubt crushed me, suffocating any sense of confidence I once had. While the perks of being in the presence of a wealthy and powerful man from a renowned family were undeniable, the way people treated me differently only highlighted my inadequacies. But I refused to let myself be dependent on him any longer - I would rather sever ties completely than continue living in this shadow of insecurity.

This date is etched into my memory with an unshakeable weight - December 2, 1992. It was the night everything changed, the night I lost my innocence and my hope. Looking back now, I know it happened because of my raging hormones and naivety, but at the time I couldn't comprehend how someone older than me, he was twenty-one. A man I trusted, would betray me in such a despicable way.

As the month approached, Caesar's attention towards me became increasingly special. Even though I felt a sense of guilt, I couldn't deny the excitement that coursed through my body whenever he touched me or kissed me. And when I felt his hard penis pressing against me, even through our clothes, I knew deep down that I was ready - ready to explore this new desire for him.

My heart raced with anticipation as December finally arrived - a month known for extravagant events in my city, where high-class people would gather and bask in luxury. Caesar spared no expense for me, buying me expensive clothes and sending me to his aunt's luxurious hair salon where I was pampered with impeccable hair, nails, and makeup. As I dressed in a red dress that hugged my curves and slipped on golden high heels to match all of my gold jewellery, I couldn't help but feel like a different person - confident, alluring, and eager for what the night would bring. That night before I left for a party, my Mum said to me "Angelina, tonight you can enjoy the night and you can stay until the party finishes but I want you home by three in the morning." Little did she know that by then, I would have already lost everything.

As soon as we were alone in the car after the party, Caesar's true intentions were revealed. He showed no mercy as he forced himself upon me. Fear consumed me as I worried about becoming pregnant, but he reassured me with cruel words - "No problem, trust me. I will cum outside of you." Nine months later, on September 1, 1993, my first son was born. I was just sixteen years old, robbed of my youth and forced to face the harsh realities of adulthood far too soon.

I stumbled into my house, shattered and broken. The memories of his rough hands and forceful actions still lingered on my skin, aching with every touch. As I gingerly made my way to the bathroom, each step feeling like shards of glass cutting into my raw and tender flesh, I suddenly felt a searing pain. Blood stained the toilet bowl as I collapsed onto the floor, crying out in agony. The pleasure that my friends promised was nowhere to be found, only replaced by a brutal violation that left me scarred and traumatised.

It took two and a half troubled months for me to register I was pregnant. My body felt like it was being invaded by an alien force, constantly nauseous and peeing blood. While walking with my sister Rebecca, I collapsed on the hot and humid street, I knew something was terribly wrong. Desperately clinging to her kind words "I'll take you to see a doctor, he's my friend and won't charge you anything," I tried to remain calm despite the panic coursing through my veins. But deep down, a voice inside me screamed in warning - a dream just two days ago had shown me, my future son.

"No, no, I don't want to go to the doctor," I protested weakly, trying to deny the inevitable truth. But as the days passed, my condition worsened. Vomiting relentlessly, my stomach felt like it was on fire while my head throbbed with pain. I could barely stand, let alone function. Yet my sister was resolute, and determined to get me medical help.

"Jesus Angelina, we're going to the doctor tomorrow at 6 am," she declared with unwavering determination. And true to her word, she dragged me out of bed at that ungodly hour and led me to her friend's clinic. Doctor Paul - tall and intimidating with his Lebanese heritage - greeted us solemnly. Despite his gentle demeanour, his commanding presence only added to my fear and anxiety.

As he began asking me questions about my symptoms, he already knew the answer before I could speak - "Do you have a boyfriend?". His words made me freeze with fear. "I am accustomed to this situation," he said, "and please do not be afraid as this is a normal routine." My heart raced with fear and confusion as he instructed me to lift up my blouse, demanding to see my breasts. I couldn't believe what was happening. "What?" I asked, my voice trembling with shock. But he only repeated himself, "Please, I have to see in order to know what this is, child." As he examined me, his calm temperament only added to the unease that gnawed at my gut.

Then, without warning or explanation, he delivered the news. "You are pregnant, my dear." My mind reeled as I denied it vehemently. How could this be? How could I not have known? But he persisted with his questioning, taking notes of every detail about my menstrual cycle and body changes. I felt violated.

As tears stung my eyes and threatened to spill over, he showed a rare moment of compassion. "I will not do a full gynaecological review," he assured me, "you are just a child and I know this is traumatic for you." But his words did little to comfort me as he described the physical signs of pregnancy that were evident in my body. He had noticed things that even I hadn't picked up on - the swollen veins in my breasts and their flushed redness that resembled a feverish heat. With every detail he pointed out, I sank deeper into despair.

And then came the final blow - an ultrasound would confirm everything. He dismissed me with promises of a nurse coming to take me there to confirm things, but in reality, he knew all along. And now there was no denying it - I was pregnant, and everything was about to change.

The ultrasound machine hummed as the gel coated my swollen belly. The pressure of the probe made me squirm, and I couldn't hold it in any longer - I peed on the table. My eyes were fixed on the screen, waiting anxiously for confirmation of what I already knew deep down: I was pregnant with a baby boy. When we left the room, Doctor Paul delivered the news to my sister with a heavy heart. "Rebecca my friend, your sister is indeed pregnant," he solemnly announced. My sister's face contorted in disbelief and she cried out, "No! You're lying! My little sister is pure and innocent, she still plays with dolls!".

But her wails turned into sobs as Doctor Paul confirmed the truth: "You will be an aunt to a baby boy." Tears streamed down my cheeks, as Rebecca began to comprehend that her once-innocent little sister was now carrying a child within her - a child conceived in sin and shame. In a fit of shock and agony, my sister collapsed to the ground, requiring immediate medical attention.

The following day, Doctor Paul made an appointment for me to have a thorough blood test and agreed to cover the expenses for my treatment. He also arranged for me to undergo comprehensive tests to check for any diseases.

My sister was very worried about breaking the news to my parents. She had grief for one week before she had digested the situation. She knew she would be the one who would act as a go-between me and my mother. She was afraid of my mother's reaction.

On the day of the big reveal, we were cramped in the tiny living room, with only enough space for a single couch and a TV. My sister said to both of our parents, "I have something very important to tell you about Angelina." My mother immediately blurted out, "What the fuck trouble is she in?" My father, who resembles an Egyptian man with his features, looked puzzled and asked, "What is it?" My sister took a deep breath and said, "It's serious. She was really sick. Didn't you notice? I took her to my friend Paul, who's a doctor, and he confirmed it: she's pregnant!" Then she turned to our parents and said, "So, what do we do now?" My father paused for a moment before saying, "Is this true? Because if it is, my son" (he always called me his son) "will not stand for it. The child can be born, but the boy will be registered as my own and be her brother." My mother chimed in, "Well, at least she won't end up in jail. It could be worse; she hasn't killed anyone. Bringing life into the world is better than taking it away." My sister shook her head and muttered under her breath, "You've both, have lost your minds."

Every week, I had an appointment with Dr. Paul, who generously agreed to cover all my treatment costs. As our interactions continued, I found myself increasingly drawn to him-- not just for his kindness and support, but also for the growing feelings of love and lust I now felt for him. Despite this, I knew that our relationship was purely platonic; after all, he was a married man with a beautiful, caring wife but no children of their own. Yet, as he accompanied me to my gynaecology appointments and had promised to pay for the anaesthetist, I couldn't help but look forward to seeing him every week and feeling cared for by him.

When it came time for my child's birth, Dr. Paul was there in the delivery room, patiently waiting. When my baby boy made his grand entrance into the world, Dr. Paul exclaimed proudly to the room, "I have never seen such a beautiful baby." At that moment, as he held my son in his arms and playfully joked about taking him home with him, I knew deep down that his words held some truth. Though he may have been playing around, there was an undeniable love and connection between us - one that went beyond any physical attraction or simple friendship. But even so, I respected his marriage and understood that our relationship would always be just as it was: doctor-patient and nothing more.

Chapter IV

Throughout my pregnancy, I experienced constant growth inside of me. Despite the daily vomiting episodes, I continued to indulge in excessive eating. My mother, with her limited medical knowledge, self-medicated me. I consumed a plethora of vitamins and indulged in rich foods. My size was undeniable; I was beautiful but as big as an elephant.

I was confined to watching Hollywood television, unable to partake in my usual active lifestyle. On-screen, actresses would gracefully give birth and emerge from the hospital with bodies as slim as supermodels. Naively, I believed that once I gave birth, I too would immediately bounce back to my pre-pregnancy weight, before my one and only sexual experience. However, the harsh reality quickly set in when I still had a belly reminiscent of a six-month pregnant woman. As if that wasn't enough, I also suffered from constant headaches due to the non-stop stream of visitors at the hospital. Despite having undergone a cesarean delivery, which meant I should have been resting and limiting my talking due to the anaesthetic, I couldn't help but engage in conversation with those who came to see me.

One of my friends remarked with a teasing smile, "Look at you now, finally joining us normal women with your post-baby belly. No more ridiculous six-pack abs for you! Because before we could use your stomach to wash our clothes." We all laughed uproariously at her joke, but little did I know it would lead to an explosive outcome. The forceful bursts of laughter caused four stitches on my still-swollen belly to burst open, leaving me in even more discomfort.

As the visitors eventually left and the painkillers began to wear off, the true agony set in. The sharp pains from the cutting and pulling during the cesarean were almost unbearable. I longed for some relief as time seemed to stand still in the lonely hospital room.

Dr. Paul had promised that I would receive the highest level of care from everyone, but even with this knowledge, the wait for medication to ease my pain felt like an eternity. I lay in the hospital bed, trying to feed Niklas, while my insides were being shredded by waves of agony. As the hours ticked by, I could feel my energy and willpower draining away.

Finally, at 10 pm, the nurse made her rounds and it was my turn to be seen. With a kind smile, she administered more painkillers and immediately I felt a wave of relief wash over me. Exhaustion quickly replaced the pain, as I knew I would be here for two days and needed all the rest I could get.

To my surprise, the nurse returned with some liquid food for the baby, giving me a brief respite to close my eyes and drift off into much-needed sleep. The steady rhythm of the machines around me mixed with the soft cooing of Niklas created a peaceful lullaby that helped me slip into a deep slumber.

As I prepared to return home after two days, I felt a mix of emotions swirling inside me. I couldn't escape the fact that my marriage was not based on love and had been forced upon me at a young age. Yes, I forgot to tell you I am married. On my wedding day, I was so nervous and four and a half months pregnant. All the decisions were made by Caesar's mother. The dress wasn't white because I was not considered pure, but rather a champagne colour to hide my supposed impurity.

Five hundred people attended the wedding, split between our two families. In the midst of it all, I couldn't help but think about the nuptial night and honeymoon ahead with dread, because deep down, I knew there would be no sweetness or happiness in those moments. As we were married in both a church and by a notary, everyone from around Brazil came to witness the event, on that Friday evening.

My mother was crying, but as I approached her thinking she was emotional about me, I said "Mum do not cry about me, I will do my best to make this work and be happy" but she replied in a sharp tone "Fuck me, I am not crying about you. I am crying because I have not seen my sister Angela for twenty years and she is here".

My sister Rebecca and father were also crying, but their tears were for me and the loss of my teenage years to this unwanted marriage. The weight of it all hit me, as I understood how much I missed my hero, my grandfather who had passed away three years prior. Knowing him, even he would shed tears if he were still here because he would see through this facade of marriage and understand the pain it caused me.

The wedding seemed to stretch on for an eternity, with a never-ending line of guests to shake hands with and kiss three times on the cheeks. My pregnant body was exhausted, my feet aching in the uncomfortable shoes that were chosen for me. The ring on my finger pressed uncomfortably against my swollen skin, weighed down by the liquid in my pregnant body. The pain radiated from my back to my legs, making each step feel like a feat. And yet, I knew there were still six more hours ahead of me, the evening party beckoning. For now, I just had to power through the fatigue and discomfort, smiling through it all, as I was showered with congratulations and well wishes.

As the evening dragged on, I remained trapped in the same dress that had become a prison of discomfort. The 9cm heels of my shoes felt like sharp daggers, stabbing into my swollen feet with each step. The music was just background noise, drowned out by the overwhelming pain and anxiety consuming me. Every moment spent in this uncomfortable situation only fuelled my obsession with the unknown horrors awaiting me. Memories of discovering my pregnancy flooded my mind, along with the awareness that I hadn't seen or heard from the father of my unborn child until today. His absence only added to the fear gripping me tighter and tighter.

The moment had arrived - it was time to leave. We got into the car and drove forty-five kilometres to the hotel, our honeymoon destination. I couldn't help but feel disappointed as we pulled up to a mediocre-looking building that resembled more of a cheap motel on the side of the road. As we entered the room, I was hit with a wave of exhaustion and relief. I could finally take off my heavy wedding dress and slip into a comfortable silk nightgown. But as I tried to settle in for some much-needed rest, a sense of dread overcame me. Tomorrow would be a new day, but I couldn't shake off the feeling of being trapped in this situation. My throat tightened and a fever consumed me, almost as if the very circumstances were suffocating me.

Caesar aggressively stripped off his clothes and marched into the shower, determined to wash away any remnants of his previous conquest. He returned to the bedroom, his naked body glowing with a sense of power as he stood before me with a rock-hard erect dick (he was always a dick). I told him I wanted to sleep, but his ego wouldn't have it. "No," he growled, "You are my woman, my wife. We are going to have sex tonight. I am going to fuck your pussy."

My protests fell on deaf ears as he forcefully pulled me into his body, his grip tightening around my chest as he stood behind me. With one swift movement, he lifted up my gown and bent me over the bed, this is the moment he raped me. Penetrating me without a second thought. I couldn't fight him, he was also a fighter. He was just as strong and ruthless as I was, and I had our baby to protect.

So I shut off all emotion, numbing myself to the pain and disgust as he ravaged my body. When it was over, he collapsed onto the bed with a smug smile on his face, completely satisfied. While I felt like nothing more than an object to be used for his pleasure. It was only the second time he had forced himself upon me, but it would be the last.

As I cleaned myself in the bathroom, tears streaming down my face, I couldn't help but feel a deep sense of shame and self-loathing. Exhausted from both physical and emotional turmoil, I lay awake in bed knowing that this was now my new reality - a life filled with fear and abuse at the hands of the man who was supposed to love and protect me.

As I left the sterile, white walls of the hospital, my heart sank at the realisation that my husband had not visited me once during my stay. Instead, it was my mother who would be staying with me for two weeks in our marital home. Despite my disappointment, she welcomed me with a warm embrace and began to take care of me and my newborn son, Niklas. Her cooking was filled with an abundance of healthy vitamins, helping me shed the extra weight gained from pregnancy. As I fed Niklas, she bathed him and stayed up through the night to watch over him so I could get some much-needed rest. My husband, however, remained present in the house but offered no assistance whatsoever. He seemed disinterested in our baby and did not interact with him at all. His absence was palpable and only made my mother's presence and devotion even more appreciated.

After two long weeks, my mother finally left us, leaving me to face the harsh reality of my new life. My mother's parting words to me were "You cannot divorce, you have to accept everything". The once cosy house now felt like a prison, with bars on the windows for security, but I was locked in every day when Caesar left for unknown reasons. Caesar forbade anyone from visiting me at the house, so even my concerned aunts had to resort to checking on me through the small speaking hole in the door. Caesar had no job, and I was not allowed to leave the confines of our home. Sleep became a luxury that I couldn't afford as Niklas cried incessantly, both day and night. In addition to caring for the baby, I also had to clean the house, hand wash the diapers, and cook, all while being subjected to Caesar's nightly beatings. Each time, it seemed his anger stemmed from my very existence and his own frustrations in life. My world had become a never-ending cycle of pain and despair within the confines of my home.

This cycle continued for eleven months, and Niklas was nearly one. His family would buy food from the supermarket for me and then give this to Caesar, as they knew Caesar did not work or provide enough food for the family. That evening Caesar returned to the house after being absent all day. He was on the rampage and more brutal than ever. He said "Who came here today" and I replied, "No, one". He was insecure and believed I had another man. Why else, would I not want to have sex with him? He beat me hard, so hard that night. He punched me in the face, chest, hips. As I fell he pulled my hair and kicked me in the back and legs. I was demobilised and my eyes were purple from the hits.

Caesar's eyes blazed with fury as he glared at the boy, his face twisted in a mad rage. He knew I had no affection for him and it drove him into a violent frenzy. Without warning, he lunged for the one thing that meant everything to me - our innocent son Niklas, resting on the bed. I moved forward to stop him but I was violently shoved to the ground by Caesar's brute strength. In an instant, his inner pain consumes him and he flung Niklas against the wall with a sickening thud. My heart shattered as I watched my child lying silent and still where he fell. A primal scream escaped my lips, echoing through the house as I ran to the kitchen and grabbed my grandfather's prize possession I had hidden there - a massive 60cm blade known as 'the butcher'. I had spent weeks sharpening it, fuelled by thoughts of revenge, and now it would finally serve its purpose.

The sound of pounding footsteps and enraged voices filled the air. My cacophony of chaotic screams and panic had been heard throughout the street. The neighbours had gathered outside the door, their eyes full of suspicion and fear as they demanded to be let in. Caesar's heart raced as he realised the mob was growing larger by the minute, fuelled by rumours and hearsay. He knew he had to act fast before things spiralled out of control.

I rushed towards the door from the kitchen, my heart pounding in my chest. But before I could even reach it, I saw that it was already flung open. The room was flooded with people now, their faces contorted with anger and concern. "Are you okay?" they asked, but all I could do was stare at them with wide eyes, my mind struggling to process what was happening.

Caesar's words were a jumbled mess of excuses and lies, but I knew the truth. And when I finally found my voice, it shattered into sobs as I fell to the ground. After eleven long months of being held captive by this man, I couldn't take it any longer. "You have to help me," I cried out, barely able to form the words through my tears. "He killed my son! Please, we need to get him to a hospital!"

As if on cue, the police arrived, along with more concerned neighbours. The house was now filled with even more people - women holding onto their children tightly, afraid of what horrors may lurk behind closed doors. But amidst the chaos and confusion, no one noticed that I hadn't even touched my baby boy. They didn't know that he was still breathing, fighting for his life. It wasn't until someone finally took him away to the hospital that they understood the gravity of the situation.

And as I sat there on the floor, shaking with grief and fear, all I could think about was how much time had been wasted, and how many warnings had been ignored. But at that moment, all I wanted was for my son to be safe and alive.

My mind was in a state of delirious shock as I found myself being whisked away to the hospital. I cannot even remember who had taken me there or how I had ended up in this chaotic situation. Tears streamed down my face, my body trembling uncontrollably with fear and desperation. In the midst of it all, I could only scream for my son, wondering where he was and if he was safe.

The hospital was a frenzy of activity, with people rushing around and numerous questions being thrown my way. The entire community seemed to have gathered there, trying to make sense of what had happened. Someone administered me a calming medication, but it did little to soothe the panic and worry that consumed me.

Amidst the chaos, my Aunt Lucy appeared by my side, a comforting presence in the storm. "Niklas is alive, my child," she said, her voice filled with relief. "He's being looked after, but his hips are broken." Her words brought both relief and fear - at least my son was alive, but the thought of him being injured made my heart ache.

Aunt Lucy went on to explain that I would need to go to the police station to file a report about what had happened. In the meantime, she promised to stay with Niklas at the hospital. My family had all been notified and were making their way there - aunts, uncles, cousins - they were all arriving now.

Feeling dazed and confused, I agreed to go to the police station with my parents who had arrived after travelling three hours from their house in another state to save me from this ordeal. As I walked into the station, I couldn't help but feel overwhelmed by the love and support of my family.

My fingers trembled as I signed my name on the final page of the police report. My body ached with exhaustion, but there was no time to rest. My parents refused to let me return to my own home, so we dropped off the keys with my aunt, and my son and I moved to their place like refugees. Finally, we would be safe.

A week later, I returned with a sense of dread, knowing I would have to face the remnants of my shattered life and I now had to begin the painful process of divorce. At just 16 years old, I was still a child in many ways but forced into adulthood by the horrific trauma of rape, motherhood, marriage, and now divorce. Each step forward felt like walking through quicksand, but I had to keep moving to survive.

Chapter V

With a mix of dread and determination, I set out on the long journey to my parents' new farm. Memories of my brief marriage flooded my mind, but I pushed them away as I focused on the task at hand. We had arranged to meet a lawyer to discuss my divorce, and as my father and I sat in his office, my mother waited in the car with Niklas.

The lawyer, with an unsettling resemblance to politician Eneas Carneiro, began calculating the exorbitant cost of representing me, my father's face paled with shock. "That's far too expensive!" he exclaimed. Panic crept into his voice as he asked, "What am I supposed to do? How can we afford this?"

But then, with a slick smile reminiscent of the corrupt politician, the lawyer turned to me and suggested, "Perhaps your father should wait outside while we have a private chat. Maybe we can find a way to lower the price."

Once alone, his true intentions were revealed as he leered at me and said, "We can make things easier for you if you let me touch and lick your pussy. We'll start the process today and have plenty of opportunities to fuck discreetly throughout.

No one needs to know, and you'll be free from this burden. Everyone wins." My ears burned with disbelief as the words spilled from his putrid mouth. I was disgusted but also cornered, trapped by my financial limitations.

My entire being shook with shock, feeling like I was trapped in a nightmare. Insecurity and fear clawed at my gut, knowing that my future was now uncertain. The vile man sitting across from me took advantage of my vulnerable state, making a disgusting proposal that made my skin crawl. Every fibre of my being screamed to lash out and inflict pain upon him, to break his neck and leave this wretched office behind. But thoughts of my innocent son and worried parents held me back as I stormed out, refusing to dignify his offer with an answer.

As I stumbled towards the car, my emotions were a chaotic mess. Tears streamed down my face as anger and fear consumed me. My father's concerned voice pulled me back to reality, "Why are you crying? What has happened?". I hesitated before telling them, knowing it would only result in rage. He was determined to confront the person who had caused me such pain. All I wanted was to escape, so I begged that we just leave. We drove for hours, seeking refuge and safety.

As we pulled up to a sprawling farm, I couldn't help but feel a sense of unease. My parents had been working here as hired hands and now I was expected to live on this property with them. The large farmhouse loomed in front of me, promising comfort. But as my mother led me to what was to be my room, with its rustic decor and inviting bed she said "Change the clothes the boy, have a fresh bath, and then come to help prepare dinner". I of course assisted my mother but how could I focus on the menial task before me, when my ex had just taken everything from me? My thoughts were also consumed by the events with that bastard lawyer, and I struggled to push them away, as I went through the motions of getting dinner ready.

Fatigued and drained, I yearned for a moment of respite and shelter. The small room seemed like the perfect sanctuary, a place to finally rest my weary body and mind. But as soon as I entered, Niklas began his usual routine of screaming and crying. The never-ending barrage of noise not only kept me awake but also tormented every living soul in the farmhouse. The chaotic symphony raged on, its discordant notes echoing through every room and seeping into every crevice, rendering rest impossible. It was evident that my arrival had brought chaos and disruption to all who resided here.

As the morning sun crept over the horizon, I knelt and prayed with tears streaming down my face, begging for a glimmer of hope in my bleak situation. The weight of the world felt heavy on my shoulders as I longed for an end to this dark tunnel I found myself in. Hours later, a crackling voice echoed through the farmhouse radio, breaking the silence that had consumed the air. It was my father-in-law, his voice trembling with remorse as he apologised for being unaware of the chaos that had engulfed our marriage. He expressed his disgust at his son's behaviour and offered to handle the separation without any financial burden on me.

However, he explained that obtaining a divorce would take longer than we had hoped, due to his son's refusal to sign the paperwork. A bittersweet relief washed over me as I listened to his words, knowing that justice would eventually prevail, even if it would take three long years. The conversation had been broadcast over the open radio channel, reaching many ears in the surrounding area and adding another layer of humiliation to my already messy situation.

Rumours began to circulate in the small village near the farm, whispered words about Valente and his beautiful daughter, a single mother at the farm. As time passed, these murmurs transformed into full-blown gossip, spreading like wildfire to the wider area. Suddenly, I was the talk of the town, my name on everyone's lips as if it were a juicy piece of fruit ripe for plucking. It seemed that no one could resist the temptation to partake in the scandalous tales surrounding me.

Before long, I had become a welcome addition to the community and was on friendly terms with everyone. With newfound hope in my heart, I believed that my problems would be resolved. My desire for a fresh start led me to yearn for a simple job - perhaps as a cleaner or a shop assistant. The thought of being able to support myself filled me with determination and motivation.

I spent days wandering the town, desperately searching for any job opportunity. But one by one, every door seemed to close in my face. I couldn't understand why until I overheard people whispering about me being too pretty and feared by wives and desired by husbands. The thought made me sick - was this small town really that backward and judgemental?

Anger boiled inside of me as I felt unfairly judged for something I had no control over. But then a twisted idea crept into my mind - if they wanted a promiscuous woman, then I would give them one. I began to flirt with anyone and everyone, determined to show them that their prejudice wouldn't hold me back.

For three fucking years, I trapped myself in this small town, suffocating under the weight of toxic relationships. My parents supported me as I struggled to find a job, and my status as a single mother made me nothing more than an easy target for men seeking quick satisfaction. And then alcohol became my crutch, numbing the pain of my desperate situation.

Despite having no money, the wealthy elite still sought me out for my wit, beauty, and cooking skills. The party culture here was centred around drinking, barbecuing, and recklessly indulging in all sorts of vices on secluded farmland. I was always invited – the source of entertainment, the life of the party.

But deep down, I knew I was just an object of desire for these men, ones who had slept with me once and wanted more or those who would do anything just to taste me once. I was aware of their intentions but pretended not to see them, drowning myself in alcohol and putting on a facade of false happiness just to survive each day.

If there was a local newspaper, I would have been on the front page news every fucking week. Then I met a boy called Sebastian and our attraction was immediate, a tall and handsome boy who lived in the bustling city of Rio De

Janeiro. His father was famous throughout Brazil a brilliant lawyer. Their wealth was undeniable, with a mansion in Rio and a sprawling farm in my small town. Maybe it was because he was an outsider, or maybe he truly had a kind heart, but there was an undeniable chemistry between us from the moment we met. He visited three times a year - for Christmas, July, and his birthday month April - and each time he came, I couldn't help but be enamoured by his good looks, charming smile, and alluring scent. It wasn't just me who noticed him though; all the girls wanted him too.

But despite his charm and popularity, Sebastian only had eyes for me. From the very beginning, he made his intentions clear: "You are going to be my girlfriend," he declared confidently. "I know you are a naughty girl, but if you agree to be mine, I don't want you to go with anyone else. I will treat you as a pure and special girl." And with those words, he stole my heart.

We became an inseparable couple, spending every moment together when he would visit for six weeks at a time. However, despite our strong physical attraction, we refrained from having sex for one year out of respect for my son and my own personal values. But even without physical intimacy, Sebastian's mere touch and passionate kisses were enough to drive me wild. He called me every day on the farm's new phone when we were apart, always wanting to know how my son was doing and making sure I was okay.

But things were not easy for us. Sebastian's snobbish sister and friends from Rio viewed me with disdain because of my status as a single mother and my lower social class. Despite this disapproval, Sebastian proudly introduced me as his girlfriend and fought to include me in their group. And for a year, we were a beautiful couple - him with his dark hair and dazzling smile, me with my son by my side. But behind our fairy tale lies the struggles of social barriers and societal expectations, making our love all the more precious.

With a sudden shift, his attitude turned cold and distant. Days passed without a word from him, leaving me in a state of anxious uncertainty. Finally, he called with a foreboding warning: "Be ready for bad news." My heart was anxious as I waited for him to arrive, knowing deep down that something was terribly wrong. When we met at our usual spot in the bustling piazza in Pirajuba City, the atmosphere felt off. No warm embrace or tender kisses like before - instead, his eyes were filled with sadness and regret. Despite it all, I could still see love lingering in them. This was a man of honour and honesty, who wasted no time getting straight to the devastating point that would change everything.

Sebastian's voice trembles as he spoke "I can't do this anymore. You're the most stunning woman I've ever been with, but there are things happening that I have no control over. My family holds too much power, and I am nothing without their support. My father controls every aspect of my life, from my education to my finances."

He then recounted what his father had told him 'Sebastian, my son. You are too emotionally involved with that woman. She's more suited to someone like me, a wealthy man who can buy any girl he desires without regard for their value or future. - she's a single mother, low class, no degree. These types of women are just playthings, not to be taken seriously. I, on the other hand, can have any woman I desire with my money. I'll never leave my family for some worthless mistress like her. You will put an end to this madness, or suffer the consequences. If you dare to continue down this path, I will not hesitate to cut you off from your degree and your entire future will be nothing but ruins!'.

My heart stopped as his words sank in. I was frozen, unable to even speak. Sebastian blurted out "You see, Angelina, this is my curse for the next three and a half years - studying, being tied to my father's demands! But after that, I will break free and become a successful man. And it doesn't matter if you're no longer perfect or have another child by then. You deserve to be free, but know this: I am deeply in love with you and I will propose to you. I'm not asking you to wait for me while your life passes you by. But at least when those four years are up, you'll belong to me once again." His words hit me like a tidal wave.

My voice froze in my throat, trapped by fear and disbelief. Every muscle in my body tensed as I struggled to maintain even a shred of dignity. My gaze fell to the ground, refusing to meet his piercing eyes. Without a word, without a single glance back, I turned on my heel and walked away with trembling steps, my heart pounding like a drum.

I sunk deeper into alcohol addiction, with no way to recover the sadness that engulfed my soul. Then I was coerced into a weekend getaway in Campo Florido by my friend Rafael, the only person among us with a car and some cash to spare. I made sure to dress to make an impact, wearing a short black leather skirt that accentuated my long legs. Along with a stylish black silk blouse detailed with silver and high-heeled boots, I was ready to turn heads.

We made a pact - if an unsavoury man approached me, he would pose as my boyfriend; but if there was a potential romantic interest, he would pretend to be my cousin. And just for added excitement, we agreed that if he got stuck talking to a dazed and confused woman, I would come to his rescue by acting insanely jealous and claiming to be his girlfriend. But of course, if the girl seemed promising, I would switch roles and play the supportive cousin. "Deal?" he asked with a grin. "Deal," I replied with a chuckle.

In every town, there is a bustling piazza surrounded by bars filled with social drinkers. The air is alive with the sound of chatter and laughter, as boys drive around like idiots in search of their chosen target. The streets are crowded with people, creating a frenzied atmosphere that intensifies as the night wears on. It was well past midnight, but the culture here starts late and the courting continues until the sun rises.

The alcohol coursed through our veins, igniting a wild sense of recklessness. Our laughter echoed through the busy street as we stumbled towards the next bar. In the darkness, I leaned close to his face and whispered, "Who is the most desirable man in this town? Because tonight, I will be with him." He paused and smirks, gesturing towards a sleek car across the street. "That's him," he declared. "A young and successful vet with looks that make all the girls swoon." I declared with determination, "Well then, by the end of tonight, he will be mine." Our laughter turned into a shared understanding of our game, one that will only end when we both find our chosen conquests.

My friend Rafael and I stood outside a busy bar on the corner of the square, sipping our drinks. As a newcomer to the area, I quickly became the focus of attention for many of the young men. The local vet had also seen me and was now making his move, pulling his car up close to us.

Stepping out of his car, he confidently made his way to the bar opposite ours. I watched as he took a seat at a small table all by himself, ordering a bottle of beer. I couldn't help but feel drawn to him, shining like a beacon of light.

As it turns out, I already knew a few girls in this town and they were all familiar with the charming vet. Seizing an opportunity, I invited them to join me at the bar across from us, offering to buy each girl a drink if they would come along.

I nervously asked the girls to introduce me to him. With reluctant smiles, they obliged and I found myself sitting at his table, my heart racing with excitement and nerves. The chemistry between us was electric, the conversation flowing effortlessly as he challenged me with his intelligence.

His name was Francesco, this twenty-four-year-old was not like the other wankers I had met. He may not have been tall, but at 5'8" he exuded a quiet confidence. His smile was like a ray of sunshine, his big eyes twinkling with mischief behind his black cap. As I gazed into his light brown hair, the same shade as his captivating eyes, I couldn't help but notice the deep dimple on his cheek when he flashed that irresistible grin.

The hours flew by and our conversation never faltered. I couldn't resist inviting Rafael to join us, and he eagerly took a seat at our table with the two gorgeous girls we had brought to the bar. Rafael was content to have the close company of these two women and happily covered the cost of all the beers.

As the sun began to rise, Francesco and I found ourselves in an intense and intimate discussion, drawing closer and closer until our faces were mere inches apart. Our eyes locked, but instead of meeting gazes, we were fixated on each other's lips. The realisation that I had a child waiting for me at home crept into my mind, and this could no longer be silenced even by the overwhelming desire coursing through my veins. "I have to go home," I whispered breathlessly. "Okay," he replied, his voice low and urgent. "But I can't kiss you here with others watching." Without hesitation, I agreed, only to have him lean in immediately and capture my lips in a fiery French kiss.

My legs trembled, my cheeks burning with embarrassment. I let out a loud "Wow" before turning to my friend Rafael and saying, "Let's go home, man." We still had a long 30km drive ahead of us. But Rafael replied, "Sure, but first I have to drop off these girls at their house. You stay here and talk some more, I'll come back for you." Francesco quickly interjected, "No, no, no. I'll take Angelina home. You can take your time with the girls." His suggestive tone made it clear that he wanted to kiss me again, maybe even more. Rafael then asked, "Is that alright with you, Angelina? Or do you want me to come back for you?" He turned to face me with a charming smile. I responded, "Yes, you can take the girls. We can talk later and I'll go with Francesco." The tension between us was palpable as we exchanged glances filled with desire.

Francesco's eyes hungrily scanned my body. The world ceased to exist and it was just the two of us, consumed by an intense desire. He drove me home at a reckless speed. As we reached my town, he abruptly stopped the car and pushed back his seat, revealing his true intentions. Our lips crashed together in a frenzy of need and our hands roamed wildly across each other's bodies. But I made my boundaries clear, refusing to let this escalate any further despite the overwhelming temptation pulsing between us.

The haze of alcohol slowly lifted, leaving behind a sharp pang of guilt and responsibility. I knew I had a crying baby waiting for me and all my duties as a mother. The harsh reality of my life hit me like a ton of bricks, suffocating me with the weight of endless tasks ahead, with no sleep.

As we pulled up to my house, his lips pressed against mine with a searing intensity that sent shivers through my body. A surge of adrenaline filled me as he whispered in my ear, asking if he could call me later and see me again. My heart raced with a mix of excitement and fear as I replied "Yes, you can call me. I would love it".

As I tried to escape the car unnoticed, a shadow loomed over me and I froze. My mother's face appeared in the window, twisted with disgust and disapproval. Her words were like daggers as I entered the hallway, piercing my heart with every accusatory question. "Who is this man? You left with Rafael and now you're with another man? And kissing?" Her voice was a whip, lashing at me for my perceived promiscuity. "I hope he wants something serious with you because your name is dirt in this town. You've been with too many men." Her words stung like acid, burning my ears and making my stomach churn. "Your actions reflect on me too, so I should care about your reputation." But I could only muster a tired response, pleading for her to let me be. Yet she continued her onslaught, mercilessly reminding me of my responsibilities as a mother and daughter. "Take a shower, you reek of alcohol.

Your son is waiting for you. And don't expect to sleep like a princess today - you're going to help me prepare lunch." Each of her words crushed my spirit.

My father emerges from the shadows with Niklas cradled in his arms, his voice hushed and soothing as he instructs me, "Go take a shower, son. Ignore your mother."

In the late afternoon, just as the sun began its descent below the horizon, I received a call from Francesco. His voice was warm and familiar but tinged with a hint of urgency. He asked if he could come by my house to see me, and without hesitation, I replied that I was sorry, but not able to do so. Exhaustion now controlled my weary body, and despite my best efforts, I had yet to find sleep that day. His response was one of disbelief - "What, seriously?" he questioned. With a heavy heart, I explained that my life differed greatly from that of other girls; I was a single mother with countless responsibilities that demanded my constant attention. But still, I apologised for being unable to see him. In return, he too expressed his regret - "I am sorry too," he said softly. "I really wanted to see you today, but tomorrow is Monday and I have to work." I reassured him that I understood and offered to see him at a later time when I had more energy. As we spoke about our conflicting schedules, he suddenly exclaimed "Right! Monday after work, I will come to your house and we can talk." His words filled me with hope and joy - the thought of seeing him again brought butterflies to my stomach and a smile to my face.

The next morning, he called with a sense of urgency in his voice and said he couldn't wait to see me later. My heart fluttered at the thought of seeing him again. As evening approached, I took extra care in getting ready. My hair was artfully styled and my perfume wafted around me like a delicate cloud. The dress I chose was long and flowing, reminiscent of a dress worn for a high-end beach party. On my feet were cute, strappy sandals that made me feel elegant and confident. When I caught sight of him stepping out of his car, my heart skipped a beat, and a lump formed in my throat as excitement and nerves intertwined.

I nervously asked if he wanted to come inside or talk in the car. To my shock, he expressed his desire to meet my parents and my son, if possible. I was taken aback, expecting a different response, this was not like all the other boys before him. But Francesco, despite his youth, exuded a strong sense of confidence and charm. As we entered the house, I couldn't help but feel anxious about my mother's reaction. But her warm and immediate approval of him left me pleasantly surprised and relieved.

I reluctantly introduced my father and son to Francesco, knowing the gravity of the situation. My father, always the joker, tries to lighten the mood but Niklas is already crying, as if sensing the tension. However, Franscesco remained resolute, his gaze fixed on me with determination as he expresses his intentions. Every night without fail, he visited me after work, becoming a familiar presence in our household. The bond between him and my son is immediate, and Niklas becomes uncharacteristically quiet in his presence. He earns the trust of my parents and on Friday night, he arrived with an air of sophistication.

He presented my mother with a box of expensive chocolates and a bouquet of red roses for me, accompanied by a card expressing his feelings. Before anyone could offer him a drink, he cuts straight to the point, addressing my mother with a directness that took me aback. "I would like to take Angelina out for dinner and show her my house," he said confidently. "If this is possible, would you be able to care for Niklas until tomorrow afternoon?"

My mother's response was sharp as a blade, as she calmly said, "So you're asking to sleep with my daughter? Fine, but only if you promise to take care of her and not just tonight, but from this day forward." My face burned with embarrassment as I can't believe this conversation is happening right in front of me.

I couldn't help but feel torn between my excitement and apprehension as I prepared to leave with this man. My mother's warnings echoed in my mind, reminding me to be cautious and guarded. I quickly packed a bag, unsure of what the evening held in store for me.

I forced myself to kiss my boy goodbye, my heart aching with the guilt of what I am about to do. My mother's embrace feels suffocating as I can't shake off the image of the man waiting for me in his car outside. As we drove, my mind screams in protest, knowing that I have to give myself to him in the most intimate way and I am consumed by shyness and fear.

As we approached our destination, the sound of a nearby river made me relax. He lived in a studio apartment tucked behind his bustling veterinary surgery where he worked. But what caught my eye was the massive chilli pepper tree standing in front of the building. Its vibrant red fruits seemed to pulsate with an otherworldly energy. Involuntarily, I exclaimed, "I have never laid eyes on a chilli tree this stunning before. It's like a magnificent Christmas tree!". My feet carried me towards it as I reached out to touch the peppers, feeling their smooth skin beneath my fingertips. The intensity of its heat burned through me, leaving me breathless and trembling.

Francesco beckoned me inside, the space was cramped and cluttered with only a single bed to accommodate us. The memories of that night were a blur, a hazy whirlwind of wildness and passion. It was a night of liberation, the first time I experienced a truly intense and fulfilling orgasm. His touch was gentle yet firm, his hands caressing my face with every move. His kisses were insistent, filled with an intensity that made me forget about everything else in the world.

Nothing mattered but the overwhelming feeling of being wanted by this man. The doubts of my mother's disapproval and my insecurities faded away as I completely let go. Every touch, every kiss, fueled the fire of desire within me and I surrendered myself to the pleasure without hesitation. It was a night unlike any other, one that I would never forget for the rest of my life.

The morning after our passionate night together, we leave the apartment and I freeze in my tracks. My heart drops to my stomach as I see the once lush tree now barren and lifeless, its branches stripped of leaves and fruits. Francesco's face contorts in shock as he exclaims "Jesus Christ, this is the tree that our entire town has come to for two years to gather the chill for their celebrations. And now it's dead." His accusatory gaze falls on me as he adds, his voice trembling with anger, "You touched it last night, didn't you? Are you a witch? You've killed my beloved tree!" I am overcome with a mix of shame and confusion, unable to comprehend how this could have happened.

But deep down, I know the truth - when I was inexplicably drawn to that tree and touched it, I felt an intense surge of energy and saw lights dancing around its fruits. Now, as we make our way back in silence, I can't shake off the guilt that gnaws at my conscience - I am responsible for killing his precious tree.

My pulse quickens as he drops me off at home, promising to come back for me later. For the next three weeks we were inseparable, for only one weekend he was absent as he had to leave to visit his family in a different state.

He had declared me his girlfriend, I felt a sense of validation and excitement wash over me. It was mid-day on a Friday and I was at his apartment, Francesco was at work. Suddenly, the phone rings, shattering the eerie silence that always lingers in this place. This was the first time the phone had rung since I had been staying here. My heart races as I answer it cautiously, not wanting to break the illusion of bliss that I have created in my mind. My hand trembled as I answered it, only to have a woman's voice questioning me, "Who is there?" I replied "Angelina". She continues "What are you doing there? Are you the new cleaner, I know the voice of the cleaner and it is not you. What are you doing in my fiance's apartment?".

My blood runs cold as it dawns on me what she is insinuating - that I am just another one of his conquests, playing house in his love nest. My vision blurs as panic sets in and all I can do is mumble my name before hanging up the phone, feeling like a fool for ever believing in his lies.

As soon as he stepped into the apartment, flames of anger consumed me and everything turned red. Without hesitation, I spat out each word with venom, "You think I'm a fool? You made me feel special, called me your girlfriend, while you had a fucking fiance all along. I demand an explanation!"

My hands shook with rage as I awaited his response. "I was going to tell you," he stuttered, "but I couldn't find the words. I know how quick to anger you can be and I was afraid. But this weekend, I plan to take care of the situation. I've known her since I was twelve and we have been together for nine years. Many times, I have tried to leave her but it is a difficult and complicated situation. Her father is a powerful and wealthy politician."

His weak excuse only fuelled my fury. "And now you expect me to believe that you'll just go and fix things with her this weekend? How convenient for you to have two women ready to fuck whenever it suits you!" My voice rose to a shriek as I declared, "I never want to see you again. And don't even think about trying to contact me if you somehow manage to 'fix' this mess." With tears streaming down my face, I added, "If by some miracle we both end up single in the future, maybe then we can try again. But until then, I do not want to see you and please do not call me"

My heart sank as I entered my parent's home, defeat pressing down on me until tears poured from my eyes. My mother's disapproving gaze spoke volumes without a single word uttered. A thick fog of sadness enveloped me, suffocating me with its heaviness. And all weekend long, I was trapped in a never-ending cycle of menial tasks and relentless weeping, feeling utterly broken and alone.

Francesco showed up at the house on Monday night, catching me by surprise. "I know I didn't call ahead, but I didn't think you would listen to me if I did," he said. "Listen, on Saturday I went to see her and it's over. I want you back. My mother and her father are mad, but I don't care." He looked at me with hopeful eyes. "Remember when you said you'd give me a second chance if I was single again? Well, I am. Will you marry me and come live with me and your son?" He promised to find a new place with two bedrooms so we could start our life together.

Chapter VI

With a heart full of both excitement and trepidation, I accepted his proposal. But there was one condition that hung heavily in my mind: I was technically still married, separated but not yet officially divorced. He had gotten us a house - two bedrooms, a quaint kitchen with a window overlooking the backyard, a cosy bathroom, and a sunlit living room. It was simple but charming. My mind raced with thoughts of starting anew in this little home, but the reminder of my unresolved marriage lingered in the back of my mind. Nevertheless, I couldn't deny the warmth and promise that radiated from our new home.

My son Niklas was with us, but he cried constantly and always wanted ack to me. He was a handful, bouncing back and forth between us for two years.

On his fourth birthday, he told my mother that he wanted to stay with me his mother permanently. My mother Laura couldn't help but cry; she had been a constant presence in his life since he was born, but she knew it was best for him to be with us.

As I spent more time with him, I began to unravel the intricacies of his behaviour and needs. It became clear that Niklas was a peculiar child. In our backyard, banana trees swayed in the breeze and rich soil covered the ground. But every day, I would hear Francesco scream that he had to stepped in Kakka - the Brazilian term for poop - as if it were some kind of ritual. Niklas my son, refused to use the toilet and instead preferred to leave his faeces hidden in obscure corners of the garden, like a mischievous cat. This habit drove Francesco absolutely mad, and I couldn't help but shake my head in disbelief.

It took a whole year to train him on proper toilet usage, but it was mostly due to the fact that we had moved into a new house without a backyard and with a standard bathroom setup. It was definitely the banana trees that were the problem.

The spacious three-bedroom, two-bathroom house exuded a comforting warmth and beauty. A lush garden with vibrant flowers and a soothing shower nestled in the corner added to the serene atmosphere. As I settled into the house, I began having vivid visions of another son - a little boy with dark, straight hair and delicate pale skin. With each vision, I could feel the overwhelming love emanating from him, leaving me wondering who this child could be. However, I knew it couldn't be possible for me to be pregnant - I felt too healthy and was still having my monthly cycle. It was all so perplexing, especially when compared to my experience with Niklas, where I was constantly sick and miserable. These thoughts were both delightful and puzzling at the same time.

Francesco had generously gifted my own car, a shiny silver Ford Ka, which I drove with skill despite not having a valid license. But one day, as I was carefully manoeuvring the vehicle out of the steep garage and onto the street, my vision suddenly blurred. My body goes limp and I lose consciousness, only to awake to the sound of crunching metal and shattering glass. Frantically, I look around and see that I've ploughed the car into our neighbour's wall.

Panic sets in as I rush to the doctor's office, desperate for answers. It's there that I learn the shocking truth: I am three months pregnant, a revelation that explains my sudden fainting spell and fills me with both fear and excitement for what lies ahead.

Francesco had left work early and picked up Niklas from school. Their arrival at home was greeted by a demolished wall, with the car still hanging over it. Francesco immediately asks, "What happened here?" His mind jumps to the worst scenario - he knows I must have caused some damage again, and now he has to pay for it.

I explained what had happened and showed him the results of my blood test. I told him I was pregnant, and his face transformed from anger to pure joy. He turned to Niklas and exclaimed, "You're going to have a new brother or sister, little man!" I smiled and corrected him, "No Niklas, you are going to have a brother." The dream of the boy suddenly made perfect sense.

As the days passed, my belly swelled and grew, a physical representation of the unbreakable bond between Niklas and the Khan. Every morning, as soon as he woke up, Niklas would come to me with a smile on his face and greet me with a cheerful "Good morning Mum" before turning to my swollen stomach and whispering "Good morning Khan. I can't wait for you to join us." It was heartwarming to see how much Niklas had changed - no longer the difficult toddler, but now a kind, loving, and helpful young man. Francesco too seemed to have transformed, becoming more caring and attentive towards me. He would kiss my growing belly every chance he got, a reflection of his excitement for our first child. As the days went by, I could feel myself getting bigger and rounder, but I embraced each new change, feeling like a beautiful pregnant goddess.

As Khan's due date inched closer and closer, every passing day brought more intense signs of his impending arrival. Suddenly on a hot June afternoon, my contractions began with such force that my waters broke instantly, sending Francesco into a panic. After fumbling to pack my emergency bag, he raced us fifty kilometres to the nearest hospital. But as we arrived, the contractions intensified, becoming unbearable and relentless. Despite my efforts, I was not dilated enough for a natural birth and the doctors urged me to opt for an emergency cesarean. With intense fear gripping me, I made the heart-wrenching decision to undergo surgery and bring my baby into the world by any means necessary.

They rushed me to the delivery room. After what felt like an eternity, Khan came into the world and landed on my chest. But when I caught a glimpse of his squished-up face, I nearly passed out. Turning to Francesco, I exclaimed, "Have you been watching an alien birth? Because this can't be our child!" The poor little thing looked like a cross between a wrinkly old man and a puffy-eyed potato. And even when he wasn't bawling, he still had the grumpiest expression on his face. I couldn't help but burst into laughter and tears at the ridiculousness of it all - this ugly baby was supposed to be mine!

As I held my child in my arms for the first time, I couldn't help but notice his lovely temperament. He had not cried once since being born, and I marvelled at how this tiny, ugly creature could have such a peaceful aura about him. So different from his brother Niklas who cried all the time.

After two days I was allowed to return home, and my mother arrived to stay with me. She remained for one week, she cooked meals. She cared for both me and my newborn son and offered words of wisdom and comfort. Then my mother left, it was the turn of my Fancesco's mother to stay with us and she stayed for three fucking long months. I was crazy to fuck with Francesco but could not as the house was too small. I had to resort to using my hands on him and holding back the moans. All I wanted was his penis inside me. Throughout it all, Khan remained a blessing, sleeping through the nights without much fuss and only needing minimal nourishment. Holding him in my arms, I felt as though I could have ten more children just like him. Despite my urges and lack of sexual satisfaction, I was feeling happy and blessed.

The two boys, Khan and Niklas, bond was strong from their early days of childhood. They spent their days playing together happily, always looking out for one another. Francesco, was a kind and loving parent who took on the role of school drop-offs and pick-ups with enthusiasm. He also made sure to attend every parent's evening, showing his dedication to their education. Niklas was fortunate to have Francesco as his stepfather, he took on the role of a father figure effortlessly, assisting with school assignments and offering unwavering support.

He would treat them to long trips to the major shopping centre, where he would buy them fancy clothes and shoes, even though it was over 100 kilometres away. The boys behaved impeccably, especially during family dinners at restaurants. But the best days were spent at the pool club, where we made friends with other families and played all day long. Though Francesco had received a higher education than myself, we remained incredibly close. He even took it upon himself to teach me proper grammar and etiquette, correcting me whenever I spoke in my common local dialect. With his guidance, I learned to speak like an upper-class individual.

As a housewife, my days were filled with the mundane tasks of caring for the house and our children. My husband, Francesco, provided me with a monthly allowance of 100 Reais to cover all expenses. While I appreciated the comfortable life this afforded us, I couldn't ignore the restless feeling inside me. I yearned for something more, something beyond the walls of our family home.

But Francesco was fiercely jealous and refused to let me work for anyone else. Instead, he suggested we open a business together. And so, at twenty-four years old with our two boys aged eight and two, we took on the venture of opening a DVD rental shop in the heart of our local small town.

My days now consisted of working from 9 am to 5 pm, Monday through Saturday. After school, I would bring the children to the shop where they would play under my watchful eye in the bustling Piazzo. When Francesco finished work, he would take over managing the shop until late into the night, leaving me with little time to see him.

The days were long and tiring, but I poured my heart and soul into making our business successful. Yet as our shop thrived, our relationship suffered. With each passing day, I saw less and less of Francesco as we both dedicated ourselves fully to our work.

Each day brought new and interesting encounters as I met and conversed with local people, many of whom were investors in the thriving industries of the area. Among the numerous individuals I encountered, one man stands out in my memory - a peculiar character standing at about 5'11", with a deep tan, large protruding belly, and long curly hair just starting to show signs of greying. This man, who appeared to be in his mid-forties, would stop outside my store every single day and utter the same words: "Good day my gypsy of the gold, tell me the number of the lottery." His name was Jerome, and despite my repeated attempts to shoo him away, he would always persist with his pleading: "You have the luck! What's your problem? Let me have a bit of your gold." It became clear that Jerome had a gambling addiction, which I later learned had driven him to sell his television while his wife was at work. Despite this unfortunate fact, Jerome's daily visits still managed to bring a bit of lightness and laughter into my days.

One bright and bustling day, Francesco and I ventured to the big city for a family photo shoot. The owner of the prestigious modelling agency was immediately taken with me, offering a tantalising proposal to become one of his sought-after models. He painted a vivid picture of the industry's inner workings and displayed glossy photos of the other stunning individuals he represented. My eyes gleamed with excitement, despite my love for our quaint shop, I knew the potential for financial gain from it was limited. I also regretted how little time I was now spending time with my partner. The thought of only having to work a few days each month and earning four times more than I did at the store was alluring and would allow me to be at home more often with Francesco. But he was not keen on this idea, his reservations clear on his face. This golden opportunity was both thrilling and daunting, as it could potentially change everything.

Within a week, I found myself fully immersed in the world of modelling. My first task was a personal photo shoot for marketing, where every inch of my body was measured and documented - from my waist to my height to my breast size. Surprisingly, my first job wasn't in fashion, but rather for a car company. It wasn't as glamorous as a fashion shoot, but it paid well and was a good starting point.

But soon after, I landed my dream job in the fashion industry. It required me to be away for more than two days at a time. At first, I was excited to learn how to walk with grace and move my hips just right. But as time went on, I understood that modelling is not all glitz and glamour. It's filled with endless stress and constant pressure to always look perfect.

My schedule quickly became packed with jobs - sometimes up to eight in one month. This meant being away from my family for long periods of time, sometimes having to travel over 250km for work. I found myself staying in hotels instead of the comfort of my own home.

Gone were the days of my humble job at the local DVD store, where I would interact with real people and feel a sense of genuine connection. In this new world of plastic and superficiality, everything felt different and unfamiliar. Enough was enough for me when I attended a private party where all the models were invited. It was brimming with rich and influential individuals, each one seemingly more shallow and insincere than the next. It quickly became clear that we had been invited there to be used as prostitutes - just another form of commodity to be bought and sold.

If you wanted to advance in this industry, it was expected that you would sleep with someone in a position of power. This exploitative norm was not surprising to me, but what truly shocked me at this party was seeing young girls, some barely eighteen years old, stumbling around drunk and being objectified by older men. And while the guests mingled and indulged in decadent pleasures, the hired waiting staff circulated among them with silver trays in hand. But these trays didn't hold drinks; they were full of cocaine and an assortment of pills. It was like a self-service buffet of drugs, with no regard for the consequences or repercussions. As a mother and 'wife', this dark underbelly of the fashion industry was too steep a price to pay for success and validation.

After that night, which I left alone, I decided that this was not for me. This decision made Francesco very happy and also my boys. As I settled into the normal routine of home life, I still felt the desire to have my own success. I now drew on my experience as an eighteen-year-old. This was the year, I conquered the role of the Queen of The Rodeo - a prestigious and competitive position. That week crashed into my memories as hard as the neighbours wall did.

In the summer of 1994, my heart yearned to be a part of the biggest event in our city: The Rodeo. I dreamed of being the Rodeo Queen but as a struggling young woman, I had no means to afford the expensive clothes I needed 250 Reais, for the costume alone. My friends, all from wealthy families, including Rafael, urged me to enter the competition for Rodeo Queen. "You are stunningly beautiful," he exclaimed. "Why not give it a try?" I sheepishly replied that I simply could not afford it. Without hesitation, they banded together and proposed a plan: "Let's finance her! If we each contribute 50 Reais, we can help her conquer this dream." They knew that winning this title would grant us all VIP access for the entire two-week event - an exclusive opportunity to rub shoulders with famous singers, have backstage passes, and attend the highly coveted rodeo shows where millionaire cowboys from all over came to compete on the bulls and horses. It was truly a sight to behold, and having free VIP access for everyone would be a rare privilege. My friends were fully aware of this and were determined to help me achieve my goal.

Tears streamed down my cheeks as I listened to their words, unable to believe what they were saying. But then, a rush of excitement filled my chest and I couldn't help but hug everyone around me. "I have to go put my name in!" I exclaimed, already planning my next move. "One of you has to take me to Barretos City, so I can pick out and rent my outfits for the two weeks." There was only one man in all of Brazil called Marcello, who made the special Rodeo cowgirl costumes, and that's where I needed to go now.

With each step, anticipation grew inside me. The cowgirl outfit would be my armour, my weapon in the arena. And it had to be perfect. After browsing through racks and racks of vibrant fabrics, I finally chose a stunning gold and purple ensemble adorned with shimmering stones. It was pure bling, designed to catch every eye in the crowd.

The top was fitted and resembled a bra, with long tassels swaying with each movement. My stomach was exposed, showcasing my toned abs for all to see. The bottom half consisted of a bikini bottom covered in tassels and jewels, leaving little to the imagination. And of course, no cowgirl outfit would be complete without a pair of golden boots that hugged my calves just right.

But the accessories were what truly brought the entire look together. Four-inch gold bracelets on each arm added an extra touch of glamour. And perched atop my head was a magnificent cowgirl hat in matching gold and purple.

In preparation for the rodeo, I spent every day practicing with the traditional instrument of country culture - a longhorn used to call cattle. Its three-foot length seemed daunting at first, but after hours of training, I began to master its sound and feel confident in my ability to use it flawlessly during the competition.

As the big night arrived, a knot of nerves twisted in my stomach. Marcello, the renowned costume designer, was there to do my makeup. He swept his skilled hands over my face, muttering praises about my beauty and confidence. "This title is already yours," he declared with conviction. "Look at your legs, your bottom, your fucking amazing face. You must go out there and shine." His words were both reassuring and intimidating, as I knew he expected nothing less than perfection from me.

As the other girls got ready around us, Marcello finished my makeup and left to prepare them. I was alone in the dressing room, struggling to calm my racing heart and trembling hands. Just as I managed to squeeze myself into my outfit, the loudspeaker blared: "And now Angelina."

I grabbed the horn and took a deep breath, I climbed the stairs onto the stage. The lights blinded me momentarily as I made my way through the crowd. My heart pounded in my ears as I moved with precision and grace, performing my fashion walk around the arena. But then they upped the stakes by building a raised walkway that took me in front of seven judges.

I played my horn expertly, flipping my hat in perfect synchronisation before catching it effortlessly on my head. I completed the fashion display as choreographed to perfection. Faking a smile and waving to the crowd, the crowd was going wild they were all upstanding and chanting my name. I left the stage feeling both exhilarated and exhausted after giving it my all. I took a final bow, I had pushed myself to the limit and left everything on that stage tonight.

As I undressed in the quiet dressing room, I suddenly felt a breeze on my backside. Confused, I looked down and saw that I had accidentally put on my underwear backwards in the frenzy before the show. And now my underwear, was like a skimpy Brazilian-style micro bikini. No wonder the crowd was going wild and cheering my name - they were all admiring my assets! Who knew my butt could steal the show?

The head judge thrusts the microphone into the air, his voice booming with finality. "And the winner of the 1994 Rodeo Queen is Angelina!" My heart races with exhilaration and I try to hastily fix my dishevelled underwear. But Marcello's voice cuts through the cheers, commanding me to stay as I am. "No, beauty," shoving me forward onto the stage. "You go there exactly as you were. You go there and give your show again. Like a Queen!" Panic rises in my chest as becomes apparent that this nightmare is far from over.

It was a night that would be etched in my memory forever. Winning The Rodeo title and my short experience as a model, presented an opportunity. I now had the chance to bring something new to The Rodeo event in my new city, to introduce them to the party and Queen competition that they were missing out on. Somehow, I ran with this brilliant idea and became their promoter.

With my new job as an event planner, I had a vision but lacked the knowledge and resources to make it a reality.

Undeterred, I turned to my hardworking sister Rebecca for assistance. Together, we poured our time and energy into creating the perfect evening that would showcase local talent and bring a touch of glamour to our city.

It all began with recruiting the girls - black, Asian, blonde - from all corners of the area to compete in our event. They were all stunning and beautiful in their own way. However, most of them came from impoverished backgrounds and needed help to afford the clothes and accessories required for the show. So, not only did I have to teach them about fashion modelling, but also helped them earn the necessary funds.

All of the girls were under eighteen and inexperienced in walking in high heels. It became my mission to train them in the art of graceful movement. With books on their heads and sticks up their backs to improve posture, I pushed them to be the best versions of themselves. We even created a makeshift catwalk for them to practice on.

But beyond just training the models, there was an entire event to plan and execute. Rebecca and I meticulously decorated the venue with a 'Wild West' theme, transforming the venue into a bustling frontier town bar. It had hey on the ground and bull skulls on the wall. Rebecca helped with everything from ordering bottles for the bar to recruiting and training the staff, everyone was dressed like cowboys and cowgirls. With her help, I even managed to secure judges, set ticket prices, coordinate with fire officials for safety precautions, and conduct thorough risk assessments.

Thanks to Rebecca's support and hard work, everything was prepared down to perfection. As I watched each girl grow and improve through this process, I couldn't help but feel a sense of pride and excitement at the challenge that lay ahead of us.

The night was a blur of success, money pouring in and the excitement palpable. As I took a swig of beer, the familiar burning sensation seemed like a small price to pay for our achievements. My sister Rebecca sat next to me, sipping water as she always does, while I drank for both of us. Suddenly, a voice rose above the chatter, someone was shouting "Speech, Speech, Speech" in an insistent chant.

My sister turned to me with a mischievous glint in her eye and urged me to take the spotlight as the face of our victorious night. Panic set in, I had not prepared a speech, but my sister's words echoed in my head: "You are the poker face here".

I climbed into one of the judge's high chairs and felt the blinding light shine down on me as I grasped the microphone. What followed was a chaotic outburst, resembling a drunken Russell Brand rant more than a formal speech. The room erupted with laughter and cheers as I stumbled through my words, desperately trying to keep up with my racing thoughts. But at least everyone was having a good time. As for what exactly I said? I have no idea. All I know is that it ended with a wild declaration: "Let's all get another drink, let's dance and lose ourselves in this party, and don't forget to give me even more money!"

The night was a wild success, but little did I know my world was crumbling around me. Francesco and I had begun to have vicious arguments filled with cutting words. His affection dwindled, replaced by his nights out drinking with his friends, excluding me from his plans. One evening, he told me he was going to play football. Maybe, it was the way he said it or the look in his eye but my intuition screamed that something was off. I knew in my heart that he was playing me for a fool.

With trembling hands, I called up one of his friend's wives and asked if her husband was with Francesco. When she confirmed his presence was still at home with her, I couldn't hold back any longer. "Your husband is supposed to be playing football with Francesco," I spat into the phone. "But instead, he's out betraying me, my man is a fucking liar!" She begged me not to stir up trouble, but it was too late. My world had already been torn apart by his deceitful games.

Raging, I strapped my two children into the car and sped towards the football field where he was supposed to be. My heart races with anxiety as I leave my kids alone in the car and run to check if he's there. But he's not. Blinded by anger, I race back home, barely keeping control of the car as I swerve through traffic. My mind is consumed with thoughts of revenge. The weapon of choice? A baseball bat.

After tending to my children's needs, I send them to bed before patiently waiting for a further forty-five minutes until that bastard comes home.

With a primal scream, I launch myself at him from behind the door, shouting "Fucking, bastard!". Catching him off guard as I slam the bat into his legs. He crumples to the ground, writhing in pain. Through sobs and screams, my children witness their mother's descent into madness, due to his noise they have been woken from their sleep. And yet, even as Francesco threatens to call the police and declares our relationship over, I am unapologetic. I am filled with emotions of pure anger and betrayal, nothing else matters but making him suffer for his actions.

I knew he was lying and had no explanation, he had been caught, and it was over.

Chapter VII

Francesco's betrayal was a deep wound that festered in my chest, pulsing with every thought of him. The separation was painful, he left and rented a small studio, taking both cars and his prized motorcycle. Desperate for some clarity and stability, I sent my children to my parents for the school holiday, while I attempted to rebuild my life and get my thoughts clear. But things were different now. He had cut me off from our joint bank account, leaving me penniless. I needed to find a job.

A week later, he appeared at my doorstep, his limp a new addition, begging for us to reconcile. Against my better judgement, I agreed and to let him move back into the family home. He knew I was dependent on his good graces. He immediately expected me to fulfill my wifely duties. Every day he would come home, demanding sex as if it were his right.

I felt trapped, suffocated by his presence and his expectations. It seemed like we were giving things another chance, but it was just a cruel facade. But I didn't see a way out - not without money or a job to support myself and my boys. He would retreat to his bachelor's den he still rented, where he could continue his deceitful ways without consequence. I was trapped in a never-ending cycle of false hope and manipulation, unable to break free from his grasp.

For four agonising months, the rumours and whispers swirled around me like a thick fog. But it wasn't until one chilly November evening that my goddaughter Rose called. "Godmother," she whispered urgently, "I have to tell you something. Francesco is in this bar with another woman." My heart stopped as I demanded, "What woman? Who is she?" In a trembling voice, Rose revealed, "She's from out of state, a nanny for some wealthy family. Her accent...it sounded like Rio de Janeiro." Instantly, my vision went red with fury. I transformed myself into a picture of perfection, slipping on my highest heels and storming towards the bar where they were supposedly entwined in each other's arms.

My canary yellow long skirt was pulled up over my breasts, the belt cinched tightly around my waist. It was a bold statement, impossible to miss. With each step, my heels clicked loudly against the walkway, announcing my presence from 100 meters away. Francesco sat at a table outside the bar, his attention captivated by a Rio girl with fake blonde hair and dark eyes. His car was parked absurdly close to the table, its open boot displaying the over-the-top sound system he had installed just to impress this bimbo. As I approached, he spoke to her in a hushed voice, but loud enough for me to hear: "It's time for you to go. The trouble is coming." His arrogance and blatant disrespect for me only stoked the fire burning inside of me as I walked towards them with determination and fury in my eyes.

I strode past Francesco, my heart racing as I entered the bar. Feeling lost and alone, I spotted my friend Marco sitting in the corner, nursing a drink. "Can I sit here, Marco?" I asked with a trembling voice. He looked up at me with concern and replied, "Of course." As I took a seat next to him, tears welled up in my eyes and I fought to keep them from spilling over. "What did that bastard do to you?" he asked, his voice laced with anger. Through sobs, I explained the horrific ordeal I had just endured.

Marco's face grew dark with rage and disbelief as he listened intently. "You have no money now, do you?" he asked, already knowing the answer. My shoulders shook as I cried once more, unable to control the overwhelming emotions flooding through me. In a kind gesture of true friendship, Marco reached into his pocket and handed me two hundred Reais. "Take this money," he said firmly. "You'll need it." Through blurry eyes, I gazed at him in disbelief and gratitude. "I don't know when or if I can pay you back," I whispered. "Or if you want something from me in return. Be clear that is something I will not do" Marco interrupted me. "I am a real man," he declared with conviction. "Obviously all men would love to sleep with you and maybe some women. But I am honourable and happily married. I would also never take advantage of you in your vulnerable state." His words brought comfort to my shattered soul as he assured me that there were still good people in this world. "Please pay me back when you can," he added with a gentle smile.

I sat with Marco for a few minutes, seething with rage. In this place, secrets didn't stay secret for long. I forced myself to sit and watch her laughing and drinking with my man Francesco. I could not believe they were doing this in front of me. My heart felt like it was being stabbed repeatedly, as I realised the whole town would soon know of their affair.

I made a quick decision and bolted out of the bar, eyes stinging with unshed tears. They could laugh at me all they wanted, but I wouldn't give them the satisfaction of seeing me crumble. But as I aimlessly wandered the streets for what felt like hours, desperation gnawed at my stomach. Finally, I remembered Josy's party at the club nearby and stumbled towards it, praying for a distraction from my torment. Yet as I stood outside, penniless and powerless to enter, my mind raced with thoughts of Francesco and his new conquest. Every person who entered the venue was a potential threat, causing a mix of hope and dread to consume me. If he had any shred of decency left, he wouldn't dare show up here with her on his arm. But deep down, I knew better - the cruel bastard always loved to flaunt his infidelity in public.

Josy saw me, she grabbed my arm and practically dragged me inside, not taking no for an answer. Embarrassment flooded through me as she led me to the bar, announcing to everyone that I was her guest and would be drinking for free. My face burned with shame as I accepted a drink from the bartender, who gave me a sympathetic look. "Don't worry, darling," Josy whispered in my ear. "I saw your man earlier. I know your situation." Each word felt like a dagger in my heart. I meekly retreated to a corner of the bar, watching the lively crowd with envy. The music thumped loudly, drowning out any coherent thoughts in my head. But then, among all the chaos, I spotted it - a VIP area filled with fancy tables and expensive champagne. And there he was, Francesco, sitting with the same woman from before, laughing and flirting without a care in the world. My stomach twisted into knots as I watched them together, feeling completely alone in a room full of people.

I stumbled backwards, feeling faint and unsteady. But just as I regained my composure, Josy's voice cuts through the air once again. "You know," she sneered, "I hate that woman too. She always goes after taken men." My blood boils with anger as Josy made a twisted proposition. "I'll give you twenty bottles of beer if you go up there and do something crazy." The words shatter any sense of morality or self-control I had left that night.

I stormed over to their table with a murderous look in my eyes. The colour drained from their faces, leaving them as pale as death itself. With a primal growl, I slammed my hands down on the table and leant in close, spitting out my words between clenched teeth: "You fucking bastard, you will regret crossing me tonight!" In a fit of rage, I hoisted the table into the air with such force that they are both frozen in shock. I then thrust it towards them, shattering the champagne bottle and glasses on impact with the floor. They tumbled backwards in a desperate attempt to escape, but they were foolish to sit so closely together. I advanced on them like a wild animal, driving the table into their bodies until they collapsed onto the ground like two helpless prey. One of them pleaded for help, but Francesco just shook his head with knowing fear in his eyes and whispers, "No, she's insane. Let her do what she wants."

The adrenaline that had coursed through my veins faded, and in its absence, reality came crashing down on me. As a mother with obligations and responsibilities, I was horrified by what I had just done. The security team descended upon me, their voices raised in a furious argument over my reckless actions. But before things could escalate further, Josy stepped in, she was laughing as she called the guards off. She was the boss and had everything under her control. In a hushed tone, she leaned in close and whispered into my ear, her lips curving into a sinister smile, "Tomorrow, twenty bottles will arrive at your doorstep."

I stormed out of the place, a mix of devastation and satisfaction coursing through my veins. I walked with purpose, oblivious to anyone or anything around me. Suddenly, I collided with someone and look up to see a breathtakingly handsome man standing before me. He towered over me with his tall, athletic frame and perfect physique. His brown skin glinted in the moonlight and his black hair was styled in a way that exudes confidence. But it was his square jaw and dazzling smile that truly captivated me. "Careful, beauty," he said, catching me by the waist as I stumbled back from our collision. Heat radiated from his touch and I felt a surge of desire within me. I noticed Francesco leaving with the blonde woman on his arm. Our eyes met for a split second before he turned away and walked straight to his car without a word.

With a mischievous glint in his eye, this man named Fabio extended an invitation for me to come inside for a drink. I couldn't resist the temptation and accepted with a coy smile on my lips, knowing that revenge was within my reach. Josy, my friend, approached me with curious eyes and asked what was going on. I explained my plans of sweet retribution. She let out a low whistle and said "Wow, he is hot". My heart raced as Fabio led me inside. His scent enveloped me like a warm embrace - a mixture of musk and cologne that only added to his irresistible charm.

As we danced, I couldn't help but be drawn in by his masculine energy. The way his hips moved and pressed against mine ignited a fire within me. And when he whispered sweet nothings in my ear, it only ignited my desire. It was like magic, the way we moved together on the dance floor and the electric chemistry between us. As the night drew on, Fabio offered to take me home and we exchanged telephone numbers before parting ways.

The morning after, my phone rang twice. The first time I was greeted with Fabio's voice early in the morning, wishing me a good day and asking to see me that evening. I eagerly accepted, already looking forward to the evening ahead. But then Francesco's voice filled my ear, full of anger and accusation. He wasted no time in attacking me, yelling "You are not a respectful woman! We have not even separated yet and you were dancing with another man!" His words stung as he continued, "I heard you almost had sex with him on the dance floor, the way you were dancing was scandalous." I couldn't help but burst into laughter at his absurd accusations. "Don't be ridiculous," I retorted. "I didn't even know we had broken up. And don't forget, you showed up in public with that blonde woman!" His double standards enraged me further. He continued "Men can do whatever they want, but women can't? Don't confuse yourself. And last night your behaviour was vulgar and cheap." But his words frustrated me. "Fuck off!" I yelled before hanging up on him. He called back every ten minutes, but I ignored them and eventually pulled the phone cord out of the wall for some peace.

As the evening approached, my anticipation grew for my visit to my friend Josy's nightclub. The theme of the night was 'Cowboys and Cowgirls', a celebration of the arrival of Rodeo season. With excitement coursing through me, I took extra care in making myself presentable. My nails were meticulously polished and my outfit was carefully selected. My children were safely staying at my parents' house, where I had spent a joy-filled afternoon playing with them in the warm sunshine.

As the sun began to set, I turned my attention to the upcoming night out. I adorned myself in light blue faded jeans that hugged my curves perfectly, paired with a form-fitting white button-up shirt that accentuated my ample bosom. To complete the look, I donned a black cowboy hat and leather boots. My cowgirl belt, adorned with a large heart-shaped buckle, added just the right touch of flair to my ensemble.

My mind was solely focused on enjoying the night ahead; I didn't want to think about Francesco and the stress he had caused me. Fabio on the other hand was a temptation, that I could not wait to taste. As I held the warm hair curler in my hand and attended to my hair, I started to have dirty thoughts about the man I was going to meet.

Fabio had extended an invitation for dinner, but I had explained that I wouldn't be ready in time. In true gentlemanly fashion, he arrived at my doorstep at 9 pm to pick me up. We planned to stop at a bar first to grab some snacks and drinks before heading out. As we climbed into his sleek black pickup truck, Fabio couldn't help but comment on my appearance, saying "Wow, you look hot tonight!". I simply smiled and replied with a gracious "Thank you". But secretly, that was exactly what I had intended all along.

My heart swelled with joy and anticipation as I got to know him more deeply. Our conversation was filled with intellectual depth, each word dripping with intelligence and charm. He was the epitome of a true gentleman, dressed in tight blue Wrangler jeans that hugged his toned legs, paired with sleek black cowboy boots. His shirt, a stylish mix of blue and black stripes, complemented his rugged look perfectly. And atop his head sat a black cowboy hat, adding an extra touch of ruggedness to his alluring appearance.

But it wasn't just his looks that captivated me. As he spoke, I found myself only able to absorb half of what he was saying, completely enthralled by his incredible scent. It was drawing me even closer to him.

His voice was like music to my ears, smooth and velvety, making my mind wander to thoughts of passion and desire. And when I looked at his face, I couldn't help but feel drawn in by his handsome features. It was almost impossible to focus on anything else when he was around.

We sit outside the bar, we had barely settled into our seats, sipping on our second beer. When a deafening screech interrupts our conversation. The driver spun the wheels and did a doughnut in the road before suddenly slamming on the brakes in front of the bar, its tires leaving behind thick skid marks on the road. I can feel the driver's intense gaze fixed on us. My heart drops as I recognise those demon-like eyes, belonging to none other than Francesco, my estranged 'husband'. Francesco repeatedly revved the car engine, its roar filling the air.

Fabio, who had heard all about Francesco during our conversation the previous night, turns to me with a complete lack of concern for the strange circumstances we currently find ourselves in. "Is this him?" he asks. I nod silently, knowing that a storm is brewing. But Fabio's words surprise me "I hope he does not dare to cause me and you trouble tonight. I don't know if I told you but as you I am also a black belt but in Jujitsu. I am not afraid of him at all.". Fear was now replaced warm wave of vengeful emotion washing over me, and I couldn't help but feel a grin spread across my face.

We try our best to ignore Francesco, his predatory gaze fixed on us from the safety of his precious car. Fabio and I exchange a look and silently agree to leave for the night club. The moment we walked in, we were hit with the sounds of lively music and raucous laughter. The atmosphere was electric as a famous Country and Western band played on the stage, their music filling every corner of the room. We throw back drinks with abandon, laughing and dancing without inhibitions.

The nightclub club was packed to capacity with cowboys and cowgirls letting loose. Amidst the sea of people, I catch a fleeting glimpse of Francesco's face before it disappears into the crowd. But I don't let him dampen my spirits as Fabio and I continue to dance, bodies pressed together, hips swaying in time to the music. Our kisses are passionate and consuming as we lose ourselves in the moment.

And even when I became aware of Francesco standing alone, drinking and staring intently at us, I couldn't bring myself to stop dancing or pull away from Fabio's touch. Every move we made my sent my heightened senses excited and I couldn't deny the heat building between us.

The lively band began to play a popular tune that had everyone on the dance floor following a synchronised routine. The air was filled with pulsating beats and infectious energy as people moved in perfect rhythm. It was a mesmerising sight to behold. However, Fabio, not knowing the dance steps, suggested heading to the bar for more drinks. I turned to my friend Rogerio, who is openly gay, and we started dancing together. The nightclub was packed wall to wall with men from out of town, their colourful outfits adding to the vibrant atmosphere. The Rodeo event had become a huge attraction for cowboys from all over the country, and it was evident with the unfamiliar faces that filled the room.

A menacing presence approaches from behind, a towering cowboy with a sculpted physique and an air of cocky dominance. His breath tickles my neck as he growls "You're gonna be mine tonight." In a flash of fury, I slam my elbow into his ribs, screaming "Get the hell away from me, you crazy bastard!" Before Fabio can even react from across the bar, Francesco emerges from the shadows shouting "Hands off from her!" and charges at the giant cowboy with drunken determination. But it's no match - the cowboy easily evades his clumsy punch, he is too short. The cowboy retaliates with a devastating blow to Francesco's face. The cowboy stands over him, seething with rage and ready to strike again.

As Fabio swaggered into the ring, the tension between the cowboys close by reached a boiling point. Friends on both sides were now involved in the escalating fight. I beckoned the trouble-making cowboy, towards me with a curl of my finger, inviting him closer. He swaggered over, his arrogance oozing as he leaned in for a kiss, assuming I would be his conquest. Little did he know, my clenched fist was ready for action. Adorning each of my fingers were rings with sparkling jewels, giving my hand the intimidating look of a "knuckle duster." But with slyness and cunning, I placed one hand behind his head and pulled him towards me before delivering a powerful punch directly to his nose. The satisfying sound of bone crunching echoed through the air as he stumbled back, blood covering his face.

I shouted "Don't you dare mess with my husband again!" The man looked at me, confusion evident in his bloody face. It's no surprise he wouldn't recognise me as an unavailable woman; I had tossed my engagement ring into the bushes just the day before.

The tense atmosphere was shattered by the sudden intervention of burly security guards, who quickly stepped in between the two groups. We were all ushered outside to the street, where an extraordinary scene unfolded. The sound of the band could still be heard, playing to the empty dance floor inside. As the lights flickered on, the music came to an abrupt halt. It was like a wild west town, everyone frozen in anticipation of a gunfight. Francesco, Fabio, and troublesome cowboy were still at odds, their fight reignited and spiralling out of control. But instead of guns, fists were flying and more people dressed as cowboys began to join in on the melee.

Amidst the chaos, I found myself face-to-face with an angry cowboy, his fists clenched and ready for a fight. In a moment of desperation, I ripped off my belt with its large heart-shaped buckle and swung it wildly in his direction. But it wasn't just him I was fighting against - my kicks and punches landed on anyone within reach, friend or foe alike.

When my old friend Rafael came running towards me, I didn't even recognise him in the heat of the moment. My adrenaline was pumping and as I struck out at anyone who came near, I accidentally kicked him in the balls before continuing to defend myself with my belt.

The fight soon spread, drawing in more people from neighbouring establishments. Now it had escalated into a full-blown street brawl involving at least fifty people. Kicks, punches, and belts were being thrown from every direction. It was like a chaotic dance of violence.

The shrill wail of a police siren pierced through the air, jolting everyone to attention. The brawl momentarily froze, giving me a small window of opportunity to slip into the shadows and vanish. The darkness welcomed me, swallowing me whole as I made my escape. The flashing lights and blaring sirens grew fainter with every passing moment, until finally fading into the distant night. Relief washed over me as I became aware I had successfully evaded capture. Even though I should have been upset, I couldn't help but burst out laughing. The night that was supposed to end in wild sex had turned into the craziest fight the town had ever witnessed.

I later found out that Fabio, Francesco, and the rest of the group had been arrested. They were held in jail overnight and for the whole next day. Meanwhile, I was safe at home and enjoying a good night's sleep. "Ha Ha Ha," I thought to myself, reflecting on the absurdity of the situation.

Sadly, Josy banned me from the nightclub, I was truly sorry for the situation but right now I did not care. The whole town was gossiping about what had happened. Some people were furious with me and others were laughing themselves to death, everyone thought I was really fucking crazy. I decided to lay low for a while.

In the days following our encounter, Francesco's calls became incessant, his presence at my doorstep uninvited and unwelcome. He seemed to stalk me day and night, desperate for a chance to speak with me. After a week of this persistent behaviour, I finally allowed him to approach me. "I am ashamed of what happened between us," I told him, "and I cannot be seen with you in this town so soon." But he persisted, suggesting we meet somewhere unknown to avoid prying eyes. We settled on Uberaba City, a bustling metropolis where we could blend in and converse freely without fear of judgement or gossip.

We met on Saturday evening, he picked me up and left our town like criminals. In Uberaba, we decided to go to a Japanese restaurant so we could talk and there we talked and talked. He made one hundred thousand promises and asked me to marry him again. Then I say, yes I will give you a chance, the last chance but I will marry him. After three years of fighting to set myself free from the father of my first son, I have no stomach for marriage but alcohol has the better of me.

As soon as I whisper the word "yes," a charged energy fills the space between us. The familiar lust and desire for him surged within me, overpowering any previous reservations. We continue to relax and indulge in more drinks, allowing ourselves to fully let go of our inhibitions. As the night draws to an end, we find ourselves at a luxurious Brazilian motel, complete with lavish amenities with a Jacuzzi bathtub, it was adorned with mirrors on every surface including the ceiling. The oval-shaped bed beckons to us, inviting us to surrender to our desires. In Brazil, these motels are known as places for married men to indulge in their infidelities, but for us, it is simply a haven for a wild and drunken night of passion.

The following day, I was consumed with overwhelming shame. How had I allowed myself to be caught up in this situation? How could I have agreed to marry a man who had proven himself to be unfaithful? I told him it was over. As we discussed the details of our separation, he grew visibly angry and distraught, but eventually accepted my decision. The mere thought of being seen with him in public filled me with embarrassment and disgust. We reached a mutual understanding regarding the financial support for his son, Khan. However, he adamantly refused to provide any assistance with caring for Niklas.

As the weeks turned into months, it became increasingly evident that I was now solely responsible for the daily school runs and raising our children. Francesco's presence grew scarce and his help dwindled, leaving me to handle everything on my own. He no longer called to check on us nor even bothered to see our children. Realising I needed to provide for myself and our boys, I began tirelessly working on my resume in hopes of finding a job. Then, my compassionate and supportive sister Rebecca, who was now three months pregnant, saw the struggles I faced and offered a solution: "Rent out your house and come live with me in Planura. I'll train you to work here at my work before my child arrives, and you can rent a small house nearby." Her thoughtfulness brought tears to my eyes as I eagerly accepted her offer, grateful for the chance at a new beginning.

Filled with excitement, I moved closer to my sister. I am really thankful for this as my parents relocated 700km away to another state. Adjusting to this new job, I immersed myself in the world of selling and purchasing crops from plantations. My daily routine involved riding my sister's bicycle to work each day. However, amidst the newness and challenges, I found myself succumbing to anxiety and stress, which manifested in my increased appetite. The weight gain was noticeable, but it was a reminder that I was far away from the temptations of alcohol and trouble that once plagued me.

After five months in this calm life, I was starting to feel suffocated and full of panic for no apparent reason. One morning as I stepped out into the heat of the day, the sun seemed to mock me. Dutifully, I took my children to the bus station and waited anxiously for them to board before setting off on my daily bike ride to my sister's office. Sweat beads on my forehead as I struggle to pedal my bike through the humid November morning. But after only a mile suddenly, a wave of dizziness hits me and everything goes black. The next thing I know, I'm lying in the middle of the street, my body battered and bruised from the fall. Blood trickles down my forehead from a deep gash, and I can barely move as I drag myself and my damaged bike to the side of the road.

My head spins as I try to make sense of what just happened. I am fighting against the waves of nausea and weakness that threaten to engulf me. With every ounce of strength left in me, I eventually managed to remount my bike and continue to my sister's office. Rebecca is waiting for me with her arms crossed because I am late. Already eight months pregnant, she was swollen with my first nephew, her belly was now like a round ripe watermelon. "What happened to you?" she gasps, her eyes widening at the splashes of blood covering my clothes and face. As I try to brush it off, she insists on taking me to the hospital, despite my protests.

The public hospital was eerily empty, her round belly bounced as we rushed through the halls towards the reception. The nurse called my name urgently. In a small room where the nurse under the supervision of the doctor cleaned the cuts on my skin while and bombarded me with medical questions.

I recount what had happened as the doctor examines me with a grave expression. "Oh my god," he exclaims, his eyes darting between me and Rebecca. "Do you have a partner?"

Shocked by his directness, I stuttered out a response. "No, I am separated." But he continues with his questioning, delving into details about my personal life and sexual activity since my separation.

Fed up with this line of inquiry, I explode in anger. "What the hell is going on here? I have come here because I fell like a pumpkin in the street and you're grilling me about sex!" My sister looks horrified at my outburst, but even that pales in comparison to what the doctor says next. "I think you may be pregnant," he states matter-of-factly, before ordering an exam and promising results tomorrow. In total disbelief I said under my breath "What fucking madness is this?".

Chapter VIII

As the sun rose over the public hospital, I stood anxiously outside, I was the first in line. I was so scared and curious I couldn't even bring myself to take my boys to school that morning. Gripped by a sense of urgency, I quickly made my way to the reception desk and blurted out, "My name is Angelina and I'm here to get the results of a test." The receptionist handed me an envelope without hesitation.

With shaking hands tore it open and unfolded the letter inside. I had to sit down in the bustling reception area as I read its contents four times before it truly sunk in. The results were conclusive - I was five months pregnant. I was in disbelief, I had been bleeding normally and had a normal monthly cycle. Memories of the first difficult pregnancy flooded back, I could not believe I had brushed the signs off including my huge tits blaming it simply on my weight gain.

Panic and desperation rush over me as I frantically call my sister, begging her to come with her pickup truck. My body is shaking uncontrollably, sweat streaming down my face and fear gripping my heart like a vice. It's ridiculous that an eight-month pregnant woman has to come to pick me up and support me because I can no longer even ride a bicycle. But I have no other options.

When she arrives in just ten minutes, her worried face tells me she knows something is seriously wrong. I load my bicycle onto the truck and show her the results letter, bracing myself for her reaction. She says nothing at first, but her eyes scream "How could you do this to me, sister?".

Her next words confirm it: "Really, sister? You couldn't let me have one moment to shine in this life? You already have two beautiful children and I've been waiting for my time to be the centre of attention in our family. And now you've stolen it from me!" The anger and resentment in her voice is palpable, seeping into every word. She takes a deep breath before continuing, her tone dripping with venom: "And look at our babies, they will be practically twins. Of course, this had to happen to the spoiled youngest daughter. You did this on purpose!" My fury rises inside me as I respond through gritted teeth: "What?! Are you serious, bitch? I'm completely fucked - two kids, no degree, no job, and now pregnant again. So yeah, congratulations, you can have this baby. You can have twins!". The tears started to fall uncontrollably from my eyes, overwhelmed by it all. I was truly fucked, I could no longer work ...now pregnant again. It was all too much for me and I crumbled into a dramatic heap on the ground.

Rebecca, the love of my life, is usually so gentle and tender, but in this moment she is like a ticking time bomb ready to explode. She clutches at her swollen belly, ready to give birth any day now. Despite her own turmoil, she comes to me with a soft touch and wipes away my tears as she whispers, "Oh dear sister, it will be okay. We will find a way."

I am just a shuddering teenager in this dire situation. My mind races with thoughts of how to break the news to that bastard who impregnated me. "How am I supposed to do this?" I blurt out, then quickly backtrack, "Not that it's bad news or anything". But my sister sees through my facade and responds firmly, "I'll call him today. He'll know everything." She continues, "We need to know the baby's gender. And you have less than four months to get your shit together". She then asks gently, "What do you want to do?". Without hesitation, I reply, "I want a bottle of Cachaça. I know I can't drink but I just want to get drunk!". My desperation is palpable as I cling to any escape from this overwhelming situation. Then she laid out our plan for the day: we did not go to work, instead, we would head straight to the gynaecologist and then have an ultrasound.

The cool, sterile air of the gynaecologist's office did little to ease my discomfort as I lay on the examination table, legs spread in stirrups. The probing fingers and instruments had thoroughly examined my most intimate parts, leaving me feeling exposed and invaded. A vaccine was then administered - a requirement for pregnant women like myself. I was left with a sharp pain that throbbed in my left arm.

Then I was led to the ultrasound room, nerves knotted in my stomach. Laying down on the bed, I shivered as the doctor applied a cold gel over my swollen belly. The room was dimly lit, but the bright screen of the ultrasound machine illuminated our faces with an eerie glow. With gentle movements, the doctor pressed a sensor against my skin, sliding it across my stomach in search of the elusive image. And then, in a moment that felt suspended in time, he pulled back slightly and announced with a smile, "It's a girl." Tears sprang to my eyes, despite all my fears and doubts about raising a daughter in this world. All I could feel was overwhelming joy and love for the little life growing inside of me.

The night before, I had a dream. A baby girl appeared as a vision of perfection - a breathtaking beauty with piercing green eyes and a perfect nose. She spoke to me and revealed her innermost desire: to simply be loved. The reality set in now as I saw my daughter's image on the screen, I was overwhelmed with tears of guilt. Asking for forgiveness, I knew raising three children wouldn't be easy but I whispered a promise and told her "You are already loved by me.". My heart ached to hold her in my arms, to see her tiny little face, and to shower her with all the love she deserved.

With renewed determination, I mustered the courage to dial Francesco's number. I knew I needed to have this conversation, it was unfair to keep my sister in the middle any longer. Following a difficult discussion, he eventually conceded to meet with me in person. He would be arriving in my city this very afternoon, and I couldn't help but feel apprehension at the thought of seeing him again.

The meeting was held at my sister's house, where I knew I would have the support and protection of Rebecca. As I poured out my heart to Francesco, he listened intently and calmly, surprising me with his understanding and willingness to honour the situation. Yet as he spoke, there was a noticeable shift in his behaviour. It felt as though he was simply going through the motions, fulfilling his duty without true emotion or conviction. He insisted that I move back in with him, but his words lacked the warmth and sincerity I had once known. In the end, I accepted his offer because I could not face this alone.

Unable to continue working, I was forced to take a break as my body began to bleed and demand rest. My sister kindly released me from her employment and I returned to Campo Florido, seeking refuge in Francesco's modest studio. Sadly, due to the distance and their schooling, I had to leave my children with my sister. The pain of separation was unbearable, tearing my heart apart with every passing moment. My time with them was limited to mere weekends, a cruel reminder of the void that consumed me during the week. Each goodbye felt like another stab in my already broken heart.

This pregnancy was not like the others, I was now weak and struggling to keep up with daily chores. I managed to clean the apartment but was forced to hire help for washing clothes as I was too ill to do it myself. As my pregnancy progressed, I sank deeper into a state of depression.

As the days passed, Francesco's treatment of me grew increasingly cold and cruel. Though I had no concrete evidence, I could feel that he was betraying me with other women. We had become estranged, our intimacy nonexistent, and I found myself retreating to sleep more frequently in an attempt to escape the harsh reality of our relationship. The toll of pregnancy showed on my physical appearance as well, as I gained an extraordinary amount of weight - 35 kilos in total. And due to the hormonal changes, dark brown marks covered my face like a mask. Francesco's words only added to my misery as he callously remarked "You're so fat and ugly...you look like a cow. What has happened to you? You are nothing like you were pregnant with Khan." As I lay there on the bed, devastated and in tears, I felt completely helpless and the sadness consumed me.

I had meticulously planned the birth, booking a Cesarean for 8 am sharp. When Nektar arrived, my heart swelled with love and pride at the sight of her perfect little face, even more beautiful than I could have ever dreamed. But my joy quickly turned to panic when it became clear that all the carefully chosen clothes I had brought for her were too small - she was the size of a one-month-old baby. In a frenzy, Francesco sped off seventy kilometres to retrieve clothes from home that would fit our precious daughter. She spent her first three hours of life completely naked, exposed, and vulnerable in this harsh world.

As I was wheeled out of the bustling maternity ward, my arms cradling newborn Nektar, I couldn't help but feel overwhelmed by the opulence surrounding me. Francesco's increased income had afforded me a private suite in the hospital, complete with a spacious room that seemed almost too grand for its purpose. The gleaming kitchenette in one corner and a pristine bathroom in another only added to the opulence of it all. But despite the lavish surroundings, my heart remained cold. I knew that Francesco's guilt and lack of connection to our daughter were the reasons behind this extravagant gesture. As much as I tried to appreciate it, I couldn't shake off the emptiness that filled me.

My heart was filled with the happy chatter and laughter of my family as they gathered to meet my newest addition. My parents beamed proudly, my sister holding little nephew Anthony who was only three months old, she stood proudly by her husband. While my two boys, Khan and Niklas, stood in awe of their new sister. Their eyes shone with curiosity and wonder as they reached out to touch her tiny fingers and toes. It was a beautiful sight to behold, and my heart swelled with joy at the way my sons embraced their new family member. I reached for my camera, capturing the precious first meeting between siblings, a photograph that would forever hold a place in my memories.

As the days passed by, Francesco couldn't hold back his excitement any longer. "I have been given a promotion and we are going to move to Conceicao das Alagoas," he announced to me with a gleam in his eye. The boys would need to adjust once again, another change and another new school to attend. But Francesco was resolute in his decision, determined to provide a better life for our family. Two weeks later, we found ourselves in the unfamiliar city of Conceicao das Alagoas. We rented a small house for the time being, but Francesco was already in negotiations to purchase a larger home for all of us. It was a big step for our family, but we were all eager for this new chapter in our lives together.

As soon as we settled into our new home, Francesco's behaviour began to change. He would come home late at night, claiming he was working, but I could smell the alcohol and perfume on his clothes. His phone became his constant companion, always ringing with unknown numbers that he refused to answer in my presence. One day, my godchild called me with a grave message: "Godmother, I have to tell you something. Francesco is not just betraying you with one woman but with many. He's been lying to you and it's not fair." She spoke of his lies and deceit, how he had clipped my wings and left me vulnerable. How could he do this to me? We had just moved into our dream house, surrounded by luxury and potential for a growing family. But now I saw it for what it truly was: a trap that Francesco had used to manipulate and control me. The furniture, the grandiose rooms, they were all just tools in his game of deceit. And I had fallen for it like a naive fool.

The moment Francesco walked through the door after working late again, I could see the guilt etched on his face. I confronted him with the evidence of his infidelity; names of other women, places he had been, it was all too obvious. He feigned innocence but when he looked me in the eye and said "I am not cheating on you?", I knew the truth. His face, once so familiar to me, was now a mask of deception. And with all the strength I could muster, I replied "I've had enough. I'm leaving." He cried and pleaded with me to stay, making promises and insisting "You're imagining things."

But I knew better, I could feel it in my bones. Calmly I replied "Why are you doing this to me? You humiliate and disrespect the good woman you have. You betrayed me!" And without hesitation, I declared "No more. Tomorrow, I'll be taking the car and leaving with the children." His response was a desperate scream of disbelief: "You're crazy! You can't drive 8 hours to your parent's house with the kids. You don't even have a driving license!" But his attempts to manipulate me fell on deaf ears. Firmly, I stated "Watch me. Staying would be madness." With that, I went upstairs to our bedroom, i closed the door behind me and stood in silence for a moment. Tears didn't come - they had long since dried up from years of heartache and disappointment.

As I loaded the car, a heavy lump formed in my throat and tears threatened to spill down my cheeks. But I held them back, not wanting the bastard to see me cry. The children were already crying, Niklas clutching Nektar in the back seat, while Khan refused to even get in the car and clung to his father's leg. His tearful pleas for us to stay echoed in my mind as we pulled away. "You're making a big mistake," were Francesco's last words. And I couldn't help but wonder if he was right. As we drove off, leaving everything behind, I couldn't shake off the feeling of insecurity that gnawed at me. What if something happened on our journey with three little children in the car? Would I even know how to change a tire?

Francesco had given me just enough money for the petrol and food, but it was barely enough to cover the expenses of the journey. He had promised to discuss splitting up our belongings later, but deep down I knew he still held onto hope that I would come back to him. As I drove 200 meters away from our old life, I couldn't hold back the tears any longer and let them flow freely down my face. My heart felt heavy and uncertain as I embarked on this new chapter alone with my children.

The trip to my parents' new house in Goias State with the children was a gruelling experience, filled with countless breaks to change Nektar's dirty diaper and feed the insatiable boys. As a single mother, driving on the hazardous roads by myself was both physically and mentally exhausting. We eventually arrived at my parents' house, located in an urban area of Goias State and not too far from the farm where my father still worked.

The direness of the situation was evident in the furrowed brows and worried looks on my parent's faces as I stood on their doorstep, three small children clinging to my sides. At twenty-seven years old, I found myself without a job and as a single mother of three children. Standing on their doorstep, I could do nothing but plead for assistance.

The gravity of the situation weighed heavily on us. The children's tear-streaked faces begged to return home and see their father. But with no money, we were stuck in this terrible predicament. Upon my arrival, I discovered the harsh reality that both of my parents were gravely sick. Yet, despite his weakened state, my father still rose at 5 am every morning to tend to the cows, earning only poor wages. The only sustenance they could afford was plain rice, beans, and eggs - there was barely enough food to feed the additional four mouths now residing with them. My attempts to secure a job and assist my parents with support had been in vain. The unemployment rate was high and opportunities were few and far between in this area.

Their small home only had one bedroom, so my children and I had to make do with sleeping on the hard living room floor.

The four of us squeezed onto a worn-out, uncomfortable mattress. It didn't bother me too much until one morning when I woke up to find slimy snail trails all over the children. Not only were we cramped and uncomfortable, but the location itself was fraught with danger - a poverty-stricken area rife with crime. I knew we couldn't continue living like this; it disgusted me and forced me to set aside my pride. I needed Francesco.

Every call I made from one state to another came at a steep cost, but I felt desperate enough to try and call him anyway. Many times, I called Francesco for help, but he always ended the call abruptly or did not answer. However, after a month of constant trying, he finally answered one evening. With my pride swallowed and desperation in my voice, I begged him to let us come back. In the background, I could hear the lively sounds of music and laughter, indicating that he was at a party. I knew it would be difficult for him to hear me over the noise, but I continued pleading "Please, we have nowhere else to go". To my dismay, he responded coldly "No, I do not want you to come back. I am living my own life now". In that moment, it felt as if the ground beneath me had opened up and swallowed me whole. Gathering all the courage I could muster, I managed to reply "Okay. Then I will sell the car. It's worth 22,000 Reais according to my father". There was a brief pause before he spoke again "No way. I won't allow it. I'll come see you tomorrow". With a glimmer of hope, I ended the call, thinking maybe we could resolve this face-to-face.

The following day, Francesco arrived at my parents' house on foot, his steps measured and deliberate. I wondered if someone had given him a lift here, but I didn't dare ask. As we met outside, I could feel my mother's watchful eyes from the kitchen window. Francesco's body language was cold and distant, his words rehearsed like a script. "Angelina, I will not let you sell my car," he said firmly. "I don't care what your father says it's worth. I will give you 11,000 Reais and I am leaving with my car." His tone was unwavering as he continued, "I am an honourable man and I want to take care of our family. I've had a lawyer draw up this document stating that after 9 years, the mortgage on my house will be paid off and I am leaving it to Niklas, Khan, and Nektar." My mind reeled as I listened in stunned silence, he produced the legal paper from his pocket and said, "All you need to do is sign this."

Although we had lived together for eleven years as partners, we had never officially married. My options were limited and I reluctantly signed the document. To my surprise, Francesco didn't ask to see our children or even say goodbye to them.

Instead, he handed me an envelope containing the agreed-upon amount and asked for the keys to his car. With a simple "Goodbye, Angelina," he got into his car and drove away, leaving me standing there feeling numb and alone.

He must have been laughing maniacally as he drove away, leaving me in a state of shock and betrayal. The next day, with my parents' guidance, I took the document to a highly respected lawyer in town. As I recounted the story, his expression changed from disbelief to horrified understanding. With sadness in his eyes, he broke the news to me: "The document is a forgery." My world crumbled around me as I collapsed in tears, while I struggled to comprehend the depth of this deceit. How could that conniving bastard do this to me? Now I had no car and only a small amount of money left to survive on, all thanks to his treachery. The rage and heartache consumed me until there was nothing left but an empty shell of the person I once was.

My mind raced in a frantic search for a solution, desperate to escape the suffocating grasp of this small town with its limited opportunities. Rumours had spread of a new land, Portugal, where work was abundant and success was within reach. Tales of a better life echoed through the streets, enticing me with promises of prosperity and endless possibilities. My family cautioned me, warning that it was a risky move to leave everything behind. But with few options to support my family and a man who had abandoned me, I made the difficult decision to leave. It tore at my heart to leave my children behind, but I knew it was the only way I could provide for them. I promised myself it would only be temporary until I could establish a stable income and bring them to join me. My parents were struggling under the financial burden of supporting us all, and I couldn't bear to see them suffer any longer. The idea of being apart from my children was unbearable, but I couldn't see any alternative.

Although I didn't even have a passport, I was determined to gather all the necessary information for travelling to Portugal. The end of October had arrived and with it, I planned to leave before Christmas. If I waited any longer, I knew I wouldn't have the strength to go through with it. Tearfully, I informed my sons and parents that my decision to leave was final. Nektar was not yet even one year old and too small to understand. My behavior changed as I prepared to depart; instead of being a loving and gentle mother, I became distant and quick-tempered, trying to make it easier for them when I eventually left. It pained me every time I lashed out at my children, but it was the only way.

I was now determined to leave and start a new life in Portugal. I had already taken care of getting my passport, but

I needed someone to accompany me on the journey. A close friend from my family Silvana, shared the same dream of going to Portugal, and she offered to help me navigate through the bureaucratic process. Being inexperienced, I didn't even have a bank account. Francesco had handled all of our finances before, but now I used some of the money from selling our car to buy the tickets for us both, Silvana hadn't saved enough for this expense. She had already done extensive research on Portugal, making her the perfect partner for this adventure and she had promised to pay me back. Silvana was leaving behind her husband and three teenage daughters behind but she was determined to join me.

As the final day in Brazil loomed, dark storm clouds rolled in, casting a gloomy shadow over the already difficult and heartbreaking atmosphere. My heart felt like it was being torn apart every day, but on this morning, the pain was immense. Tears poured down my face as I looked into the tear-stained faces of my parents, my children, and a few close friends who came to bid me farewell. Their eyes held a mournful gaze as if they were attending my funeral. I hugged and kissed each of them goodbye, trying to hold back sobs that threatened to consume me whole. A family friend arrived to drive me to the bus station, where I would then head to the capital and onward to the airport. I had begged my father not to come with us, knowing that his emotional state would only intensify the suffering.

As we drove towards the bus station, I couldn't hold back the gut-wrenching sobs that escaped my throat. I clutched a few photographs tightly in my hands, my nails started to dig into my skin. They were from our family lunch the day before, each glance I made brought a tidal wave of emotions crashing over me. My children's faces stared back at me through the tears, their innocent smiles only adding to my pain and regret. I barely noticed my kind friend driving, his attempts to comfort me lost in my own misery. His tear-stained face mirrored my own as we both silently acknowledged the horror of the moment.

The relentless rain pounded against the windshield as we drove, our destination the bus station was in sight. As we waited at a bustling junction, surrounded by honking cars and flashing lights. Suddenly, a white Fiat Uno appeared out of nowhere, screeching to a halt in front of our car. We were trapped, unable to move as the white car blocked our path. Through my blurred vision from tears, I could see my father's face in the driver's seat. The windows were rolled down, revealing the anguished expression on his face. In his arms, he held my son Khan up to the window, his tears mixing with the raindrops. In the backseat, my oldest son Nicklas cradled my daughter Nektar in his arms, both children holding up their tear-streaked faces for all to see.

The hard, cold rain beat down on my body as I stepped out of the car to face them. My hair was soaked and clinging to my face, and my clothes quickly became drenched in the downpour. I stood before them, feeling small and vulnerable against the elements. They sat in the car, dry and protected, as I faced them in the open air. My father's eyes were filled with anguish and tears as he looked at me. "Father, what are you doing here?" I asked, my voice shaking with emotion. He spoke through sobs, "I couldn't let you go without seeing you one last time. I don't know if we'll ever see you again." I stood there, tears mixing with the rain on my face, as I looked at each of my children and then back to my father in the car. I spoke with a trembling voice, "I ask for your forgiveness. I have failed you all. But please understand that I am doing this for everyone, for a better life. I love you all so much." My words were carried away by the wind and rain, but I knew they had heard me. And as I turned to leave, I promised myself that I would not allow myself to fail again.

With a heavy heart, I climbed back into the car and we drove towards the bus station. Glancing through the rear window, I saw my father's car motionless, they were watching us drive away. Tears streamed down my cheeks, mixing with the raindrops that had soaked me to the bone.

Silvana and I met at the bustling bus station, surrounded by the sounds of engines and people rushing. My tears continued to flow as we boarded the bus that would take us to the airport. In a trance-like state, I followed Silvana like a devoted puppy through the entire process of check-in, passport control, and eventually to our gate. The other travellers in the airport were mere ghosts, their bodies passing me by unnoticed. We were headed to Sao Paulo's international airport and this was my first time on a plane. Despite having some experience with travelling, Silvana seemed just as lost as I was in this unfamiliar environment. The connecting flight passed in what felt like mere minutes, and before we knew it, we were thrust into the bustling international airport, surrounded by people rushing to get to their destinations. The noise level was overwhelming.

We had arrived at this giant airport far too early for our international flight to Portugal. The busy terminal was filled with people from all corners of the world, each speaking a different language and wearing a diverse array of clothing. As we made our way through the crowd, I couldn't help but feel overwhelmed by the screens of information displaying symbols and numbers. Other passengers stood mesmerised, their eyes glued to the screens as they waited for some sort of signal or announcement. And then some inexplicably announced to no one in particular, "The gates aren't open yet." I was now lost in a chaotic and unfamiliar world.

We began to walk aimlessly through the terminal, feeling disorientated and out of place. Eventually, we joined a long line to board the plane after waiting for what felt like an eternity, I heard snippets of conversation in Italian. Suddenly I realised - we were in the wrong line. It seemed almost comical that in Brazil we have a saying that goes 'Who has mouth goes to Rome', meaning if you have the words to ask questions, you leave your ignorance behind and obtain knowledge and with this, you will can go far. And here I was, without even speaking and in total ignorance, heading to Rome.

My mind snapped out of its trance and I quickly turned to Silvana, my travel companion. "We're in the wrong line," I exclaimed urgently, adrenaline coursing through my veins. "We have to find the right one." Silvana nodded, her eyes wide with determination.

I took control of the situation and began scanning the screens for our flight to Lisbon. Amidst the sea of travellers, I blended in like a chameleon. But inside, I felt like a fool for not paying closer attention. It didn't matter now - all that mattered was finding the correct gate before it was too late.

A fellow passenger noticed our panic and directed us towards the correct direction. We wasted no time and sprinted for what felt like a mile until we finally arrived at our destination. As we caught sight of our gate, a wave of relief washed over us. Our decision to arrive at the airport early had paid off. The final boarding call echoed through the bustling airport as we made our way towards the gate.

The line of passengers slowly dwindled until we were one of the last to board the plane, our feet shuffling against the carpeted floor. The hum of chatter and excitement filled the air as we stepped onto the jet bridge and made our way onto the plane. Inside, the soft glow of overhead lights illuminated rows of seats, each with a small TV screen and an adjustable headrest. The cabin crew welcomed us with warm smiles and directed us to our designated seats, already occupied by pillows and blankets in preparation for the long flight ahead. As we settled in, the roar of engines signalled our imminent departure, and I felt a sense of anticipation mixed with a tinge of nervousness for the journey ahead.

As the plane soared through the sky, I must confess, I wasn't the most desirable travel companion. My hair was a mess from the rain, and my eyes were swollen and red from crying; even a cartoon character would have seemed more put together than me.

My thoughts inevitably turned to home. I reached for the worn photographs tucked into my bag and gazed at them longingly. As I came upon the one taken on my daughter's first day of life, her tiny form cradled gently in the arms of my sons, a wave of emotion crashed over me. Tears welled up in my eyes and broke free, cascading down my cheeks in uncontrollable sobs. Surrounded by concerned onlookers, I could feel their worried stares boring into my skin as I tried to hide the torment building inside of me. My whole body shook with a mixture of agony and despair, my heart pounding in my chest like a caged animal. I couldn't help but revel in the sheer misery that consumed me, making my existence feel like a never-ending medical emergency.

After what seemed like hours of crying, I finally surrendered to the exhaustion that had been building inside me. My tear-stained eyes drooped heavily and my body slumped into the cramped airplane seat. The low hum of the engines provided a steady background noise, the gentle rumble was like a soothing lullaby, easing all tension from my body and mind. Before I knew it, I was lost in a peaceful slumber, carried away by the steady rhythm of the plane's engines.

Chapter IX

My arrival at Lisbon International Airport was met with chaos and a sense of disorientation. The endless lines of people, all eager to pass through passport control, seemed to stretch for miles. Among the crowd were travellers from Brazil and various African countries, united by only the language of Portuguese. A shared dream of a better, more prosperous life united all the people gathered here. For me, as a first-time visitor to Europe, it was an overwhelming experience. My mind was consumed with insecurities, fear, and sadness due to my current situation. Despite the bustling energy around me, I couldn't shake off the feeling of being lost in an unfamiliar place.

We took a taxi to the city centre, Silvana had an old childhood friend, she said he would be waiting for us in the city and that he had grown up alongside her. But now he resided in the most sought-after area - Marques De Pombal Street. This bustling street was known as the heart of Lisbon, with its grand architecture, lively markets, and charming cafés.

We continued to the address written on a piece of paper Silvana had treasured from Brazil. Silvana's friend had promised us a room to stay here, the air was filled with the rich scent of history and culture and I could already feel the excitement building within me. As I imagined exploring this vibrant city from our home base on Marques De Pombal Street.

We exited the taxi and to my surprise we stood outside a rundown building with peeling paint and crumbling walls, which Silvana assured me was the correct address. Outside the building was a tall, dark-skinned man - this was her friend who was waiting for us, J.Junior greeted us kindly. A few minutes later, Mr Manuel, the owner of the building, arrived. He had a round belly and a bald head with sparse patches of hair clinging on for dear life. A thick moustache perched above his thin lips, and he wore grey trousers and a dirty white shirt that seemed to blend into his unkempt appearance. He spoke rapidly in Portuguese, but I struggled to understand even a single word. It dawned on me then that the Portuguese spoken here was different from what I was used to in Brazil - it was almost like an entirely different language. I politely asked him to repeat himself, but his immediate reaction was one of fury as he shouted, "Oh pa. Are you a donkey? You make fun in my face?".

He then informed us that there was only one room available and it would be 350 euros per month, and we would have to share it. The amount seemed steep for such a run-down place in 2004. Then he added, "We have rules here - you will be living with Romanians, Yugoslavians, Africans, and other Brazilians. This building has ten floors and no elevator." His rules caught me off guard as he sternly warned us not to use too much water when showering because Brazilians are weird and known for excessive bathing habits. He mandated that we limit ourselves to a five-minute shower and only one shower per day. In fact, he made it clear that one shower per week was enough. I looked at my friend Silvana with questioning eyes that asked, "Is this for real?" and with an embarrassed yellow smile, I could tell she was thinking the same as me.

As we climbed up the stairs to the eighth floor, the darkness engulfed us and I could feel unease within me. The steps were exposed wood, worn down by years of use, and creaked loudly under our weight. To my disbelief, a trail of mice scurried behind us as we ascended the staircase. The burden of my heavy thirty-two-kilo bag made each step feel like a struggle, as the narrow stairs seemed to wrap around the walls in an endless spiral.

Finally reaching our floor, we stepped into our almost abandoned apartment with faded magenta walls that were peeling due to their age. The small kitchen was barely functional, with outdated cupboards, a sink with a tap that dripped constantly, and a tiny fridge that we had to share. The freestanding old cooker looked like it belonged in a museum rather than in a place of residence. The apartment was suffocating.

It consisted of four cramped sleeping rooms and a shared bathroom. We were forced to share one bedroom as the other three bedrooms were occupied by a Ukrainian woman, a Romanian man, and the other shared by a Brazilian brother and sister. There was no common area or living room to relax in.

The bathroom was a nightmare. The bathtub was stained brown with dirt and age, and despite hours of cleaning with strong products, it still looked ancient and uninviting. The shower hung above it, but I refused to use it without wearing flip-flops for fear of catching some sort of disease. This place was truly disgusting and almost unbearable to live in.

While Silvana rested and slept, I ventured out into the city in search of a place to arrange a money transfer. I had brought 2,000 euros with me to enter Portugal, the minimum amount required by immigration for my supposed 15-day holiday, of course, I had lied. My plan was to keep 1,000 euros for myself and send the other 1,000 back to my family in Brazil. I had already left enough money for them to cover one month's expenses at the local supermarket and pharmacy back home, but I couldn't help but worry about their well-being. I wanted to send them as much money as possible so they could survive while I searched for a job over the next few months.

At the transfer exchange store, I carefully counted out the bills and arranged for the money to be sent to my family back home. The store was small and cramped, with shelves lined with various items for sale. In one corner sat a pay-as-you-go telephone, its keypad worn from frequent use. With a sigh, I purchased five euros worth of credit on a card for the phone, along with another for my travelling companion Silvana. She seemed indifferent towards her own family and rarely mentioned them, which struck me as odd.

I inserted the card into the phone and quickly dialled my family's number. The sound of beeping echoed in my ear as the credits began to drain rapidly. In a rush, I spoke my rehearsed words: "I am doing well and will start looking for a job on Monday. I am full of hope."

As the call ended abruptly due to lack of credits, I couldn't shake off the feeling that my words were empty promises to myself. Despite my best efforts, I couldn't convince myself that I truly was hopeful for my future.

As I walked through the bustling streets of the city, my mind was consumed with one thought: I needed to find a job. My eyes darted around, taking in the sights and sounds of this strange place. The colourful buildings with their unique architecture, the street vendors selling their wares, and the busy crowds all added to the electric energy of the city. I couldn't help but wonder which doors I could knock on to ask for an opportunity to work.

After walking for what seemed like hours, taking in the sights and sounds of this new place, I returned to my rundown room for some much-needed rest. But even as I drifted off to sleep, I couldn't shake the determination to make something of myself in this city.

The next day dawned bright and promising, and I wasted no time trying to be productive. "I'm heading to a butcher's shop," I told Silvana, eager to prove myself. "The Brazilian man living here said where they have the cheapest meat." She nodded knowingly. "We'll have to go about 6 miles away." Without hesitation, she added, "But don't worry, I know just the place."

In an effort to save money, we decided to walk rather than take a taxi. After hours of walking through the city, my skin prickled with the chill of the December air. It was a stark contrast to the warm climate I was used to in Brazil. But the coolness provided some relief from the long walk we had just taken. We finally arrived at the butcher shop, our mouths watering at the sight and smell of all the different cuts of meat. As Brazilians, we have a deep love for meat and we didn't hesitate to buy kilos of it. Our stomachs were grumbling with hunger after a full day of not eating, so we made a much-needed stop at a little cafe. The aroma of freshly brewed coffee filled the air as we ordered hot cappuccinos and indulged in a delicious mozzarella and tomato sandwich. Although grateful for this quick refuelling, we were both looking forward to returning home and preparing a proper meal - after all, a simple sandwich is just a snack to us Brazilians.

As we stood up to leave the quaint cafe, our eyes were met by a group of Portuguese men gathered across the street. Their stares were leering and they pointed to us, their voices loud as they shouted, "Look, more Brazilian prostitutes!" Their raucous laughter and playful shoves towards each other made it clear that this was normal behaviour for them. Their words hit us like a powerful blow, leaving us feeling deeply uncomfortable and insulted. The disgust in our hearts grew with every step the men took away from us, their vulgar comments staining the air around them. How could anyone think this type of behaviour was acceptable in public? It left us feeling worthless and disheartened by the lack of respect shown by these men.

After making a quick stop at the bustling supermarket, we made our way back to the apartment. The sun was high in the sky, casting long shadows on the pavement as we walked. As hunger gnawed at us, we set to work preparing our dinner in the claustrophobic apartment we were staying in. During our cooking, we were greeted by an unexpected visitor - the Brazilian man who was also staying in the apartment. His sister and he shared one of the other rooms, however, we had not yet met his sister. She worked nights and slept during the day, while he worked.

Silvana immediately struck up a conversation with him, her playful flirting causing him to laugh and open up to us. As they chatted, she couldn't help but vent about the terrible behaviour we had encountered during our time here. To our surprise, he simply shrugged and replied, "This is normal here." With a wry chuckle, he added, "Especially when it comes to how they treat Brazilian women." This comment piqued our interest and we eagerly asked for more insight into the cultural dynamics at play. He chuckled again before giving us a warning: "If you think Brazilian men are chauvinistic, you haven't truly experienced Portuguese men yet!"

With smiles and gentle gestures, we extended our hospitality to the man to be polite. We ate stood up kitchen and shared a simple meal together, exchanging stories and laughter. As the night wore on, I felt my eyelids growing heavy and excused myself to retire for the evening to pray and sleep. But before leaving, I whispered to Silvana, who remained with our guest, "Please try not to disturb me when you return, and do be mindful of the light."

The next morning, I woke up early with determination in my heart. Silvana chose to stay in bed, but I couldn't let her reluctance deter me from finding work. As I made my way out the door at 7 am, the city was already bustling with activity. I wandered through the streets, stopping at every open establishment in search of employment. But by midday, as the shops began to close for their afternoon break, I had only received negative responses. Frustrated and disheartened, I continued my search, trying cafes, bars, and shops - asking for any type of job available. Kitchen work, cleaning duties, anything to make some money. With no luck and my energy fading, I returned to our apartment feeling defeated.

But Silvana was awake and had prepared a meal for us to share. As we ate, I recounted my fruitless attempts to secure a job. We decided together that it was time to widen our search, even if it meant travelling further away from home. With tickets for the tram in hand, we set off in the afternoon with no specific destination in mind, determined to find some form of employment.

Each day, we fell into the same monotonous routine, repeating our actions for fifteen long days. There was no work to be found, and my hard-earned money seemed to slip through my fingers like grains of sand. Silvana, my companion, had no money of her own, leaving me to endure the burden of providing for us both. This financial strain was becoming increasingly difficult, a weight that I could not afford to carry. If it were only me alone in this struggle, perhaps I could have persevered longer. But with Silvana relying on me, I felt an immense sense of responsibility weighing down on my shoulders, making each passing day feel like a battle for survival.

Silvana had only recently left her husband behind, but that did not stop her from starting a relationship with the Brazilian man who shared their apartment. I couldn't understand or agree with her actions - after all, her husband was handsome, fit, and had a steady job. In contrast, this Brazilian man was small in stature, with a scarred face that gave him a dangerous air. His missing teeth only added to his rough appearance, and it was clear that there was no future for Silvana with him. But as much as I disapproved, I had to respect her choices and remember that I was also there for my own personal reasons - to find a job.

It became evident that Silvana saw me merely as a source of financial support and was only interested in having fun. As I watched her indulging in this reckless affair, I couldn't help but feel resentment and gradually became more selfish in my thoughts and actions towards the situation. Finally, it had become clear she was just a fucking lazy, opportunistic bitch.

She even stopped staying in our shared room, she had almost entirely moved in with the Brazilian man. But one Sunday morning, as I was making coffee in the kitchen, the Brazilian man's sister Eliza caught me off guard with her words. "What's going on Angelina?" she questioned. "You two came together and now you barely speak." I could feel the anger boiling up inside of me as I explained the painful truth. "I'm about to kick her out of my room," Eliza spat with venom. "She's always leaving her clothes everywhere and my brother only cares about one thing - pussy." My cheeks burned with embarrassment as I revealed that while she was at work at night, the apartment was full of their animal-like fucking noises, and then Silvana would try to sneak back into my room once the sun rose. I recounted I had had enough and I had started locking my door at night. "I'm disgusted by her,"

I confessed, raising my voice in frustration. "And this morning, when she kept knocking on my door, I threatened to punch her in the eye and break her neck if she didn't leave me alone." It all clicked into place, the pieces falling together like a perfectly solved puzzle. Eliza had discovered Silvana sprawled out in the hallway, devoid of any sense of self-worth. And that was the only reason why she was standing here and talking with me.

The early morning sun shone down on the bustling city street as I ventured out once again in search of a job. As I turned the corner, my eyes caught sight of a colourful Chinese shop. A sense of hope and determination filled me as I thought, "Why not?" Making my way inside, I asked to speak with the owner who emerged from a back room. He had all the appearances of a typical Chinese man, his features reflecting years of hard work and dedication. With a friendly smile, I greeted him and explained that I was searching for an opportunity. His first question was whether or not I had any documents, to which I replied that I did not but I was working on obtaining them. To my surprise, he simply shrugged and said, "You start tomorrow, be here at 7 am." My heart swelled with joy and disbelief as I thanked him profusely. Without wasting a moment, I rushed to buy a phone card and called my family to share the good news -

after weeks of struggling, I had finally landed a job! It felt like a Christmas present come early, bringing with it the promise of stability and success.

The following morning I arrived at work promptly at 7 am, eager to tackle the day ahead. However, as soon as my boss began speaking, I knew it would be a challenging one. His thick dialect was even more difficult to understand than that of the Portuguese people I had encountered before. Despite my best efforts, I struggled to grasp his instructions and found myself constantly asking for clarification. I didn't want to offend him by continuously asking him to repeat himself, so I tried my best to listen intently and follow his every word.

The small shop was always full of customers, presenting a new challenge for me every day. Despite the long hours, I worked from 7 am to 10 pm, I was content with my job. But as soon as the doors closed, the real work began - cleaning up and putting everything back in its place. The customers were always making a mess, touching and rearranging items on display. It was always midnight by the time I made my way home, exhausted and longing for rest. As I worked through my first eight days, I eagerly awaited my first month's salary.

But on day eight, work was even more exhausting than usual. The shop was constantly packed with impatient customers demanding my attention. By closing time, I could barely keep my eyes open. After closing and cleaning the shop every night, he would inspect my wallet and bag to make sure I hadn't taken anything before we could leave.

During tonight's security check, he became uncomfortably familiar, crossing boundaries that should never be crossed. His hands roamed over my body, pretending to conduct a pat-down before eventually making their way between my legs.

Shocked and paralysed with fear, I couldn't believe what was happening. But then something inside me snapped and I found my voice: "I have had enough! You will never touch me there again. I don't need this abuse. And I will not be coming back tomorrow. Just pay me for the eight days of work!"

My boss just laughed in my face and uttered words that cut deep into my already bruised soul: "Leave. I will pay you nothing because you are illegal here anyway. Leave now, you bitch. And if I see you anywhere near this place again, I'll call the police and have you arrested for being illegal."

My heart racing and mind clouded with fear, I hastily left without looking back. Devastated and exhausted, all I could think about was taking a long shower and collapsing into bed, trying to wash away the feeling of violation and betrayal.

The next morning, I struggled to wake up at 10 am but found myself unable to move until 1 pm. My body felt heavy with fatigue and my mind was filled with a deep sense of despair. I had no appetite and just wanted to escape outside for some fresh air. I made my way towards the Marques De Pombal piazza, the sun beating down on my skin as I walked. As I reached the piazza, I collapsed onto a bench and gazed up at the towering statue of the Marques De Pombal mounted on his majestic horse. The bustling sounds of cars passing by filled my ears, but they were drowned out by the overwhelming heaviness of my emotions. Tears streamed down my face uncontrollably as I concluded I had no more ideas or plans for my future. The world around me seemed hazy and uncertain, with no glimmer of hope in sight. At that moment, I felt like a lost child crying out for help.

As I sat lost in my thoughts, a statuesque woman strode past me. Her tall, slim figure was accentuated by her perfectly proportioned curves, giving her the appearance of a model straight off a runway. Her long, flowing blond hair and piercing emerald eyes were enough to make anyone stop and stare. At first glance, she appeared to be from Russia, but as she spoke directly to me, I could hear a hint of Brazilian accent in her voice.

"What are you doing there, little fool?" she asked, her tone both playful and challenging. I turned my gaze to the ground, trying to ignore her intruding presence. But she persisted with another question, "Are you Brazilian or Portuguese?" With a sigh, I replied, "Brazilian." She let out a peal of laughter before confidently plopping down next to me without any hesitation.

"I'm sure you're crying over money," she said bluntly. I was taken aback by her brazenness and rudeness, but also strangely curious about what prompted her assumption. "How do you know? Why do you think my problem is money?" I asked her, hoping for some rational explanation. She just laughed again as if this were all a big joke to her.

"Because money," she declared with a smirk on her face, "is the problem for most people around here. Not me though; money is not an issue for me." As if to prove her point, she gestured toward the luxury building across the street where she apparently lived.

"I only have one problem at the moment," she continued nonchalantly, "I'm looking for a dark-haired beauty to work with me as a luxury companion at a gentlemen's club." My mind immediately went into alert mode; this had to be some kind of trap or scam.

But then she dropped the bombshell. "You could make a minimum of 500 euros per night," she said with a sly smile. I couldn't believe what I was hearing. My instincts screamed at me to walk away, but my curiosity got the better of me and I found myself considering her offer.

The woman's incessant chatter filled my ears, drowning out any thoughts of my own. She talked on and on about the girls and the gentleman, their names and preferences, their schedules and earnings. I felt trapped, with no options but to listen and comply. I was desperate, only ten minutes earlier I had been thinking of desperate measures like robbing someone or even a bank. My mind raced as I tried to come up with a way out of this situation.

Finally, unable to bear it any longer, I blurted out, "What do I have to do? Are you going to pimp me out? Do I have to pay you some sort of commission?" The woman laughed, a harsh sound that made my skin crawl. "No, don't be stupid," she replied. My heart sank at her nonchalant response.

Feeling defeated, I spoke again. "I have no experience in this job, you know that?" The woman shrugged, not showing any sympathy. "Well, you have children, don't you? Then you know how to fuck".

As she spoke, her voice was soft and reassuring. "I will be your guide, all I need is for you to have black hair so we don't miss any potential customers. You see, I often lose out on jobs because I refuse to travel to far-off hotels and apartments. But with two of us, it will be much easier," she explained.

I nodded in understanding and reassured her, "It's okay, I'll go with you."

She wasted no time and immediately said, "We have to leave now. Let me try and book an appointment for you to get your nails done and hair fixed before we go. Then we can stop by my apartment to see if any of my many dresses will fit you. I also have some nice shoes that might work. And if nothing fits or suits your taste, I'll buy something just for you." She paused and added, "This club is exclusive and filled with models; not everyone can get in. But with me by your side, that won't be a problem at all. I bring in a lot of money for the house."

Her words oozed with confidence, and I was taken aback. After all of this preparation, I couldn't help but worry that I would be turned away at the front entrance. I didn't fit the typical model - carrying an extra 12 kilos of baby weight and still sporting a prominent brown butterfly melasma on my face. I voiced my concern to her.

She spoke up with determination in her voice. "No, with foundation, we will transform your skin into a flawless canvas. To me, you are already beautiful." Her words were sincere and full of conviction.

I now noticed her perfectly applied makeup and elegant dress that accentuated her features. "My name is Gabriela," she revealed, "But it's not my real name. None of us use our real names here. You'll need a new name too. What do you want to be called?"

Without hesitation, I replied confidently, "I am... Angelina. That is my name and I won't change it."

At this moment, I knew that the new Angelina was born.

Chapter X

As the sun began to set, fear crept into my bones once again. The chilly December air seemed to seep through my skin, causing my spine to shiver. Determined to provide for my family, I steeled myself and decided to do what was necessary to earn some money. Gabriela had offered to assist me, and she directed me to a salon where I had my nails expertly manicured and painted. It had been quite some time since I had experienced such a luxury. My hair was styled in a new way, as I gazed at my reflection in the mirror, I felt a glimmer of confidence returning - no longer did I feel like a worthless, broken piece of garbage.

Once our beauty treatments were complete, Gabriela invited me back to her place nearby. Her magnificent apartment was adorned with colourful paintings and vibrant plants, instantly lifting my spirits. Her apartment was actually close to mine, yet it felt like a completely different world. Situated on the entire seventh floor, accessible by a modern lift, her home exuded luxury and elegance.

My eyes were immediately drawn to the beautiful dark wood furniture that stood out against the stark white walls. A plush beige sofa sat in the centre of the living room, surrounded by tastefully chosen decor. Her bedroom was just as elegant, with matching beige tones and a wardrobe unlike any I had ever seen before. The eleven doors of the wardrobe were made of the same rich dark wood as the rest of the furniture, and upon opening them, I was greeted with rows upon rows of dazzling dresses. But it didn't stop there - at the bottom level were shelves overflowing with shoes in every style and colour imaginable, while the top shelves proudly displayed an array of designer handbags. It was truly a sight to behold.

In the middle of her bedroom stood a grand, intricately carved wooden table with smooth, polished glass on its surface. The drawers on either side were adorned with delicate gold handles and filled to the brim with treasures. Through the glistening glass top, I could see a dazzling collection of watches, rings, necklaces, and designer sunglasses. The room seemed to radiate opulence and extravagance, like a secret treasure trove. Startled by the display before me, I couldn't help but marvel at this place, it was unlike any I had ever seen before.

With a smile on her face, she beckoned me inside the wardrobe. "Help yourself to whatever catches your eye," she said warmly. My gaze fell upon a dazzling display of designer clothing, each piece more luxurious than the last. The rich fabrics and intricate designs seemed to call out to me, begging to be worn. She gestured to the accessories as well, her long fingers gracefully pointing to sparkling jewellery. I was aware that her height exceeded mine, so it was obvious the shoes wouldn't fit someone with smaller feet. Undeterred, she quickly called a friend who sold high heels and bikinis and asked her to bring over some items. "Come quickly," she urged. "I need them for tonight." Within minutes, her Moroccan friend arrived with two large bags overflowing with boxes of shoes. Excitement bubbled within me as I searched through the boxes, trying on different styles and colours. In the end, I chose a shiny classic black high-heel shoe - versatile enough to go with any outfit and sophisticated enough for any occasion.

The sun had already set, painting the sky in shades of dusky purple and pink as I made my way back to my apartment. As I stepped into the shower, I couldn't help but worry about ruining my perfectly styled hair, meticulously done earlier at the hairdressers.

As I walked through the corridor, Silvana stopped me in my tracks. Her eyes were fixed on my new dress, lying on the bed. A look of curiosity filled her expression. "What is this? Where did you get money?" she interrogated. I rolled my eyes and responded coolly, "When I feel the need to justify myself to you, I'll let you know where I'm going tonight." With an indignant huff, she retreated back to her man's room. In my room, I carefully slipped on the new dress.

With her wisdom and foresight, Gabriela had thoughtfully prepared a large bag 'The Hooker Kit' filled to the brim with everything I would need for my night as a hooker. It contained a variety of condoms, different shades of lipstick, just enough cash for a taxi ride if necessary, a vial of alluring perfume, lubrication, and a long coat to conceal the tight-fitting, light blue dress that now clung to my body.

As the clock struck 8 pm, Gabriela was already waiting for me outside. She had insisted on doing my makeup, I was ushered back to her apartment. Her skilled hands expertly applied cosmetics to my face like an artist creating a masterpiece. And indeed, when she was finished, I looked in the mirror and was taken aback by how beautiful I looked. It had been years since I felt this glamorous. With a satisfied smile, Gabriela revealed our evening plans - dinner would be at the club at 10 pm, where they always served a lavish meal to the girls who arrived early. She even produced a travel toothbrush and toothpaste for me to freshen up after dinner.

As we stepped out into the night air, the bustling city sounds surrounded us. The dim streetlights cast an eerie glow on the pavement as we walked, there was no need for a taxi. I was full of nerves as she turned to me and spoke in a voice laced with confidence and reassurance. "When we get to the club," she said, "I'll buy you two glasses of wine." Her offer brought a small smile to my face, but I could feel the fear still lingering within me. I needed a stiff drink for courage and she seemed to understand that. "Angelina," she said, "just one week will be difficult, but soon you will be accustomed to the job. I already know you are smart and capable. You're going to make a lot of money." Despite her words of encouragement, I still couldn't believe what I was about to do. But I took a deep breath and followed her lead as we made our way through the bustling streets towards our destination - not too far from her apartment, but worlds away from anything I had ever experienced before.

We now approached the grand and famous gentlemen club 'Elefante Branco', also known internationally as 'White Elephant'. The building had a Gothic appearance, complete with grand steps leading up to a massive wooden black door, to me it looked like a castle entrance. Two giant figures, dressed in black suits, guarded each side of the door with an intimidating presence. My companion, Gabriela, confidently strode up to these men and spoke assertively, "Please call the manager for me, this new girl is going to start work here tonight." One of the giant men immediately followed her instructions and disappeared inside to retrieve the manager, Roberto.

As we waited, I couldn't help but feel nervous about my first night at the club. But Gabriela's cool demeanour and commanding presence reassured me. Finally, Roberto emerged from the club's doors and Gabriela wasted no time introducing me, "Roberto, I have brought Angelina here to work with me. I hope I have your permission for that."

Roberto's eyes lit up with recognition as he gave Gabriela a knowing smile, "You are such a troublemaker, Gabriela. But of course, you have my permission. Welcome Angelina, come on in." With his blessing, I followed Gabriela into the luxurious establishment that was sure to bring many changes to my life.

As we entered, the sight of a beautiful buffet greeted us. My stomach grumbled at the sight and smell of the delicious food, but my nerves were too overpowering for me to even consider eating. I followed Gabriela's lead and sat by her side as she calmly enjoyed her meal. Slowly, gentlemen began to trickle into the club, each one dressed in their finest attire. Gabriela excused herself to freshen up and returned with a determined look on her face, uttering the words "Work, work, work, girl. First lesson."

Despite having only one glass of wine, I was still completely sober as I followed her, my entire body trembling with nervousness. My hands were freezing and covered in clammy sweat, shaking uncontrollably.

Gabriela confidently approached the men, introducing both herself and me, I could only manage to confirm my name. I couldn't speak or even imagine doing what she was doing. The men seemed disinterested in anything other than drinking and enjoying themselves during this 'happy hour'. They were Portuguese and had come here solely for that purpose - to drink and maybe flirt with some girls without rejection.

I inquired of her, "If you are aware that these men come here every night just to drink, why do you bother speaking with them?" Her response was quick and confident, "You never know what could happen. It's important to make connections. Besides, I wanted to introduce you as the new girl. Perhaps one day they will surprise me." As we talked, the rest of the girls in the club seemed uninterested and disconnected, gathering in small groups around the booths. Some were sipping on drinks while others were eating. In this environment, I felt like a child amongst adults, out of place and uncertain of my role.

As the clock chimed 1 am, two elegant gentlemen sauntered into the club, their suits perfectly tailored and their body language exuding confidence. Within seconds, two other girls pounced on them, eager to do business. Gabriela turned to me and sneered, "Those fucking bitches, you have to move fast Angelina." My heart raced as I replied, "Okay, I will try." But deep down, I knew I couldn't do it. One by one, the girls tried to charm the men but were all quickly dismissed. With a determined look in her eye, Gabriela turned to me and said, "Now is our chance." I shook my head and responded, "No if every girl in this club has been turned away, why do we think we'll have any luck?" But she persisted, "Because we have to try Angelina. We have to try." I took a deep breath and mustered up the courage to approach them, but only close enough to discreetly gaze at them from afar. I refused to be humiliated like the others. The most I could bring myself to do was stare intently at them with fake longing.

After ten minutes of flirting close to them, the guys approached us. They introduced themselves as Portuguese pilots, Sergio and Pedro. Despite my nerves, I was driven by the thought of earning some much-needed money. My companion, Gabriela, seemed unfazed by this exchange - she didn't need the money. The pilots invited us to their hotel and I nervously accepted, knowing that this could potentially be a lucrative opportunity.

As we waited in the reception area of the hotel, Gabriela made an agreement with me - whoever finished the job first, would call the other to signal that it was time to leave.

Sergio with his polite demeanour and handsome features, appeared to be around thirty-five years old and exuded confidence and charm. After I had completed my duties. He showed a genuine interest in getting to know me. He even asked if I was a mother and about the children, which brought back bittersweet memories and caused tears to well up in my eyes. To my surprise Sergio then was exceedingly generous, slipping me over 1000 euros before we parted ways, not the 500 euros we had agreed. He had also asked for my phone number and mentioned that he would be in town for a few more days. I never could have imagined making such a large amount of money in such a short period of time. It all seemed so unreal to me.

As we left the hotel and headed towards home, the city lights glittered around us. Gabriela suggested that I stay over at her apartment for the night to rest. I eagerly accepted, knowing that her place was a little slice of paradise. I knew the evening would not be filled with alcohol, drugs or cigarettes because Gabriela prided herself on her clean and healthy lifestyle. But that didn't mean she couldn't enjoy the finer things in life - her apartment boasted a wine fridge, its glass doors revealing rows of perfectly aligned bottles, each one glinting in the soft light. "Tonight, let's make an exception," she declared with a mischievous grin. "Let's have a toast and open a bottle of good champagne." With a pop and a fizz, the golden liquid poured into two crystal glasses. We clinked our glasses together, she then said "Angelina, you have done well tonight, I think you are going to make a lot of money". Savouring every sip we relaxed into the comfortable silence of her chic apartment.

My stomach grumbled loudly, reminding me that I had skipped dinner because of my nervousness. But then she appeared, holding a tray full of delicious-looking snacks. "Help yourself!" she exclaimed cheerfully, motioning towards the well-stocked fridge and inviting oven.

We talked until the first rays of sunlight peeked over the horizon, signalling the start of a new day. Feeling tired from our deep conversation, I excused myself to change into something more comfortable. Borrowing a pair of well-worn jeans and a faded t-shirt, I made my way back across the street to my apartment, still wearing my sleek high heels that now seemed out of place in the early morning light.

As I entered my apartment, a feeling of unease washed over me. Silvana, my roommate, was like a ghost lingering in the hallway. She had been sleeping on the floor again, her body curled up in a sad attempt to find comfort on the hard surface. The sound of my footsteps must have stirred her awake, as she sat up and rubbed her eyes before speaking.

"I want to sleep in your room," she declared, her voice wavering with emotion. I paused, unsure how to respond to this unexpected request. After all, I had locked my bedroom door for a reason.

She explained she no longer wanted to stay with her man in their shared room. She said what I was doing to her wasn't fair. Not wanting to argue at such an early hour, I promised we would talk more when I woke up later, right now, I had other plans that needed my attention and I needed sleep.

As the harsh ring of my phone jolted me awake at 2:30 pm, I rubbed the sleep from my eyes and answered the phone, Sergio's voice on the other end. He wanted to see me again, but first, he wanted to take me to dinner. He mentioned Pedro and Gabriela's plans for the evening and the dinner would be the four of us. "Of course," I replied, "I would love that." This was a lie. After hanging up the phone, I barely had time to process the call before Gabriela called me. She wanted to confirm my participation in their scheme. I explained I had already agreed, and that I was eager for the chance to change my circumstances. "Then you must come to my apartment," she instructed firmly, "so we can plan your outfit for tonight." The only thought that consumed my mind was of the money I would receive, perhaps it would be enough to finally escape my rundown apartment and rid myself of Silvana, that parasite who lived off me.

Since the Portuguese people tend to eat dinner early, we also chose to dine early. We sipped on a few glasses of wine and enjoyed a meal with the two pilots, to be fair the conversation was interesting and the food was exceptional. Our arrangement was two hours for dinner and one hour for intimacy at their hotel, all for 500 euros. Once the task was completed, we met in the lobby of the hotel as agreed, Gabriela proposed, "Elefante Branco has already been open for an hour. It's too soon to call it a night, with just 500 euros. Why don't we go there directly?" So, we hailed a taxi from the hotel and headed straight to the gentlemen's club.

As we pulled up to the club, a group of men were already gathered outside. Their distinct Portuguese accents and loud laughter filled the air. We entered the club and I immediately noticed there were not many women around, as it was December and most had returned to Brazil or Africa for the holidays. The men from Scandinavia, America, and England were busy 'playing happy families', so they wouldn't be frequenting the club during this time of year. It was known as the quiet season for girls in this business, with fewer clients and less hustle and bustle compared to other months.

The air was thick with the sounds of music and laughter, and the smell of cigarette smoke lingered in every corner. The men were regulars and they knew that Gabriela lived just around the corner, and she would always arrive at exactly 10 pm. We were late, it's become clear to me that a significant portion of the clients have a fetish for paid sexual encounters with women who have already been with another man. It seems that many of them are fascinated by the details of our past interactions and the actions of other men in the same situation; this particular kink is quite popular.

Amongst the bustling bar area, in what seemed like mere moments after our arrival, two boisterous Portuguese men waved us over to their table. I can only recall the name of one man who spoke to me - Jorge.

Reluctantly, I agreed to accompany him to a nearby room. Jorge's voice was smooth and persuasive as he tried to negotiate the price down to 300 euros. But I knew deep down that we were at their mercy; they saw us as nothing more than workhorses, not deserving of any kindness or leniency. Gabriela's eyes flashed with determination as she interjected, "Let's get this over with quickly and get the hell out of here. We'll take 300 euros from this disgusting, bloated pig." My stomach churned at her words, but I knew we had no other choice.

As the dim lights flickered in the dingy hostel corridor, Gabriela and I made our way to separate rooms. We had agreed to meet again later, but this time she had whispered "Quickly, Quickly, yeah" in my ear before disappearing into her room. We always operated by the rules she had taught me: never kiss, not because of fear of a bond with the gentleman, falling in love was an impossibility but for fear of disease. And always use protection and never let them perform oral sex on us. If they insisted on bareback, we would take their money and make a run for it. We couldn't risk getting caught or worse, infected. The air in the room was thick with the smell of cheap perfume and sweat, reminding me that this was just another transaction in our line of work.

As I stood there, preparing for what I thought would be a simple and easy job, my stomach turned at the sight of him.

He was repulsive - overweight with odorous sweat emanating from his body. His teeth were stained and discoloured, adding to the grotesque image before me. When he removed his clothes, I was even more appalled by the sight of thick, black hair covering his entire body like a gorilla. To make matters worse, he was short and stout, making him appear even more disproportionate due to his size.

As he pulled down his trousers, an overpowering stench of unwashed skin filled the room. I couldn't bear it any longer and insisted that he take a shower before we began. "No, you not gonna give me the time I have paid for. I am not going to waste time with a shower" he argued. So I reluctantly grabbed some towels and wet them with warm water to clean him off. And then came the shock - as I reached for a condom to put on his penis, I realised it was the first time I had seen a micro penis in person. I gasped out loud at how small it was, it was a struggle to put a condom on such a small member.

At my reaction he was now seething with anger, his grip on my hair tight, and forcefully he pulled my head towards his groin. His words were degrading and commanding, demanding that I perform oral sex without a condom and receive his ejaculate in my mouth. The smell emanating from his penis was nauseating, making me want to retch. I reluctantly looked at his small, unimpressive member and defiantly stated "No way." In response, he lashed out with an open-handed slap but I swiftly blocked it with my hand. Gathering all of my courage, I firmly told him to "Fuck off" and threatened to punch him in the face. Surprisingly, he calmed down and said "Okay, okay, you have fire, I like this." He then reached into his pocket and quickly handed me some crumpled notes, which were as filthy as he was. Without hesitation, I stuffed them into my bag, desperate to rid myself of any association with him.

He then spoke, "I want to suck your nipples and then you can go". I pulled my dress off and unclipped my bra, exposing my full breasts. His words repulsed me as his lips made their way to my breasts, I closed my eyes and prayed. I could feel his hot breath on my skin as he eagerly placed his tongue on my right nipple, causing me to gasp in displeasure. But as he moved on to my other breast, I felt a wave of disgust wash over me, this was the vilest thing I had ever experienced. He pressed his body against mine, and I could feel his bulging stomach against my skin. The thought of it made me want to vomit. Yet, he continued to fondle and lick my breasts with an insatiable hunger, covering them in saliva and making me cringe in revulsion.

His hands roamed my body, this made my skin crawl. Then the shock of his teeth biting down on my nipple jolted me, this sharp pain caused me to recoil in horror. At the same moment, his other hand crept towards my most intimate area, and in a reflexive reaction, I pushed him away with all my strength. "You dirty bastard!" I screamed, anger and fear mingling in my voice. "I am going to fuck you up!" He seemed momentarily taken aback by my outburst, giving me just enough time to hastily grab my clothes and bag before bolting towards the door.

Pounding on Gabriela's door, I shouted for her. "That's it, I've had enough!" I exclaimed, panic and rage coursing through me. "That disgusting, vile bastard is horrible! I am getting out of here." Immediately Gabriela burst out of the door, frantically adjusting her dress. She knew from the urgency in my voice that something was wrong.

But before we could make our escape, the fat man came charging into the hallway, bellowing obscenities and demanding that I come back and finish what he had paid for. Gabriela and I linked arms, determined to make a quick escape from the revolting, naked man in the corridor. Despite our high heels, we were able to outpace him easily as we ran away together. As we fled from the nightmare unfolding behind us, I turned and defiantly thrust my middle finger in the air towards the raging maniac. "Fuck you!" I yelled at the top of my lungs.

Exiting the hostel, we turned to each other and burst into uncontrollable laughter, our bond solidified as partners in crime. As we strolled down the street towards home, I couldn't help but replay the experience in my mind. But now, the feeling of disgust and repulsion flooded through my body, erasing any trace of humour. Making an excuse to leave Gabriela for the evening, I hurried back to my apartment. Without a second thought, I headed straight for the bathroom. Turning on the shower, I shuddered with revulsion as memories of that man's tongue running over my body flooded back. Sitting in the tub, water pouring over me, I desperately tried to scrub away the filth and shame that clung to my skin. But even with soap and a harsh pad, I couldn't seem to get clean enough. My arms and breasts became raw and red from my frantic scrubbing until finally, blood mingled with the soapy water. Tears streamed down my face as I wept in disgust at what I had become.

The following day, I met Gabriela and she exclaimed, "What on earth have you done?" I recounted my actions to her, and with a heavy sigh, she responded, "I understand, but you must learn to be more neutral. Not all men we spend time with are princes. You will learn to navigate this." Despite her wise words, my heart still refused to block out the overwhelming feelings of disgust.

Gabriela then suggested, "I will talk to Madam Marta and see if you can move into the apartment below mine." She went on to explain that Madam Marta was an elderly woman who used to work as a prostitute. With no children of her own, she now owned the entire block and many other properties thanks to a politician who gifted her property in the area as payment. She was known as the 'Golden Pussy'. Gabriela mentioned that Madam Marta enjoyed hearing stories, as she was often bored with nothing else to do. "She will adore you," Gabriela assured me with a smile.

Gabriela had arranged for us to meet Madam Marta outside her apartment building later that day. As we approached, I could see a petite figure waiting for us at the entrance, it had to be Madam Marta. She exuded elegance and grace, despite her advanced age of late seventies. Her short curly hair was a beautiful shade of grey, framing her kind face. And although she may have been small in stature, she radiated warmth and kindness. As we approached, Gabriela introduced me with a smile,"Madam Marta, this is Angelina." I greeted her politely, "Hello Madam Marta." Without hesitation, she took control of the situation and suggested with a smile,"Let's go for a coffee."

The vibrant sign of 'Mane Coffee Bar' beckoned us inside. As we settled into our seats, the smell of the coffee was strong and alluring, filling the air with hints of caramel and roasted coffee beans. I ordered my usual cappuccino, Gabriela ordered the same, while Madam Marta opted for a strong black coffee. As we talked, her gaze kept drifting to my arms, which still bore fresh scratches from the shower. Concern was etched on her face as she asked about what happened. Knowing she was open-minded, I shared the events of the previous night with her. She comforted me by wrapping her arms around me and pressing a gentle kiss to my forehead, murmuring "Those pig bastards...I'm so sorry this happened to you." I responded with a resigned tone, "I'm just trying to follow Gabriela's teachings and stay neutral."

As we sat and chatted, our talk soon shifted to business matters. I expressed my desire to rent an apartment and the woman nodded, her face alight with interest. She informed me that she had a smaller, yet perfectly located and fully furnished apartment below Gabriela's, which was not occupied. The thought of living in such a prime location with all the necessary furnishings made my heart skip a beat with excitement.

Madam Marta's voice was calm and reassuring as she addressed us. "You will be working closely together, so it would be beneficial for you to live near each other as well. You make a great team. I also have a studio on the first floor that may interest you. It may be small, but it has all the amenities you need - a living room, a fully equipped kitchen, a comfortable bedroom, and a luxurious glass shower room. You both can rent it." Her smile widened as she continued, "It would be perfect for hosting guests and it is also secure. I also live on the top floor, I see by the cameras who gets in and who gets out, I never sleep. No more trips to the hostel for either of you." As Madam Marta spoke, Gabriela and I exchanged glances before nodding simultaneously. "Yes, why not? Thank you".

As we entered what would become my apartment, the first thing that struck me was the warm, inviting colour scheme. The bed was adorned with snug blankets and pillows in shades of red and orange, while the bathroom towels were a soft cream colour. The furniture, all made of dark wood, gave off a sophisticated and elegant vibe. My favourite features were of course now I had my own 11-door wardrobe and a wine fridge, all adding a touch of luxury to the space. I couldn't help but notice that my bedroom lacked the jewellery centrepiece that Gabriela had in hers, but it was still a charming apartment. However, my favourite thing was the stunning marble flooring throughout. It was love at first sight and I couldn't wait to move in. The monthly rent was agreed at 700 euros plus an additional 200 euros for the studio below. I used the money I had been saving up some money to send back home to my parents, who were expecting funds from my previous job at the Chinese shop (which they believed I still had). But I knew that next week I would earn a lot more.

With anticipation and excitement, we then made our way to the studio on the first floor. Madam Marta had meticulously designed the space with tones of warm beige and a hint of red. The atmosphere was both elegant and sensual, perfectly suited for the task at hand. It seemed as though Madam Marta had been expecting us, almost like Gabriela had planned this encounter for some time now. Eventually, I bid them farewell and returned to my place to tackle the issue with Silvana.

As I walked across the street, the transition was jarring - like leaving the luxurious streets of Beverly Hills and stepping into the gritty, run-down neighbourhood of the ghetto. It felt like going from paradise to hell in a matter of seconds. When I entered the apartment, Silvana was in the shower. I could hear the water running and steam billowing out from under the door. I waited for her to finish, my eyes scanning the surroundings. I reminded myself Silvana had done nothing for the past six weeks but party. Finally, she emerged from the bathroom, her face stormy and tense. It was clear that something had upset her deeply, despite her carefree lifestyle.

I had begun gathering my belongings, preparing to leave and start a new chapter elsewhere, but she suddenly interrupted me. "You're leaving me?" she exclaimed with a mix of surprise and hurt in her voice. "I never said I had any obligation to you," I replied firmly. "I know you've been spreading rumours about me in Brazil, accusing me of hooking up for money with transsexuals because you couldn't get into the exclusive club 'Elefante Branco' and I know you have tried. You don't like that I spend time with Natasha, the beautiful transsexual woman who stands on the corner with her loyal German shepherd each morning as the sun rises. But let me be clear, the only truth in your accusations is that I do talk to her - I am not selling my body on the streets. Unlike you, I have no problem with transsexuals. It's your words that are causing problems, labelling me a street hooker. You should know better than anyone that I have been actively trying to find legitimate work. And don't think I haven't heard about your attempts to get hired at the 'Gallery' and 'Hippo' gentlemen clubs - both of which turned you down."

I declared, "I'll rent you a room for one month." I reached into my bag and pulled out 200 euros. "If you're smart with this money, it can last you the month. Now take your fat ass and go back to bed with that Brazilian bastard." I was not finished. "Maybe you'll learn to do something by yourself!" In my final angry rant, I shouted, "You know more about legal papers and working visas than I do, yet you refuse to explain or help me get them. And then you dare to ask for 30 euros for a process I do not understand? Screw you! I hope I never have to see your face again!".

As she angrily marched off towards the Brazilian bastards' room, she spat out, "Fuck you! You think you're better than me? You're just a daughter of a bitch!" I simply shook my head and thought to myself, there's no point in wasting words on someone who holds no significance. I focused on finishing packing, knowing that the next day I would be moving into my new apartment and starting a better life.

Chapter XI

As we sat in a cosy cafe, sipping on steaming lattes one afternoon, Gabriela and I made a decision - it was time to up our game. The year was now 2005, and the Internet was rapidly gaining popularity. We were forward-thinking and we needed professional pictures to showcase our services and attract clients online. Through one of our connections, we obtained the phone number of a highly recommended photographer and quickly booked an appointment for our photo shoot.

On the day of the shoot, we arrived with small suitcases in tow, each filled with carefully selected items. Our outfits ranged from sexy lingerie to stunning bikinis, accessorised with delicate jewellery and fun props like hats, sunglasses, and of course, the signature high heels. We were ready to shine in front of the camera and capture our beauty and confidence for all to see.

The studio was a stark contrast to traditional photo shoot locations. Instead of bright lights and white walls, it resembled a tattoo studio with its dark, Gothic aesthetic. Skulls adorned the shelves on the wall, adding to the edgy atmosphere. To make the situation even more surreal, the photographer's wife was going to be present for the shoot and watch as we posed for these photos. Surprisingly, I found myself feeling a bit self-conscious as we walked in. Gabriela must have sensed this and confidently took the lead.

She announced, "I was born in a brothel, raised in a brothel, and I have spent my entire life in a brothel, being naked is normal". Her words jolted me, like a sudden clap of thunder on a clear day. I was caught completely off guard, as it was the first I had heard of this. It was true what she had said, and she effortlessly struck provocative poses in a variety of outfits without a care in the world. Her body moved with fluidity and confidence, drawing the attention of the camera lens.

As I stood there, uncomfortably sober, I couldn't help but feel self-conscious under the gaze of the photographer's wife. Her piercing eyes seemed to bore into me as if silently judging my discomfort. Meanwhile, my companion continued to revel in her natural talent for modelling, her every move exuding sensuality and allure. I could only watch on, feeling like an outcast in this seductive world.

It was finally my turn to take centre stage, standing nervously under the watchful eye of everyone in the room. I had chosen to start with a sleek black trikini, determined not to fully bare myself for the camera. Memories of my past modelling experiences flooded back, and I channelled that professionalism as I posed effortlessly for the shoot. Every movement was deliberate and precise, every angle carefully calculated to capture the perfect shot. Despite my initial hesitation, I felt myself slipping into the familiar role with ease. I moved through the different outfits I had prepared, and finally, I struck my most seductive pose while donning a sleek black cowgirl hat, its brim casting a shadow over my alluring features.

After the intense photo shoot, we made our way back to our apartments and dropped our suitcases off. We wasted no time and went straight to the shops, determined to elevate our appearance with fresh clothing, hairstyles, and manicures. This was just another day in the life of a high-class hooker - a relentless routine of maintaining a polished appearance. Your perfectly manicured nails and expertly styled hair were essential elements in attracting wealthy clients and commanding top dollar for your services.

After a few days had passed, we once again made our way to the photo studio, eager to select the perfect photographs and pay for them. Without a computer of our own, we had to rely on the agency that ran the website for call girls catering to wealthy clients. Their office was sleek and modern, using a large computer screen in a box, that resembled a massive old TV. They expertly handled everything from creating the online advertisement to adding our carefully chosen photographs to the site, ensuring we stood out among the competition.

As our online presence expanded, we were filled with hope for the potential success and wealth it could bring us. Only two days after our launch, while strolling through the bustling city streets, Gabriela's phone rang. On the other end was a man named Ruy, his Portuguese accent dripping with opulence as he offered us a tempting proposition. He claimed to be incredibly wealthy and was seeking a few ladies to accompany him and his friends on his yacht, willing to pay us each 1,000 euros per hour for our company. A glance at Gabriela's face confirmed that she had hit the jackpot.

As the conversation about money grows, her eyes widen and a faint flush spreads across her cheeks. She momentarily loses her mind in the possibilities of how much money we could make for a few hours of work. Her voice becomes animated as she starts rattling off information over the phone to this mysterious man - our city, neighbourhood, even our street, and where we work 'Elfante Branco'. I can't help but find it strange that she is divulging so much information to a stranger, but I know she is the one with experience in these matters. The corners of her mouth turn up in a self-assured smile as she continues to negotiate, her confidence radiating from every word she speaks. This is what makes her the leader among us, able to navigate these situations with ease.

He asks if there are more girls available, or if it is just me and her. She replies calmly, "We work together, yes, and currently it is only me and Angelina. However, our street, Marques De Pombal, is known as a haven for prostitutes. It is where all the girls live, as it is conveniently close to where they work being 'Hippopotamus', 'Gallery', and 'Elefante Branco'."

Her voice was low and smooth, promising something illicit. "If you want," she said with a sly grin, "we can arrange for more girls." I could tell she was already thinking about pimping out some other girls, always looking to make a profit. But she was never like this with me. She did anything I asked of her without hesitation. She genuinely liked me, never asking for repayment of the money she had invested in me at the start. The dresses she gifted me were mine to keep, she never asked for them back. She even refused to accept any money from me, no matter how much I insisted on repaying her. It wasn't until later that I discovered she truly liked me and was simply a lonely person. As for the other girls, she was tough and unyielding with them.

The conversation comes to an end with a definitive agreement. He promises to call Gabriela in the coming days, finalising details for the number of girls needed and the location for the day trip on his luxurious yacht. The thought of this adventure fills us with excitement and anticipation. As life carried on, the memory of our conversation faded into the background and we focused on the present moment.

The following day was a pamper day, we started with food shopping, and we strolled through the brightly lit aisles of the bustling supermarket, filling our cart with fresh produce and artisan treats. Afterwards, we stopped by a quaint cafe for a steaming cup of coffee and indulged in some delectable pastries. As the morning turned into afternoon, we decided to treat ourselves to a delicious lunch at a nearby restaurant. The flavours danced on our tongues as we savoured each bite. But the best was yet to come - we had an appointment for a luxurious massage and of course expert hair styling. The soothing scents and gentle touch of the masseuse left us feeling relaxed and rejuvenated, while our newly styled hair added a touch of glamour to our day.

As we made our way back towards home, I couldn't help but notice the stares and whispers from the people around us. It was like all eyes were drawn to us, and their voices carried with excitement and intrigue. "Do you see that?" I whispered to Gabriela, feeling self-conscious under the intense gazes.

"Of course, they're staring," she replied with a confident smile. "We are two very pretty girls, and we look fabulous."

But as we continued walking, the attention only seemed to grow. People turned their heads to watch us pass by, some even openly pointing and whispering to each other. And then there was the group of teenagers in the distance, huddled together and bursting into laughter as they looked our way.

"This is getting ridiculous," I exclaimed to Gabriela. "What's going on?"

She chuckled, her voice dripping with amusement. "This, my dear, is our magnetism at work. We have a certain energy that draws people in."

I couldn't deny the thrill of it all, the rush of being the centre of attention. But there was also a growing sense of unease, wondering why we were suddenly attracting so much attention and what it could mean for us. "Magnetism or not," I said firmly, "this doesn't feel normal."

Gabriela simply shrugged her shoulders and grinned mischievously. "To me, this is just money coming our way."

As we entered the lobby of the apartment building, the lift beeped and the doors slid open. Madam Marta was standing there, a copy of the Lisbon City newspaper clutched tightly in her hand. Her face was a mix of gossip and urgency as she exclaimed, "Look at this! You and Angelina are on the front page of this newspaper, naked!" Her words hung in the air, heavy with scandal and shock. "You two are the talk of the town," she continued, "all the girls are buzzing, all the bars are abuzz. And they all know that you are working girls, thanks to Gabriela spilling your names." Madam Marta's tone was equal parts disapproval and delight. "Everyone in this area now knows about you two," she concluded with a knowing look.

The bold, black letters of the newspaper headline read 'The Glamorous Sick World Of Prostitution'. In one of the accompanying photos, Gabriela was captured in all her exposed vulnerability, posed on all fours with her body completely bare. However, in an attempt to censor the content, her most intimate areas were blurred out, leaving only a glimpse of her smooth blonde hair and a small portion of her delicate side profile visible.

The article delved deep into the conversation with Gabriela, leaving no stone unturned. With Gabriela's thorough input, it laid bare everything, it was a compelling expose.

I, on the other hand, had two pictures on the front page. One was a side profile of me standing tall, proudly displaying my curves in lingerie. The other showed me straight on, baring everything from head to toe in a sleek black trikini. My entire face was visible for all to see. As I looked at these images, I felt my hands begin to shake, and my mind raced with fear. If Silvana got her hands on this newspaper and shared it with my family in Brazil, she could potentially destroy my life as I knew it.

A flash of disappointment flickered across Gabriela's face as she studied the newspaper, her lips pursed in a thin line. "Why couldn't they have used a better photo of me?" she exclaimed with frustration. "I feel so humiliated here, and on the front page, my god. That bastard Ruy could have had a little more consideration and picked a better photo of me!" We couldn't help but burst into laughter together; only we could find ourselves in such a ridiculous situation.

If I had any sense I would be worried but since I don't, I laughed a lot at this situation. After two weeks, I was still receiving stares from everyone on the street. One night while having dinner with Gabriela at 'Elefante Branco', a member of the waiting staff approached me and began gossiping without hesitation.

"Do you know what I heard girls?" Gabriela said no we have no idea "Last night we had a group here from England and they were talking about the newspaper article. They wanted to know where you were. They had heard about the famous Gabriela and Angelina in their national newspaper all the way in England but you had gone with some clients". I couldn't believe it when I heard that our magnetism had made international headlines and people were talking about it all around the world. It was starting to annoy me. I had endured weeks of attention and stares from strangers. I had reached my limit. The next morning, I woke up and immediately made an appointment to chop off my long hair.

After struggling to secure an appointment for the next day, I finally found a hairdresser who could fit me in. As soon as I sat down in the salon chair, the stylist's fingers ran through my long, with a look of sorrow on her face. She asked if she could keep 60cm of my hair, but I declined. This was no ordinary haircut - I had already decided I was going to keep my locks to donate to a public cancer hospital in Brazil's Barretos City. I knew it had potential to be sold, but I wanted it to go towards making a wig for someone in need.

The result of my haircut was drastically different, yet I couldn't help but love it. My once lengthy locks were now transformed into a short, Chic Channel cut with a fringe. The lady from the salon couldn't contain her excitement and exclaimed, "Wow, you look fantastic! You remind me of Cleopatra." While I didn't quite feel like the ancient Egyptian queen, I did feel confident and stylish with my new hairdo. I also knew that people on the street would no longer recognise me, and that was exactly what I had hoped for. Later I did donate my hair, as I had planned and I couldn't be happier with the outcome.

My excitement was palpable as I gazed at my reflection in the mirror, admiring my new hair style. Everyone around me couldn't help but compare me to the legendary Cleopatra, and I felt like a queen with my bold, daring look. Despite not being able to speak English fluently, my appearance seemed to captivate a new breed of man that frequented the gentleman's club and these were the rich English. I relied on an old English-American dictionary and managed to pick up a few key phrases to communicate with them.

As January settled in, the job became increasingly quiet. Days passed by without any work, for any of us and it wasn't until the end of the month that things picked up again. For 15 long days, I had no work. The scandal had died down, but because of it, I was no longer featured on that infamous website and was relying on the club for my income.

Every day, I persisted in going to the club, hoping to 'fish' something for a profit. But as each day passed, my savings dwindled. Despite having my expenses and responsibilities here, I also sent money back home to my family in Brazil. The desperation set in until one evening when I found myself at the club once again. Gabriela chose not to even show up for work - she knew it was a slow and struggling time for the establishment. Instead, she took some personal time to rest and recharge.

The club was nearly empty, with only a handful of clients and girls lingering in the dimly lit space. The air felt thick and suffocating like the weight of unfulfilled desires hung heavily in the atmosphere. I had been on the verge of giving up and heading home, my eyes had begun to glaze over from hours of staring at the same spot on the wall. But then, at the end of the bar, I saw a figure that would stay etched in my memory forever. He was a man, not much taller than me but with an athletic build and piercing blue eyes that seemed to shine even in the low light. As soon as he entered the club, his gaze locked onto mine and he headed straight towards me, perhaps realising he didn't have many other options that night.

His sympathetic manner and offer of a drink couldn't mask the underlying intentions in his eyes. I chose Champagne, I did not like this drink but it was expensive and a way to thank the club for the dinner they provided every night. As the bubbles danced in my glass, he cut right to the chase, asking "How much would the rest of the night with you cost?". I named my price - 600 euros - and asked which hotel he was staying at. His response made my blood run cold - a rented house on the beach. I shook my head and uttered those familiar words, "I'm sorry, but I don't go to clients' houses." But he wouldn't take no for an answer, tempting me with 1,000 euros and the offer to leave whenever I wanted. A voice inside me screamed 'Don't do it, it's too dangerous', but desperation took over after 15 days without work. He seemed harmless enough...so I agreed to go with him. Little did I know, this decision would haunt me forever.

We left the dimly lit club and travelled by taxi to his house, the city lights flashing by in a blur. An uneasy feeling settled in my stomach as I asked for the payment upfront, which he paid without hesitation. The tension eased slightly as we arrived at our destination - a small, white villa with low walls surrounding it and a gate at the front. Everything appeared to be normal until he opened the door and I stepped into the hallway. From there, I could see down into the living room, and that's when I spotted two enormous figures standing inside.

Starting to panic I asked, "What is going on? Who are they?" The man promptly locked the door behind me and replied with a sly smile, "Our friends." It was then that I understood this was a trap. With all my might, I tried to maintain a calm facade and asked, "Friends? Could you tell me their names?" I walked towards the living room and the two men, I focused on appearing confident and at ease. They had an air of mystery about them, perhaps Moroccan by their appearance - tall and muscular with dark features. Turning to the man who had brought me here, I mustered up the courage to ask, "May I use the restroom?" My mind raced with fear and uncertainty as I waited for his response.

I needed to use the restroom to send a message to Gabriela. The only issue was, I had no clue where I was. His face hardened and he sternly declared, "No, you're not going anywhere." My heart raced as I questioned, "Why not?" But deep down, I already knew the answer. So I suggested going to our room, hoping to diffuse the tension. However, his response was firm and commanding: "You are not going anywhere." And then came the ultimatum: "Take off your clothes!" I froze with hesitation, and I was full of fear of what would happen if I disobeyed.

Suddenly, one of the two men approached me and grabbed me around my arms with a tight, unyielding grip. In his eyes, I saw a glint of malicious intent. The other man circled me, his hands already reaching for the fabric of my clothing. As I screamed and cried for help, the men erupted in cruel cruel laughter, as if this was some twisted game to be enjoyed. Fear coursed through my veins as I struggled against their hold, but they seemed to only tighten their grasp. I felt vulnerable and exposed as they stripped away my garments, each layer feeling like a stripping away of my dignity. Tears streamed down my face as I realised how powerless I was in this situation. This was not a game, but a nightmare that I couldn't wake up from.

Strong hands grabbed me and forced me across the room, shoving me onto the worn sofa. Agonising pain shot through my body as their teeth sank into my flesh. I screamed as they yanked on my hair. Fingers probed at pussy, violating me in ways I couldn't even comprehend. I struggled and fought against them, but their strength was overpowering. Every punch and slap left stinging marks on my skin, a vicious dance of violence and control. I could only pray for it to end soon, to escape from this nightmare of terror and pain.

A small table sat next to the sofa, its drawer slightly ajar. Inside were items that could deliver an electric shock, knives, sex toys, and dildos. My suffering only increased their excitement as they relentlessly slapped my face with their hardened dicks, they spat on my battered body without an ounce of remorse.

One of them had grabbed a wooden broomstick and forced it into my mouth, commanding me to suck on it and spit on it. With tears streaming down my face, I obeyed their cruel game. But that wasn't enough for them; they wanted to cause me more pain. They shoved it into my ass with such force that the pain and discomfort were almost unbearable.

They used the array of toys from the drawer, each one more sinister than the last, and used them on me without mercy. As I screamed and writhed in agony, they laughed and continued their torture. Their teeth sank into my flesh, leaving behind red marks and bruises as painful reminders of their sadistic pleasure.

I shrieked for them to stop, my voice trembling with fear and desperation. I was certain that death was just seconds away. "Please, I have small children," I cried out, my words coming out in a hoarse, terrified whisper. But they paid no heed to my pleading, their cruel torment only intensifying as they shoved a massive black dildo into me. The intense force caused an excruciating tearing feeling, as my vagina and anus became one in an agonising instant. The pain was overwhelming and unbearable, and I could feel the warm rush of blood between my legs.

Then two brutal punches landed on my face, everything went black, and I drifted in and out of consciousness. My cries and screams had ceased. The thrill of violence was now gone for them, the attackers standing around me as I lay motionless. In a final act of humiliation and degradation, one of them even pissed onto my battered body, I felt the warm urine on my skin and stinging in my eyes.

They then went through my bag with callous hands, to snatch up the 1,000 euros and the emergency taxi money I had hidden away. They then proceeded to smash my phone, rendering it useless. After throwing me and my dishevelled clothing, forcefully onto the street, they shut the door. With cruel laughter from inside ringing in my ears. Lying on the ground, I tried to make sense of what had just happened. My head swam with confusion and fear as I struggled to stand, blood trickling down my face from a cut above my eyebrow. With trembling hands, I struggled to put on my dress and coat, trying to cover up the physical and emotional scars left behind by this traumatic experience. I stumbled away from that house of horrors.

Disoriented and without a sense of direction, I stumbled through the unknown terrain, my bare feet aching with each step. My once-elegant high heels dangled from my hand, now useless I was barely able to walk barefoot. In the distance, a faint light illuminated the darkness behind me, growing brighter as it approached. Fear gripped me as I thought it might be them, coming to capture me again. But I was too weak and exhausted to run, my body feeling heavy and lifeless. Blood dripped steadily from my wounds, staining my clothes and leaving a trail behind me. The bruising around my eye was beginning to close it shut, blurring my vision.

As the car came to a stop, I hesitated to turn and face whoever was inside. A deep, unfamiliar voice with a strong Portuguese accent called out to me, asking if I was okay. With shaky courage, I finally turned to look at the car and saw that it was a taxi. The driver's concerned gaze met mine as he asked, "What happened to you, my dear?" His words were laced with genuine worry and care.

I crumpled to the floor, my sobs echoing off the cold concrete walls. He rushed over, concern etched on his face, and retrieved some cloths from his car. The fabric was rough against my skin as he wrapped them around my trembling body, trying to stop the blood from seeping through my torn clothing. Slowly, he helped me up and gently guided me into the backseat of his car. Through my tears, I managed to choke out the words that had been haunting me since I escaped: I had been raped in a nearby house.

His gruff voice demanded, "Show me the house and then we'll go to the hospital." He wanted to involve the police, but I couldn't hold back my tears as I pleaded, "No, please no!" He relented for a moment before insisting, "Okay fine, but I am taking you to the hospital." Panic flooded my mind as I whispered, "No, please not the hospital. It's risky for me." Fear of being caught as an illegal immigrant consumed me. "Please take me to where I live," I begged, "but I have no money to pay you." To my surprise, he brushed off my concerns with a wave of his hand and started to drive. As we pulled up to my address, he persisted in wanting to escort me inside. My thoughts were a jumbled mess of worry about the police and fear of being dealt with as an illegal immigrant. With a trembling voice, I managed to utter a heartfelt "Thank you and god bless" I stumbled into my apartment building, using the lobby walls to steady myself, I made my way to the elevator and pressed the button for Gabriela's floor.

As the elevator doors slid open, my battered body collapsed against Gabriela's door with a heavy thud. I gasped for air, my vision blurry and my head spinning. The sound of my fall must have alerted Gabriela because she quickly opened the door to her apartment. Shock and concern were etched on her face as she took in my dishevelled bloody appearance. "Angelina, oh my god, what has happened?" she cried out, rushing to my side and helping me into her home. My voice trembled as I told her through tears that I had been attacked, beaten, and raped. "Hold on," she said firmly, "I will go get Madam Marta." Gabriela said firmly, determined to get me the help and protection I desperately needed.

Madam Marta moved with swift determination, her warm eyes glinting with a mix of compassion and professionalism. She made a quick phone call to an old friend who was a nurse, who worked local abortion clinic. This was not new territory for the nurse, she had spent many years working in secret to help women in situations like mine.

Madam Marta had explained the incident in full, her voice trembling with worry and concern. The nurse arrived swiftly, carrying a large medical bag filled with all the necessary equipment to treat my injuries. With gentle hands and a calm approach, she sutured and repaired my torn vagina and cleaned out any lingering debris. "I can fix outside the body," she murmured, her professional tone tinged with empathy, "but I cannot be sure of the damage inside. You should go to the hospital." Madam Marta's face fell at this suggestion; it was simply not an option for us.

The nurse's eyes flickered over to my swollen eye, fear etched in her features as she carefully examined it, she was concerned I would lose the eye from the impact of the punches. After a few tense moments, she breathed a small sigh of relief and stated that it should heal with time. Finally, she moved on to treating and cleaning the deep bite marks that covered my body like a painful mosaic. Despite the pain, I felt grateful for the nurse's skilled and gentle touch.

The nurse's face was etched with worry as she made a phone call, her voice trembling. The situation was far worse than she had initially thought and she needed all the help she could get. She waited for a doctor she knew to answer her desperate call for assistance. He was not known for his underground illegal work outside of the hospital, but in this dire circumstance, she knew he was my only hope.

After much persuasion, he arrived, and he examined me with a seriousness that only comes from years of experience. Prescriptions were quickly written out - strong painkillers to ease the suffering, sleeping pills to provide some much-needed rest, and antibiotics to fight off any infections.

The doctor gently placed a small bottle of pills into Gabriela's outstretched hand, his voice soft and reassuring. "These tablets will help Angelina sleep for at least four days," he continued "Her body needs rest to heal." The pills were small and white, with tiny letters etched onto the surface. Their purpose was to bring me solace from the pain and exhaustion.

For the next four days, I took refuge in Gabriela's apartment. Her unwavering support I will be forever thankful for, as I navigated through my emotional turmoil. While she tended to my needs, she put her own life on hold, choosing instead to stay by my side. She sacrificed work and any other obligations to make sure I was okay. Her presence alone brought a sense of peace and reassurance during those difficult days.

The day finally came when I could move to my apartment. Every step was agony as I navigated the journey, my body still weak from the ordeal. But Gabriela was there to help me every step of the way. She tended to my needs without hesitation, running to the pharmacy for any medication I required and making sure I had everything I needed from the supermarket. She would go to work at night, then come straight to my apartment at dawn and stay with me. She talked and cared for me constantly. For twenty-five days, I stayed confined to my apartment, slowly regaining strength and healing with Gabriela's constant support and care.

A month had passed and I was in desperate need of money, having earned nothing for what felt like an eternity. With a heavy heart, I turned to Gabriela and said, "Tonight, I am going with you to work." I knew I wasn't ready, both physically and mentally, but I had no other option. She hesitated at the idea, her frown deepening, but I persisted. That night, we returned to the notorious 'Elefante Branco' establishment together.

The lights flickered above us as we made our way through the dark streets, filled with seedy characters and the faint smell of alcohol. My heart raced as we approached the entrance. But I had no choice - it was either this or face complete destitution. Steeling my nerves, I followed Gabriela inside, prepared to do whatever was necessary to survive another day.

Chapter XII

Upon my return, I felt uneasy in my skin and was filled with fear. The thought of staying at a hotel made me shudder, so I made the decision to only conduct business at the studio apartment. Madam Marta, with her sharp eyes, would be watching the security cameras. As February continued, work remained slow. And because I refused to go to hotels, I lost out on potential income and had to rely on working with repulsive local Portuguese men.

Why do I say disgusting? To put it bluntly, I find this situation revolting. The majority of them are only willing to pay a fraction of what English, Scandinavian, and American clients pay, yet they want to stay with you and use the service for one hour. They refuse to shower, and their bodies are unclean and unkempt, with matted hair. They seem unconcerned with hygiene. But I had to face them because I was afraid to go to any other place but the studio apartment. In this place it was my rules, I had even stashed some knives there, and this time if they played me a fool, I was ready to really mess with them and to my worst.

As the days passed, my defences slowly began to crumble and by the last week of February, I found myself accompanying the Gringos to various hotels, sometimes with Gabriela and sometimes without. On a particular Wednesday, I took extra care in styling my hair, choosing to wear a sleek black dress for work. Our dinner conversation at the club was filled with gossip and laughter as we caught up on each other's lives. But when a group of five Swiss men entered the club, all the girls around me immediately became restless and agitated. It was almost comical how they behaved - as if they were starving and desperate for money. They showed no respect towards the gentlemen who simply wanted to enjoy a few drinks and maybe choose a companion for the night. Like a pack of ravenous hyenas, they pounced on the unsuspecting men. Meanwhile, Gabriela and I simply observed from a distance.

The cycle repeats itself: girls approach them in the bar, then leave; the men just want a moment of peace to enjoy their drinks. As they began to get drunk, Gabriela and I knew it was nearly time to make our move. Three of the guys beckoned three girls over to their group, known as the 'Barbie Lesbians'. These girls may look like Barbie dolls, but they are not interested in men at all. The other two guys motioned for us to join them.

As we approached, we made our introductions. The other group then separated the men from our group. Despite my limited English, I was able to communicate a little with the Swiss guys using the English language.

After buying her a drink, the man who was supposed to pick up Gabriela says, "Thank you Gabriela, but I've decided to go alone for now. If you want, you can join someone else."

Gabriela was not upset; this situation was not unusual for her and she excused herself. But before she left, she leaned close to me and whispered "Take care and be careful." We found a table near the bar to sit at, with just me and the two guys now. They introduced themselves as Hans and Max and we had a hilarious conversation while drinking. Max mentioned he was going to take me to the hotel, to which Hans responded this was no issue at all.

An hour passed, and the rest of the group joined us: the three men and the 'Barbie Lesbians'. They announced that they were leaving for a disco before heading to the hotel. I asked about their arrangement, and one of the 'Barbie Lesbians' replied, "One hour at the nightclub and one hour at the hotel." The three foolish 'Barbie Lesbians' had already settled for 400 euros, so I couldn't push for more than that. Max also wanted to go to the disco first, and he asked if I was satisfied with this agreement. I nodded.

We divided into two taxis and made our way to 'Dreamers Disco'. The music inside was loud and pulsating, the beat vibrating through our bodies as we stepped through the doors. The air was thick with the sweet scent of perfumes and colognes. As soon as we arrived, drinks were poured and passed around, their colourful alcoholic contents tempting me to indulge. I joined in the conversations, talking to everybody despite my limited knowledge of English, I managed to communicate. The "Barbie Lesbians" didn't speak English or Swiss, while the guys struggled with Portuguese. They just stood there, exchanging baffled looks and unable to communicate.

Before long, everyone was drunk. The Swiss men towered over the rest of us, and even Hans managed to find a girl who joined our party. The men wanted to show off their strength, so they lifted the girls they were with into their arms and cheered as if it was an impressive feat. Due to Max's small stature, he was unable to do that with me. But in my drunken state, I didn't hesitate to join in and scooped him up in my arms. As I held him high in the air, I was teetering on 15cm heel stilettos, completely drunk and feeling dizzy. Suddenly, I lost my balance and toppled over, taking him down with me. He hit his head hard on the floor. I grab his hand and forcefully pull him to his feet, apologising profusely. But he's not having it - furious doesn't even begin to describe the fire in his eyes. And as I turn to face the group, their laughter rings in my ears like mocking bells. The girls try to show their amusement behind fake smiles, but their eyes betray their true thoughts - 'You are beyond ridiculous, Angelina.'

Then a little bit embarrassed by what I had done and needing some time to pull myself together, I said "I have got to the toilet." The toilet was located on the second floor, so I made my way up and quickly took care of business. However, upon my return, I found that the group had disappeared. It was as if they had vanished into thin air, leaving me standing alone.

The alcohol-induced daze lifted from my mind and I found myself thinking, 'Oh Fuck, what do I do now?' My legs carried me to the entrance of the club, where the Swiss men were getting into a taxi. Hans, however, was still standing on the sidewalk, he was going to be the last to get in.

I yell out to Hans, "Wait!" He turns towards me with a mixture of confusion and amusement as I make my way towards the taxi. "Where's Max?" I ask, feeling slightly embarrassed for being left behind. "He went back to the hotel," he replies sheepishly. "And what about the girls?" I press, knowing something is off. Hans hesitates before admitting, "We paid for their time because they received a call about Cristina's one-year-old daughter having a convulsion." Shocked, I exclaim, "What? Are you Fucking kidding me? They're all lesbians; they don't have a daughter!" Hans looks ashamed and I continue, "They have played you for fools, just like Max did to me."

Hans was now in the taxi, so three men were already seated in the car and one was in the front passenger seat. I speak up, "Let me come to the hotel with you, I am going to kill Max," they started laughing, I continued "Tomorrow I am going to kill, one by one those fucking bastard pussy lickers." The guys are nearly convulsing with laughter, but they all say in unison, "Come on then!" Feeling bold, I lay down across their laps in the backseat as we drove towards the hotel. They can't stop laughing and one of them shouts, "Angelina, fuck him up!"

As we reached the entrance, I saw that it was a Marriot Hotel - a fancy five-star establishment. I didn't give a fuck about its reputation; I knew I was going to make a scandal here. The four of them guide me to the door of his room, their hushed whispers warning me to be quiet. With gentle taps on the door, they call out in unison, "Max, open up." The anticipation builds as we wait for a response from inside.

Max opened the door in just his boxers and I barged in, fuming. "You owe me money!" I demanded. "You pay me now! I want my money! You were the only one who was to have sex tonight. Bastard! Those lesbians have done a runner, and even they have been paid and they have made your friends a fool." I pointed to Max's four friends who stood in the doorway, they were watching in amazement.

I push Max forcefully to sit down on the bed, I continue "Being lesbian is not a problem, the problem is you are being an ass hole" I place my high-heeled shoes in his groin, threatening to crush his balls with the sharp heel. The Swiss men standing in the doorway watching and can't contain their laughter any longer. I grabbed his chin and made steady eye contact as I demanded, "I want my money now, Mr. Mini." His hands trembled as he reluctantly handed me four one-hundred euro notes.

I wagged my finger at him and exclaimed, "No, No, No! Because of all this embarrassment, I now want 500 euros from you." I turned to the group of guys and asked, "How much was the taxi fare?" They responded, "25 euros Angelina." I added on, "Then I also want an extra 50 euros for the ride, so a total of 550 euros." I continued, "Or else I will start spanking you, you little bastard." He reluctantly handed over another one hundred and fifty euros.

With a quick nod, I spun on my heel and strode confidently out of the room. The Swiss men at the door made way for me, parting like the Red Sea as I passed through. I paused in the doorway and turned to them, my heart filled with gratitude. "Thank you guys," I said sincerely. The tallest of the group stepped forward, "Angelina, you are the nicest and craziest woman I have seen in my life." He leaned in closer, conspiratorially. "I'll be seeing you tomorrow, my dear. At Elefante." And with that, I left the hotel and disappeared into the darkness of the night.

I stumbled home, my stomach churning and bile rising in my throat. The room spun around me, mocking my drunken state. I collapsed onto the cold bathroom floor, curling up like a helpless child as I vomited into the toilet. Darkness swallowed me whole as I drifted into a deep sleep, reeking of alcohol. I had managed to drag myself out of the bathroom and crawl into bed. When I awoke at 4 pm, I saw twenty-two missed calls from Gabriela on my phone. With a groan, I forced myself to take some medicine for my pounding headache, I knew I had to tell her the story.

As soon as she arrived, I recounted the entire tale to her. Initially, she burst out laughing but then she said "This is exactly why I don't drink," she said, shaking my head. "It's not a game or something to do for fun. This is a job like any other. Do you see people drinking in their jobs, when they work? You could have been raped, or come home with no money in your bag!" Unfortunately, I am a little bit wilder than her and never learned the lesson she gave me.

As the afternoon faded into an inky dusk, we dined at a quaint Italian restaurant, enjoying the last rays of sunlight. But as the night fell upon us, it was time yet again to prepare ourselves for another evening. There was always a sense of danger lurking just beneath the surface. We arrived at "Elafante Branco" on this Thursday night, expecting a quiet evening. Instead, we were met with a swarm of men from various European areas - France, England, and Scandinavia.

The Portuguese locals were scarce and intimidated by the influx of wealthy and refined foreigners. With their money and class, the gringos now claimed this territory as their own. The Portuguese refuse to pay what they should and treat us poorly. They should understand that if they don't want to pay, they should stay home or take their chances trying to find someone on the street with their charm.

As Gabriela and I stood in the bar, a group of four men approached us. They had an air of sophistication about them, with their well-tailored suits and hangers-on girls trailing behind them. The leader of the group was Joel, a tall and handsome French businessman from Monaco. He immediately took a liking to me and asked, "Is it alright if we go back to the hotel together?"

I hesitated for a moment before responding, "The price is 500 euros."

Joel immediately agreed and even said he was happy to pay for his three employees to have some fun too, with a girl of their choice. This meant Gabriela was also in business and thankfully would stay in the same group. After we finalised the deal, we celebrated with a round of drinks.

Then I noticed the Swiss men from the night before had arrived at the club, but Max was noticeably absent - I must have left quite an impression on his balls with my stiletto the night before. Despite being occupied with someone else, the tall Swiss man approached me and said, "Hello Angelina. I was hoping to spend tonight with you." I apologised and suggested that they should have come earlier, then I turned to Joel and told him, "You have a choice: pay me now or I will go with him!" This was a new version of Angelina, I was more romantic than ever before.

With Gabriela by my side, I felt safe and secure as we made our way to the luxurious five-star Marriot Hotel. As we entered the grand lobby, I couldn't believe that this was the same place I had been the night before. Joel had a luxurious room and we indulged in some drinks before we fucked. Despite his limited Portuguese, we managed to have a conversation.

Suddenly, he blurts out an invitation: "Tomorrow I must go to a meeting in Porto, but on Saturday I return and I want you to join me again. Will you come with me to Monaco for one week?" I responded with a noncommittal "Yeah, Yeah, Okay." In this line of work, it's hard to trust anyone or anything. The only thing that matters is the present moment; I don't have time to worry about the future or dwell on the past. Today is all that matters in my world. I could tell that Joel was a married man by the fact that he didn't ask for my phone number. It made me feel disgusted.

The following day, Friday, I woke up feeling sober and not hungover. I called my family to talk to my kids. I miss them dearly and feel a deep sense of emptiness without them. I can't wait to make enough money and leave to be with them again. I want to be there to see them grow up.

As always on Fridays and Saturdays, the day seemed to fly by, and before I knew it, I had only one hour left to apply my makeup, get dressed up, and spray on some perfume for tonight's pointless charade.

After offering a prayer for safety, it was time to start work. Gabriela, as always, was already standing in front of the building when I arrived. She is impressively quick at getting ready. I constantly found myself procrastinating, finding any excuse to delay my departure. By 10 pm prompt, she would always be at the 'Elefante Branco' club, prepared for dinner.

For this evening, I chose to wear one of the suits that she had gifted to me. It was a beautiful red suit designed for women, complete with a matching short skirt instead of trousers. I had painted my nails and lips a bold shade of red, and to finish the look I wore a tight black top under a jacket and black high heels.

The long jacket was always a part of my 'Hooker Kit', providing the necessary cover. Gabriela was also stunning, in a small green dress that perfectly complemented her emerald eyes. She strutted confidently in red high heels, she was also with red nails that we had both chosen to match for the night. Our matching lipstick completed our femme fatale look.

As we approached the entrance of the gentlemen's club, the doormen exclaimed, "Wow, you ladies look stunning tonight!" We smiled and thanked them as we walked by. We entered the club with confident smiles, fully aware of our attractiveness. As usual, we handed our coats to the woman at the coat desk. I had no idea that this night would change my life.

The clock read 1 am when, the manager announced: "Girls who speak English, go to the front line; others, back off." Gabriela cheered me on, saying "Go, Angelina!" The manager went on to explain that a group of English and Swedish men had made a reservation. Feeling nervous, I told her "I don't speak English well." She reassured me, saying "You speak better than me; I can only say how much!? Go get one for you and one for me." Reluctantly, I replied, "Yes boss, I'll do it." I hated having to approach any guy in this situation.

The club was massive and divided into two sections. The front line included the main bar and the surrounding banquet tables, while the second line encompassed the restaurant with its own bar area, and this was separated by a black glass wall.

I didn't actively engage, instead opting to stand near the bar and observe as the first group of English people walked in. The other girls eagerly swarmed around them, but I couldn't help feeling like it was all a bit undignified. I don't think I'm better than anyone here, but this level of subservience seems unnecessary and disrespectful towards the guys. There were about twenty girls gathered in this section of the bar, with even more scattered throughout the seating areas.

We were offering ourselves to the gringos, as if we were pieces of meat. The men appeared content with the attention they were receiving, basking in the admiration of all the girls gazing at them. One of them stood taller than the rest and had brilliant blue eyes, he was also dressed in simpler attire compared to the others.

While the others were dressed elegantly in suits with large, expensive Rolex watches on their wrists, he stood out in his casual ensemble of jeans, t-shirt, and trainers. He continued to stare at me, his gaze so intense it almost felt like he was devouring me.

And then a blond Brazilian fucking girl call Rachel, taller than me stepped in front of me to shield me from the guy. She was not even meant to be there, because she could only speak Portuguese and a bit of Italian. I placed my hands on her back and dug my nails in, leaning in close to her neck and said "Move out of my way! I always leave the Italians for you but now you're in my path. If you don't get out of my front, I'll wait outside and beat you. You can't even speak English." With that, she disappeared.

The casually dressed gentleman, emboldened by this sudden movement, took a step forward towards me. As if drawn by an invisible force, the other men followed suit and they all at once began to approach girls in the bar. The scene was peculiar, almost as if the first man had permitted them or set the example for the others to follow.

He approached me and introduced himself as Timotee. He was fluent in both English and French. Later, he revealed that he was born in England but his father is French. Since my English was still lacking, and he knew I was not fluent in English, he called over another member of his group who spoke Portuguese. He introduced his friend and translator, as John. It became clear that John was working for Timotee. Timotee started talking, "You are my **fate**!" I had no idea what the word 'fate' meant and he offered me a drink, then suggested that we take a seat at a nearby table.

It was now clear that the other men with him were his bodyguards. They were permitted to have brief sexual encounters, but they were not allowed to drink and only disappear one at a time, as they were still on duty. Timotee did not partake in any drinking; the only one allowed to drink was John.

He soon invited me to his hotel, and we agreed on a price. But once inside, he was unlike anyone else I had met before. He didn't seem interested in getting to know me personally, only asking my age, if I had children, and why I chose this line of work. He asked me to take a shower right away because even though I didn't personally smoke, my hair stank of smoke. At 'Elfante Branco' smoking was allowed. He had a strong aversion to the scent of cigarettes.

He had already handed me the agreed five hundred euros earlier. The original agreement was for me to be there for an hour. After taking the shower, he offered me an extra 1,500 euros and gestured towards the bed next to him, saying "Please lie down here."

Carefully, he flicked off each light switch one by one until the room was enveloped in complete darkness. The only source of light was the soft glow seeping out from under the bathroom door, reminding me that I had forgotten to turn it off. There was a complete absence of any sound or movement.

He instructed me to face away from him, and my immediate thought was that he might be a psycho about to harm me. He noticed my dolphin tattoo on my neck and leaned in to kiss it, calling it beautiful. Then he traced the words "you are beautiful" over and over with his right index finger until he drifted off to sleep. All I could think was, "Please let it be 6 am so I can leave this place. This man is far from normal."

As the minutes dragged on, I found myself constantly glancing at the phone, desperately hoping for time to pass faster. The dull, early morning light seeped in through the curtains, casting a faint glow over the room. I quietly stepped out of bed at 6 am, careful not to wake him. I gathered my things and clothes but no matter how much I tried to muffle any noise, every tiny movement seemed to echo loudly in the silence.

His voice made me jump, "Where do you think you're going?" My heart pounded as I stammered out a response, "I have to get home to shower and I have a nail appointment at 8 am." It sounded ridiculous, but it was the truth. I had carefully planned this appointment the day before, knowing that I needed to look flawless in case the meeting in Monaco actually happened. He replied, "Sure, just give me your phone number and I'll also pay for your nails and taxi fare." He handed me 150 euros. I was surprised by the amount and felt like I had hit the jackpot.

As I stepped out of the hotel room and into the bustling lobby, a wave of astonishment washed over me, I knew I could not continue to treat this man with my usual detachment and indifference. Instead, I would have to approach him with warmth and kindness, something that felt foreign to me.

As the taxi made its way through the bustling streets, I remembered I had left my long black jacket in his room. It was an essential item in my 'Hooker Kit' but I knew that this didn't matter - because soon he would call me and we would meet again. It was Saturday, and now Joel, with his promise of Monaco was no longer my target.

After my nail appointment, I slept until 3 pm. I hadn't put my phone on silent because I was waiting for Timotee to call. But the call never came. My friend Gabriela was already at my apartment and she loved hearing about all of the crazy, funny, and dangerous things that always seem to happen to me. "This guy is gay for sure?" she announced. "John is his lover for sure and he just used you to make him jealous. And I bet he gave you a fake number. You should call him." "No way!" I replied. "I'm pretty sure he's gay and a total psycho" she concluded.

I dialled his number, but it wouldn't connect. It was a fake number. I couldn't believe he had tricked me, but at least I had been paid. She laughed and taunted me, saying "See? I told you so." Now, my only hope was that Joel was telling the truth because then at least 500 euros was guaranteed. As my mother used to say 'it is better to have one bird in the hand, than two in the bush', which means that having one sure thing is better than chasing after two possibilities.

After our usual daily routine and calls to our families, we begin the normal preparations for work. It's all about survival these days. Once evening falls, we head back to the gentlemen's club where Joel is already there, waiting for me. He greets me with a big smile, and this time I don't feel ashamed as I approach him. He wraps his arms around my waist and kisses my cheek. "A few drinks and another night at my hotel?" he asks. I nod and reply, "Yes, sure." He smiles again and says, "I missed you, girl."

After a few drinks, we decided to leave the club early and go back to the hotel. Once there, he tried to get more intimate with me, kissing and using his tongue in a French style. He also wanted to perform oral sex on me and wanted me to give him a blowjob without a condom, but I refused and treated him as a client. I was still annoyed with the other crazy French guy, Timotee, because I stayed all night with Joel, I did not even ask for more money. Our sexual encounter wasn't particularly passionate or intimate; I think I was just angry with the other idiot.

As the sun rose and quickly disappeared, I arrived home only to have my phone ring. It was Joel with a slightly upset tone "What have you done, I wanted to have lunch with you before I go today. But I want you to come to Monaco and I will buy you a ticket" I hesitated, but finally, I agreed on the condition of being paid per day and receiving his contact information in case of any danger. He promised to send everything over for verification.

It was Sunday, I had made the decision to have a normal day. Gabriela and I decided to venture out to the bustling Vasco Da Ga shopping centre. Its grand entrance beckoned us with promises of endless shopping possibilities and delicious treats waiting inside. We strolled through its vibrant corridors, admiring the colourful displays and soaking in the lively atmosphere. The hours slipped by effortlessly as we explored every nook and cranny of the mall, trying on clothes and testing out new beauty products. Exhausted we left the urban paradise and headed back home.

As the evening settled in, Joel sent me a flurry of information - my ticket for Monaco, his company's information, pictures, and even his work telephone number. With the flight scheduled for Monday morning, I quickly packed a small suitcase with everything I would need for my journey.

The next morning, I left my apartment before dawn and hailed a taxi to take me to the airport. It was only my second time travelling by air, so despite my best efforts to prepare, I still encountered some difficulties at the airport. The maze of signs and gates seemed to spin me around in circles, leaving me feeling frustrated and overwhelmed.

Then suddenly, I heard my name being called over the speakers for the last call of my flight. Panic set in as I sprinted through the crowded terminal, bumping into people along the way. Finally reaching the gate, I handed over my ticket and rushed onto the plane. As soon as I sat down in my seat, panting from the adrenaline rush, I realised with horror that I had left both my phone and watch at home.

My heart raced as I stepped off the plane and scanned the crowded airport terminal. There, through the throngs of people, I saw him waiting for me. My stress levels were already high, knowing Madam Marta and Gabriela were waiting for me to confirm my safe arrival. I knew without contact from me, they would fear the worst. Turning to Joel, I pleaded with him to make my stay as short as possible - no more than five days - and asked him to buy me a ticket back home to leave on Friday. He managed to arrange this for me. With a sense of relief and gratitude, I grabbed the ticket home from his hands and took a deep breath, knowing that at least one source of worry had been alleviated.

My days in Monaco were not the glamorous and exciting experience I had imagined. Instead of exploring the beautiful city, I found myself alone for most of the day, while Joel was at work. Our evenings together were lacklustre as well, consisting only of dinners at various restaurants, dull conversation, and returning to his apartment. It was located in the bustling centre of Monaco near the famous 'Casino De Monte-Carlo'. The constant buzz of traffic and people outside seemed to mock my unfulfilled expectations for this trip. Despite its luxurious reputation, my time in Monaco felt mundane and uneventful.

Throughout the day, he provided me with money for food. In a country where Italian, English, and Portuguese were not widely spoken, I struggled to spend this money. All I could manage was a feeble "Yum, Yum", my stomach growling and my body weak from hunger. I resorted to making exaggerated gestures in hopes of communicating my needs to the locals.

With each new dish that arrived, I never knew what to expect. Some were delicious and perfectly seasoned, while others were a complete surprise. One dish in particular was heavily salted - even for someone like myself who has a love affair with salt. As soon as the first bite touched my tongue, my taste buds went into revolt against the overwhelming briny flavour. It was like a tidal wave of salt had crashed into my mouth, assaulting my senses with an intensity that left me unable to stomach any more bites. This was not just a pinch of salt, it was a mountain of it, overpowering everything else on the plate. Never before had I encountered such a bold and unapologetic use of seasoning. It was an experience I would not soon forget, but one I hoped to never repeat.

The situation was far from ideal. He had shown no interest in taking me to any of the beautiful places Monaco had to offer. I was there to dine with him and pleasure him sexually, and then he would simply discard me like a used toy. And I couldn't shake the feeling that he was already married and this displeased me. Despite the glamour of the boardwalks and luxurious boats, I just wanted to return to my home in Portugal. Instead, I felt manipulated and unimportant.

The days dragged on, but at least I had found a note in my notebook with my sister's phone number in Brazil tucked inside my bag. Thanks to that, I was able to reach out and make a connection with home while I was away. Each day had blended into the next until finally, the day came when I was able to return home. After being away, I couldn't wait to see the familiar surroundings of my apartment again. The flight back was brief, but exhaustion weighed heavily on me. However, as I gazed out the airplane window and saw the sparkling city lights below, a sense of relief washed over me.

As midnight approached on Friday, I finally arrived at my apartment. The streets were quiet, save for the occasional car passing by. My heart sank a bit as I realised that Gabriela was still at work, and our reunion would have to wait until morning.

As the first rays of sunlight stretched across the city, I made my way to the coffee shop on the corner. The smell of freshly brewed coffee wafted through the air, tempting me as I settled into a chair outside. With each sip of my warm cappuccino, I could feel the anticipation building for Gabriela's arrival at 2 pm. We had so much catching up to do, and both of us were eager to share the latest gossip. The sun continued its ascent into the clear blue sky, casting a warm glow over the bustling streets and filling me with a sense of hope for the day ahead.

Silvana's sudden appearance made my blood boil. Ignoring her would not make her disappear, and she now had the audacity to approach me with a poker face. "I know what you are," she said without hesitation. "A lowly prostitute, living off the desperation of others. I could easily ruin your life, but

I have a proposition for you. Be nice to me and I won't tell anyone in Brazil about your shameful profession."

My jaw clenched as she spoke, and I could feel the red-hot anger rising within me.

"Give me 1,000 euros," she continued, "and I will pay my rent and have enough time to find a respectable job. Then we can forget this ever happened." Her entitled tone only ignited my rage.

I looked her up and down, taking in her lazy posture and arrogant personality "Do you think I would spend 1,000 euros on someone like you?" I spat out. "A parasite who contributes nothing to society and does not even bother trying to improve their own life? If I were to spend that amount of money, it would be on someone worth investing in."

I was now standing facing her. I leaned in close, my voice seething with venom. "In fact, for 1,000 euros, I could easily hire someone to kill you. That is the value of your life – you are nothing more than a nuisance. You can tell who you want, I do not care!" With a flick of my hand, I dismissed her and walked away, leaving her standing there in shock.

After returning home from a day of feeling bored and down, I plopped down on the couch and turned on MTV. The constant barrage of flashy images and loud music did little to lift my spirits. Suddenly, there was a knock at my door. It was Gabriela, her face etched with worry. She explained she was only waiting for two more days before finally calling the police to report me missing. I explained that I had been without a telephone and unable to make contact. In an attempt to make up for my absence, I presented her with some souvenirs from my recent travels. We decided to go out for lunch at our favourite restaurant. Afterward, we fell into our familiar routine of preparing for work.

As the sun set, we were already at Elefante Branco', it was really busy. My friend and I sat at the bar, engaged in conversation without any intention of seeking out potential clients.

However, we noticed a tall man with olive skin and jet-black hair watching us intently. He exuded an air of confidence and mystery, and I couldn't help but think he must have come from Spain. With a smooth stride, he approached us and introduced himself as Mario - the organiser of a renowned Rally event. He explained this was the annual car rally from Lisbon in Portugal to Drakar in Africa.

Immediately, he spoke up and said, "I was interested in Gabriela first, but now I'm into you, Angelina." I responded, "What do you think of all three of us going together?" My friend Gabriela and I often pretend to be lesbians so as not to lose the client, but we don't actually act intimate with each other or kiss, the reality was cleverly covered by our hair. We agreed on the price of 400 euros each.

When he asked if we took drugs, Gabriela responded with a sly smile and said, "No but if you pay, we take." I was familiar with this tactic; it was how we kept the clients. Once payment was in hand, we never actually indulged in drugs and instead shifted away the conversation and our actions to maintain professionalism. He replied, "I prefer to avoid drugs."

As we exited the club, we made our way to his luxurious hotel. It was a surprise to see that he had booked the penthouse suite, and even more surprising was the interior. Every inch of the room was covered in mirrors - behind the bed, on the walls. It reminded me of a motel I had stayed at in Brazil, but the rest of the room exuded opulence and luxury. The soft glow of dimmed lights added to the intimate atmosphere as we made our way inside.

After he paid us, Gabriela wasted no time shedding her clothes. Within five minutes of our arrival, she stood naked before him. I couldn't help but comment, "I didn't even have a chance to grab a drink." Her response was firm and resolute: "Drink? We are here to work." The briskness and purpose in her voice left no room for argument. We had a job to do.

I retreated to the private confines of the bathroom, taking a moment to prepare myself for what was to come. I carefully applied the lubricant to my pussy.

With a deep breath, I emerged from the bathroom and joined Gabriela in front of Mario on the bed. We began our performance, feigning a passionate kiss while Gabriela's luscious hair acted as a veil between us. Our bodies moved in sync, teasingly close but never touching lips. Mario's eyes were fixated on us, watching our every move with mysterious eyes. The room was filled with electric energy as we continued our seductive charade, building up the tension until it was almost unbearable. We playfully touched each other's breasts and giggled like a pair of clowns.

Gabriela's body moved with sensuous grace, her eyes locked onto his as she slipped the condom on him with her mouth. But before she could proceed, he abruptly stopped her. "No, No, stop," he commanded. "Stay there Gabriela, keep going with the show." We were all stunned by his interruption. He continued, "I want to see where this 'show' goes. I can see through the mirror that you're trying to make a fool out of me. What bullshit is this?" We quickly apologised and explained that we were not lesbians.

He said, "I never asked you to be involved with each other. This whole discussion about lesbians started because of you both. I can be intimate with both of you without you having to touch each other."

At first, we feared he was angry with us, but to our surprise, this man in his late fifties remained surprisingly calm. Gabriela boldly straddled his erect penis, but even this did not seem to satisfy him. Without hesitation, a fresh condom was placed on his hard penis and he thrust himself into my waiting body, reaching a climax deep inside me. However, I could not find release in this encounter - for me to reach climax during a client session, it typically took at least a week of arousal and stimulation. The lucky partner could even be unattractive, for me to achieve orgasm was almost impossible with a client, and when it happened it was without truly enjoying their intimate touch.

After we finished our task, as we said goodbye he asked for Gabriela's phone number. The next day, he called her and told her he had a gift for her. He also asked to speak with me.

When I got on the phone, he said, "Angelina, this is awkward, I really like Gabriela. However, I want to spend the night with you before I head back to Porto. I'll give Gabriela some money as thanks and then we can go to a hotel. I need to see you before I leave to prepare for the rally event."

We had made the appointment for that evening, and I met him again. At the hotel, he had prepared champagne for us to enjoy. We talked a lot, had sex once again, and then he invited me to join him in Porto for a week. Without hesitation, I agreed and we made arrangements for the price. Two days later, he was waiting in his car outside of my apartment and we set off for the city of Porto together.

To my surprise, he drove me to his home - a sprawling, luxurious villa that sat nestled among the green countryside on the outskirts of Porto. Despite the hot weather, we spent evenings in his impeccably manicured garden, surrounded by vibrant flowers and fragrant herbs. Unlike Joel, this man showed me the true essence of the area, taking me on tours and introducing me to its hidden gems.

The physical aspect of our relationship was purely professional, but each day spent with him was filled with new adventures and deepening connections. As he prepared to drive me back to Lisbon, he surprised me with a stunning pair of Channel shoes and a special collection of replica miniature cars from his rally, every car was there with their number printed on them, neatly displayed in a presentation box. While I appreciated the thought behind the shoes, it was the miniatures that truly touched my heart - a thoughtful gift I could give to my children.

When he dropped me off at my apartment, I couldn't help but feel a pang of sadness. As I said goodbye and watched him drive away, my heart ached knowing I would never see this kind and gentle man again. He had treated me with such dignity and tenderness, and it was bittersweet to say goodbye.

Chapter XIII

A week had passed since I bid farewell to Mario, and it proved to be an incredibly hectic one. Like a tsunami, hoards of junkies flooded into 'Elefante Branco' each night at 10 pm to indulge in their vices. We would work tirelessly until the early hours of the morning, sometimes not returning home until 8 am. However, what captivated my attention more than anything else were the groups of girls who claimed they never drank or caused trouble, yet continuously judged and looked down upon those who did - including myself. These girls were also dangerously addicted to Cocaine and Weed, making them no different than the people they condemned.

It was a Wednesday night, and a large group of Scandinavian men, mostly Swedish but with a few Danish guys mixed in, arrived at the club with a craving for both women and drugs. Gabriela and I were the only ones there who remained sober amidst the debauchery.

We were allowed to join a group of girls who had made first contact, the guys had singled out for their attention. Two of them had their sights set on us, and we were asked to join in on their night of fun. The villa we arrived at was impressive, with its grand entrance and sprawling gardens. Yet, instead of being focused on the money, the other girls were there for lines of Cocaine - they were like wild animals, willing to do anything for drugs. This depravity and desperation began to stress me out and made Gabriela uneasy as well.

And then came the demand for us to strip down to lingerie or nothing at all. "Without money, no funny," I protested sternly. But Bjorn, one of our hosts, simply brushed it off with a carefree attitude. "We are here to have fun and good times," he declared. But my mind was still fixated on the payment I was promised and now I also wanted taxi money as well because this was a very remote location. As the one who spoke English the best among the girls, it was, my responsibility to take charge and make sure we were not being taken advantage of.

As the night wore on, tensions rose and tempers flared. The idiot refused to pay us the agreed-upon 300 euros each, causing frustration and anger to bubble to the surface. I was ready to take my payment and leave, still leaving enough time to make it back to the club. But I couldn't stand the Swedish guys who always thought we would give them our services for free just because they were good-looking.

The situation became more intense as I snatched the bottle of vodka off the table and warned them that I would break it and cause them damage if they didn't pay what they owed. Eventually, an agreement was reached - those who wanted to stay could stay, and those who wanted to go were free to leave. In the end, they paid the money promised, only five girls chose to leave with me, while another six chose to indulge in drugs and stay with the men. It was a chaotic and tense situation, but one that I had grown accustomed to in this line of work.

Cristini, the petite girl, had confirmed she was leaving with me. So once I gathered the money for the departing girls, I discreetly slipped it into her pocket. It was obvious that everyone assumed I had the money on me. I made sure to usher Cristini into the waiting taxi before the other girls, and then one of the men from the villa came running out, yelling "You worthless bitches, you can't just take our money! You haven't done anything to earn this money!" The other girls were now already inside the taxi, their panicked expressions reflecting my own.

The door of the taxi hung open, beckoning me inside. But before I could get in, the man grabbed hold of my waist and tried to pull me back towards the villa. In a desperate attempt to stop him, I kicked him away with all my strength. But he persisted, holding onto me while I struggled to break free. Inside the taxi, the other girls grabbed onto my legs, trying to keep me inside as well.

Just when it seemed like we were locked in a vicious tug-of-war between the man and the girls. Our driver suddenly emerged from his seat and charged towards me. With a loud thud, he slammed the car door into the man's body, shouting for him to let go. Stunned by the sudden turn of events, the Swedish man stumbled backwards towards the villa, muttering angry words under his breath. "Fucking thieving bitches," he spat before disappearing back inside.

Finally able to escape, I quickly climbed into the safety of the taxi. As we sped away from that chaotic scene, I couldn't believe how calm and indifferent the girls who stayed seemed despite the chaos that had just unfolded. They were used to situations like this - remaining for only Cocaine solely focused on satisfying their addiction. It made my stomach turn in disgust.

We returned to the club to find our plans had gone wrong. We now found the club devoid of any potential clients, the 'good guys' had already been taken care of. Our time had been wasted on travelling to and from the villa, and trying to get money from those bastards. So Gabriela and I decided to leave and head home.

As the sun rose on a new day, we went to the cafe bar across from our apartment for our usual fix of strong Cappuccino. But there was no talk of daily routines or weekend plans - instead, the buzz of gossip was about the death of a girl we knew. Her name sent chills down our spines as it appeared in bold letters on the newspaper's front page - Latifa. She was a Brazilian with Lebanese roots, working as a prostitute for her drug-dealing pimp boyfriend. We were aware of her cocaine use, caused by her toxic relationship, but we never could have imagined the depths she had sunk to. Now, our hearts were heavy with sorrow as we thought of her innocent daughter left behind in the wake of her tragic overdose on heroin. Our world had been shattered, and the darkness of reality set in.

Sadly, this is a typical story of girl's lives spiralling out of control. It starts innocently enough, with just one line of Cocaine and this leads to another until they're hooked and move on to crack or even heroin.

The lure of the money we make at the club beckons, but we resist and decide to stay in for the night instead, watching mind-numbing MTV. When not working Gabriela and I were never the type to frequent bars and discotheques; we preferred the safety of home, where we could talk to our family and try to maintain some normality.

All of our spare money went towards rent and maintaining a certain appearance for work, which included frequent visits to the hairdresser and perfect nails. In reality, the only enjoyment was indulging in lunch at restaurants. Unknowingly, whilst I was sending a large portion of my earnings back to my family in Brazil, I was slowly losing myself in this never-ending cycle.

We didn't attend Latifa's funeral, as our connections with her and those she associated with were not strong. They were all involved in the perilous underworld that encircled us, and we made sure to keep a safe distance.

The sun had barely risen on a beautiful Friday morning, filling the sky with a soft golden glow. I could feel the energy coursing through my body as I woke up, feeling completely rested and rejuvenated after a peaceful night at home. The stress and worry from previous days had lifted, leaving me feeling light and carefree. Our usual routine of cappuccino, brunch at our favourite restaurant, a quick stop at the salon, and the afternoon stroll felt more enjoyable than ever before. My mind was clear and my heart was full. As the day went on, I couldn't shake off the feeling that something great was in store for me tonight. The anticipation and excitement grew with each passing hour, filling me with a sense of invincibility. It was as if the universe was aligning to bring me prosperity and abundance. I couldn't wait to see what the night would hold, confident that it would be full of success and fulfilment.

As I sat in the darkened club, surrounded by chattering girls and sipping on my second margarita, Gabriela's words snapped me to attention. "Angelina, the psycho weird gay is back. He's here to finish the job. He's here to kill you!" Her voice was deadly serious, making my heart pound against my chest with fear. I followed her gaze to see his towering figure lurking behind the black glass, a chilling smile plastered on his face. My body froze with terror, my legs incapable of carrying me away from danger. All I could do was turn my back, unable to even utter a word as he approached.

Timotee walked with deadly purpose, his eyes locking onto me from across the room. John was at his side, but the rest of his security team was nowhere to be seen. He strode directly to the bar but then circled around the room, positioning himself in a spot where he could study my face without obstruction. I tried to ignore him, focusing on the girls by my side, but I could feel his intense gaze burning. Every nerve in my body tingled with unease as I waited for him to make his move.

With a determined glint in his eyes, he strode towards me holding a dolphin toy. As if on cue, he pressed a button, and a red laser shot out from its eyes, aiming straight for my heart. I couldn't move as the beam stretched across the room and landed squarely on my chest. He sat down next to me, while John took the other side. At that moment, I knew without a doubt that the prophecy of Gabriela was coming true and I was completely screwed.

The words tumbled from his mouth, with an intensity that made my heart race and my palms sweat. "Where have you been, woman?!" His voice echoed off the walls. "I sent my men here to find you every day for two weeks, but you were nowhere to be found! And now, on this crucial night, you are here!"

John stepped in to translate, as Timotee continued but even he struggled to keep up with the man's frenzied speech. I could see the veins bulging in his neck as he ranted about me playing games and how tonight would be the deciding factor. John made it clear to me, that Timotee had come tonight prepared with a bag of money to buy the establishment, as I could not be found. He planned to then ban all the women from ever sitting foot in here with names similar to mine - Gabriela, Angel, Angelica, Rafaela...all because of Angelina!

I was flabbergasted at the thought of being responsible for potentially ruining these women's livelihoods. As I introduced myself with the name. I said "I am... Angelina," his expression told me that he couldn't even remember it correctly. This struck me as humorous, and I couldn't help but burst into uncontrollable laughter.

He asked if I wanted to drink something, and I said "Wow, I guess tonight I need alcohol. Yes, one margarita more please." Then he drank vodka and orange juice and he said he never drank like this but he was nervous. He explained, also that my jacket was with him. He had opened all of it with a knife and checked it for microphones. He thought I had acted weird and this was not normal. I admit I was strange but this was because I did think he was weird too.

He spoke in a serious tone, asking, "Would you like to come with me? I have a proposal for you. We can go to the Algarve tomorrow morning and I am willing to pay you whatever amount you want. I will also ensure that you are back by Monday." My mind raced, thinking, 'My God. Could this be it? Is he planning to take me to the Algarve and dispose of my body in the sea?'

I hesitated, my mind racing with doubt and suspicion. But something inside me, a burning curiosity, pushed me forward to accept his invitation. His words were like a spell, luring me in with a key phrase '**You are my fate**'. A shiver crept through my body as he spoke the word "**fate**," causing my heart to skip a beat. "Why didn't you call me?" he demanded, his voice dripping with accusation.

Panic rose in my chest as I tried to explain myself. "I did try!" I protested, but he wouldn't believe me. "I stayed by my phone all day long," he continued, his eyes narrowing in anger. "I even paid for two extra days just in case you called and on Sunday I even came here to the club and you were not here!" My head was spinning as I struggled to remember every detail of that fateful day. "I called you...I called so many times," I stammered, reciting the number from memory. He confirmed each digit without hesitation until I reached the last two numbers: 62. His response was swift and crushing: "No, it's 67." My heart sank as I realised my mistake, 7 and 2 look the same to me, I am blind without my glasses. "My goodness," I whispered, feeling utterly foolish. And then the truth hit me but one that only seemed to happen to me - I am... Angelina and I am cursed with bad luck and misfortune at every turn.

His words were said with purpose. "You won't escape me tonight, I am coming with you tonight to wherever you live; you can pack your suitcase and join me at my hotel." there was a glint in his eyes, I could not put my finger on it. My heart races as I feel a mixture of fear and anticipation. This wasn't what I had planned for the night, but I could smell the euros. I hurriedly lead him back to my place, trying to ignore the unease settling in my stomach.

As we enter my tidy living room, I offer him a drink but he declines. "You can stay here while I pack," I say nervously, hoping to delay the inevitable. But before I know it, he's already standing in my messy bedroom. "Oh, you're already here, don't worry I am not going to escape out of the balcony" I stutter, scrambling to hide the evidence of my chaotic life. But with practiced ease, I transform my room into a pristine haven in just ten minutes. As I finish packing my bag, he sits on my freshly made bed, his gaze following every move I make. The atmosphere between us is intense.

I requested his address and details of where we were going. After a few moments of anticipation, he replied with an unexpected answer – his house was located in Vale Do Lobo, the most prestigious and exclusive address in all of Algarve. This was where the ultra-wealthy and famous resided, including the likes of Madonna, Cristiano Ronaldo, and even Bill Gates. My mind raced with curiosity and excitement at the thought of visiting this lavish area. With a quick tap on my phone, I sent a text to Gabriela and Madam Marta with all the details for safety. In a moment of dark humour, I concluded the text with 'Please pray for me xx.'

I arrived at his hotel and was immediately taken aback by all the surprises waiting for me in his room. There was a large bouquet of various flowers, including red roses, as well as a card, a box, and a sack. I immediately rang the receptionist and asked for a vase so I could take the flowers with me to the Algarve. The card revealed that he had been searching for me all around the world, particularly in Egypt. He even mentioned that he had dreamed about me since he was 25 years old. This was another shock for me to process.

As he spoke, my heart fluttered with anticipation. "First the sack," he commanded, and I obediently opened it. Inside was a giant dolphin soft toy, its velvety skin seeming to glimmer in the light. I pressed its belly and was rewarded with the sound of a real dolphin singing out into the room.

Next, I lifted the lid of the box he had given me. My breath caught in my throat as I beheld a beautiful white gold necklace, adorned with a large cross glittering with diamonds. I couldn't help but think back to my earlier conversation with him, where I had mentioned my strong religious beliefs. Did he remember? Or was this just a coincidence?

I was completely taken aback by his generosity. A stranger who had been searching for me for three weeks now bestowing upon me not one, but two lavish gifts and flowers. Unbelievably he also claimed to have been searching for me for 20 years, especially in Egypt. Thank God I had cut my hair!

My inner teenager, still holding onto her belief in Disney princesses and fairy tale romances, revelled in the romance and beauty of it all. But my adult self, the 29-year-old woman who had been through so much pain and trauma before this encounter, couldn't help but feel a twinge of unease. Was this too good to be true? Were there hidden intentions behind these gifts?

As much as I wanted to fully embrace this fairytale-like scenario, my instincts were screaming 'Red Flag!' All the shit that had happened to me, only seven weeks ago, I was raped and now I was really careful.

My mind was swirling with thoughts when a knock on the door jolted me back to reality. It was John, accompanied by a stunning woman from 'Elefante Branco' named Naomi, who bore an uncanny resemblance to the famous supermodel, Naomi Campbell. With a charming smile, he invited us to his room for some drinks. We eagerly accepted and soon found ourselves laughing, talking, and indulging in drinks until the early hours of the morning. Exhaustion threatened to overtake me as I collapsed onto the soft mattress, but before I could fully surrender to sleep, I forced myself up once again. It was time to leave for the Algarve.

Timotee grabbed our suitcases and we made our way to the hotel garage where my jaw dropped and stayed there. There before me was a brand new red Ferrari, its sleek body gleaming under the bright lights. I had never been so close to one in my life and I could not believe this was happening.

The four of us piled into the car, eagerly anticipating our journey to the Algarve. This was my first time visiting this famous destination, and I couldn't wait to see the sights. As we drove, the landscape gradually transformed from dry plains to lush greenery. Vineyards and olive trees dotted the rolling hillsides, and majestic cork trees towered over us.

After what seemed like hours, we finally arrived at our destination. But it wasn't just any ordinary villa - it was a palace. The sheer size and grandeur of the place left me speechless. And the property surrounding it was more than just a garden - it stretched out as far as the eye could see, resembling a sprawling farm.

As we drove through the gates, I couldn't help but notice the impressive collection of cars lining the patio. There were at least forty of them, in every colour imaginable - Lamborghini's, Ferrari's, Bentley's, Rolls Royce's, even a Bugatti. It was like a dream come true for any car enthusiast.

But what caught my attention was the presence of a limousine and a bus motor home among all these expensive cars. It was clear that whoever owned this palace had a taste for luxury and extravagance.

I glanced at Naomi and saw that she too was stunned by the opulence before us. I struggled to contain my awe and excitement - this was not something you come across every day. This was not a normal home, this was a palace fit for royalty or perhaps a rock star.

The grand house was adorned with a sprawling, lush Roman garden, filled with towering statues that seemed to watch our every move. Ascending the stone steps we entered the upper-floor kitchen, I couldn't help but feel like an insignificant being in such a magnificent place. The kitchen itself was a dream, equipped with all the latest appliances and luxurious finishes.

But what truly captured my attention and left me feeling awestruck was the gallery landing that encircled the enormous

Atrium entrance hall. Sunlight streamed in through the glass dome roof, illuminating the space and highlighting the intricate details of the bust statues placed around it. On one side stood proud figures from ancient Rome and Egypt, including Caesar and Nefertiti. On the other side were Cleopatra and Mark Antony, their expressions frozen in time. In the centre of the entrance hall, were two colossal statues standing at a towering 8 meters tall - Greek and Roman versions of Venus and Aphrodite. Flanking them were two majestic palm trees, adding to the opulent atmosphere of the space.

Despite my attempts to appear calm and collected, my body trembled uncontrollably. However, he was calm as he said, "Come, I will show you our bedroom. And if you are not comfortable sharing a bed with me, I can show you to the other bedrooms." My gaze was still fixed on the exquisite statues of Venus and Aphrodite as I followed him to the stairs that led to the other rooms.

The first door we came to was his bedroom, and as he opened it, I couldn't believe what I saw. The room was adorned in white marble, from the sitting area before the massive bed to the walls and floors. He proudly informed me that the bed was of the same brand used by the Queen of

England herself. Unable to contain my excitement, I leapt onto the bed which towered at waist height.

As I turned to take in my surroundings, I noticed a grand bathroom and two walk-in dressing rooms, one for each of us. In one corner of my dressing room was a dressing table with chairs and mirrors illuminated by soft lights. It was like something out of a dream.

He gestured, indicating that I could put my belongings there. As I unpacked and settled into the room, he suddenly called out to me, his voice laced with excitement. "Come over here, I want to show you something." He pointed to a large framed picture on the wall, a striking image of a nude woman with long black hair held by her hands which were delicately placed above her head, accentuating her curves and lines. "Do you like this picture?" he asked eagerly, "Does it seem familiar to you?" I studied the image for a moment before responding, "Yes, it's a beautiful picture. But no, I don't think I've seen it before." He smiled slyly and replied, "That's because it's you in the picture. Look at the face – it's exactly like yours." As he spoke, I couldn't help but see the resemblance he pointed out. Yet part of me couldn't shake the rational thought that it was simply a depiction of a naked woman.

Next, we descended the stairs and greeted John and Naomi. After some small talk, I finally had a moment alone with her. She couldn't help but exclaim, "Jesus Christ, Angelina. I've never seen anything like this before. How much are you charging him?" I replied, "Well when I first met him, I asked for 500 euros. But he ended up giving me 2150 euros, and has also given me some gifts since then." I proudly showed her the necklace around my neck and she exclaimed, "Wow!"

I continued "I plan on requesting 2000 euros per day and seeing how things play out." She couldn't help but show off her stunning smile, showcasing her pearly white teeth in her wide mouth. She questioned, "John isn't the one in charge, do you really think I should ask for the same as you?" I confidently responded, "Absolutely. It's not about who is the boss or who is not. This is about me and you being here to work, so we both deserve the same." Her smile grew even wider at my words.

Timotee offered us some food and asked if I wanted to rest. I glanced at Naomi, and our eyes communicated with each other. "No, I'm fine," I said, "but I could use a shower and something to eat." He nodded in understanding and said he would show me how everything worked in the bathroom. As I stood under the warm water of course I had locked the bathroom door, I heard him making a phone call and asking a woman to come over and help prepare breakfast for us.

After I finished my shower, I quickly got dressed and made myself presentable. As I headed downstairs, a tall and athletic woman entered through the front door. Her persona was softened by a warm smile as she introduced herself in perfect Portuguese as Nikita. I couldn't believe my eyes - she was incredibly beautiful and flawless. Though a few years older than me, her body was that of a goddess. Her presence was commanding, even while doing something as mundane as cooking. When she introduced herself as Timotee's friend and employee, I couldn't help but wonder if there was something more between them. But I told myself, this is not my business, I have no right to be jealous.

Nikita and Timotee kindly serve us a typical English breakfast, which adds to the already eccentric nature of this French man who seems surprisingly British. I find it a bit too heavy and unusual. We don't typically eat beans for breakfast in my country, so I can't help but wonder where the pastries and French bread are. But every day brings new experiences, and I am always open to trying new things. Then Timotee suggests, "Why don't we take my yacht to Vilamoura? We can sail to Albufeira, have lunch there, and explore the area." John agrees, saying "That's a great idea. We can show the girls some of the beautiful Algarve." Feeling overwhelmed, I turn to Naomi and say, "A yacht?" Everyone in the room laughs as I add, "I don't have a bikini."

Tomotee's smile never faltered as he turned to Nikita, his eyes sparkling with excitement. "If Angelina desires a bikini, please take her to the shops later and assist her in choosing one and buying whatever she wants," he said eagerly. The thought of spending time by the water on a beautiful yacht was too thrilling to waste any more time. "But for now, we must hurry. Our table is waiting for us at 'Castello Di Norcia' in Albufeira's stunning marina."

In three separate cars, we all set off towards the marina. The streets were lined with quaint shops and colourful buildings, the salty scent of the ocean lingering in the air.

As we approached the marina, I could feel my heart start to beat faster with excitement. The sight of the magnificent vessel before us left us both speechless. The sleek white hull gleamed in the sunlight, and the tall masts reached up towards the blue sky. For me, it would be a first-time experience sailing on both a yacht and the vast sea. But for Naomi, this was not her first rodeo - she proudly told me that she had sailed before in Lisbon, years ago.

As we sailed from Vilamoura towards Albufeira, I couldn't help but marvel at the beauty around us. Every inch of the coastline was adorned with breathtaking scenery - pristine beaches and rugged rocks jutting out into the sparkling sea. It felt like I was sailing through a painting or heading towards a mirage; the view was unlike anything I had ever seen before.

As we arrived at the restaurant, I basked in the comforting warmth of the sun's rays, whilst a gentle breeze carried the aroma of fresh herbs and delicious Italian dishes, making my mouth water in anticipation.

The manager greeted us with a warm smile and led us to our table with enthusiasm. The food was presented on vibrant, blue plates, each dish bursting with rich hues of red, green, and orange. The food was delicious and the company was not bad either. From our table, the view was breathtaking. The waves relentlessly crashed against the shore and the sun hung high in the sky, its rays drenched the scene in front of me, saturating it with vibrant colours.

After lunch, we strolled along the marina, past the luxury boats and bustling crowds. As the day wore on, fatigue set in from a sleepless night. As we sailed back to Vilamoura, Timotee kindly offered to take me shopping and purchase anything my heart desired. Despite being tired from our travels, my excitement overtook any feelings of fatigue. I eagerly agreed, not only thinking of myself but also wanting to find something special for Gabriela as a token of my appreciation for her friendship.

As we disembarked Timotee says "Whilst you go shopping with Nikita, I have a few business things to take care of" I was a little surprised that he was not coming with me but he had a sense of urgency to his words. Naomi and John went to John's house in Loule. Nikita asked me "Where would like to go shopping, which designer do you like?" I said, "I have never put my feet in a designer shop before. I have no idea". So then she said "I could take you to the shopping centre. But all the brands are not there. So I think I will take you to the fashion outlet."

Her black VW Phaeton exuded a dangerous aura, its sleek leather seats reflecting the blinding sunlight in a dazzling display. The rich and luxurious scent of leather permeated the interior, evoking images of expensive goods and high-end boutiques. As we drove towards the outlet, she received a message from Timotee instructing her to buy me perfumes, a dress, and heels for the evening.

She then bombarded me with questions about my preferences. But also explained our time was limited, and she also had instructions to buy me jewellery the next day. "Timotee is hoping you'll agree to extend your stay for another week," she stated firmly. "He has plans for the both of you." I remained steadfast, reminding her that our agreement was only for two days. But she insisted that Timotee would not take no for an answer. "You'll soon realise he always gets what he wants," she warned in a hushed tone.

Despite her words, I refused to be swayed by Timotee's influence or Nikita's manipulations. "Unless he puts me in chains, I'll be returning to Lisbon on Monday," I said confidently. Nikita's voice turns hushed as she mutters "She has a fiery temper...this is not a good sign."

Under her guidance, we perused the racks of elegant dresses suitable for the evening. Her keen eye for fashion and knowledge of Timotee's taste made the search effortless. Being from Brazil, I tend to be drawn towards things that are flashy and showy rather than refined and subtle. The concept of designer brands is lost on me. Nonetheless, she helped me choose a stunning dress and high heels that exuded both sophistication and charm. I also searched for a dress for Gabriela. I settled on a vibrant yellow, black, and red Versace dress - her favourite colours.

As we arrived back at his house, I collapsed onto the couch, exhausted. But the respite was short-lived as it soon became time to dine once again. This time, in an outrageously expensive restaurant in Vale Do Lobo. I couldn't help but feel a sense of disgust at this display of excess and wealth. The constant need for structure and following a strict schedule made me feel like a mindless robot, unable to act on my own impulses. I longed to be able to simply jump into the sea or indulge in a simple meal of bread and eggs while wearing comfortable pyjamas. But there was no room for spontaneity in this world of opulence. It all annoyed me greatly, but I had to keep up appearances and push through, pretending that I was just another cog in the machine.

As we returned to his villa after dinner, we were joined by Nikita, John, Naomi and we indulged in drinks. But when it was time for bed, Timotee showed no interest in touching me, leaving us to simply share the cold sheet of the bed together. I couldn't understand him - he was the strangest man I had ever met, but to be clear I am not complaining.

The next morning, the creature awoke at an ungodly hour of 6 am and flung open the curtains, flooding the room with blinding sunlight. If I had a gun within reach, I would have given no thought to being a guest in his home - I would have pulled the trigger without hesitation. No amount of wealth or status could make up for this man's insufferable personality.

The creature returned from the shower, naked and his penis aroused, his eyes locked on mine. My confusion only grew as he beckoned me closer, commanding me to dress and join him for breakfast. I could not understand why I did not protest, why I allowed myself to be controlled by this terrifying being. As he served me pancakes, I felt a surge of revulsion at the thought of consuming them, but I was powerless to resist. And when he whispered "I am in love with you" with such intense emotion, I was filled with fear. I could not help but wonder, how was this man in love with me? Or was it something even more dangerous?

Sunday was a never-ending cycle of mundane activities, much like its predecessor Saturday. I yearned to escape from this place and the overbearing presence of Timotee. However, we were at least able to find some solace by the poolside. We indulged in a copious amount of cocktails, his expertise of drink making was evident in every sip. The company of John, Naomi, and Nikita also helped make the day more tolerable.

Despite this, he couldn't help but constantly dictate my actions and behaviour. It was becoming clear that even after such a short time here, he had a controlling nature. I quickly learned that I could not freely express my wild side, as even wearing a Brazilian bikini was deemed inappropriate and required me to cover up with clothing, even while swimming in the pool. He maintained a stoic facade while claiming Nikita was a lesbian, only for me to discover later on that she was not. As the afternoon progressed and alcohol flowed freely, even Timotee seemed to let loose a little from his normally reserved manner.

He approached me with a look of desperation in his eyes, begging me to join him upstairs in his bedroom. He thrust a small, black long box into my hands and pleaded, "Please, stay one more week with me. I'll pay you." Before I could even respond, he commanded, "Open it now." I hesitantly lifted the lid to reveal a stunning bracelet adorned with thirty-three glistening diamonds. The light caught each facet and caused them to sparkle and shine like stars in the sky. I couldn't believe my eyes. It was clear that Timotee was trying to buy me, with this extravagant gift.

Feeling overwhelmed and uncomfortable, I mustered the courage to speak up. "Thank you for the beautiful gift, but I cannot accept it," I stated firmly. "I am not staying another week and our agreement was only for two days." Timotee's face turned from pleading to shock as he asked, "Why not?" I responded calmly, "Because I have other responsibilities and a life outside of this arrangement. I hope you will honour your word and fulfil your part of the deal by taking me home tomorrow. Otherwise, I will have no choice but to walk to the bus station in Quarteira and return home."

Tension filled the air as we stood motionless, both unwilling to give in to the other's wishes. Finally, Timotee let out a deep sigh and reluctantly nodded in agreement. "Fine, I'll do whatever you want. But please, keep the bracelet; it would offend me if you didn't. And I really, want you not to go to Elefante this week, I'll pay for your week and we can talk before next weekend. Can you agree to that?"

I needed to come up with a solution quickly, and I thought that taking a one-week break and getting paid by this man would be a good idea. In my most girlish tone, I responded, "Sure, I can do that for you and for myself." I then initiate a sly, manipulative, and untrue conversation with him "Because I also have started to have some feelings about you".

It didn't seem like he was very content, since the situation was out of his control. But for me, it was pure happiness. I was going to receive 2,000 euros daily without having to work at all. My only thought was if Gabriela agreed, I would give her 500 euros a day, so she could stay at home too. Although I couldn't fathom this man; my behaviour towards him shifted greatly. From that day on, I became less aggressive in my responses and even started treating him with a bit more kindness. However, he still had something off-putting about him - his presence was unnerving and I couldn't shake the feeling of fear around him.

The next day, he drove me back to Lisbon in his black Cadillac Navigator. As we cruised down the winding roads, his hand reached for mine and gently squeezed it. "You are so precious to me," he said, his eyes never leaving the road ahead. "Next weekend, I have a surprise for you...and it won't just be diamonds and jewellery." It was no secret that he was fifteen years older than me, a well-travelled man with an abundance of wealth. He knew he could win me over with material possessions.

As we pulled up in front of my apartment block, he leaned in, his hand cupping the back of my neck before pressing his lips to mine. It caught me off guard, stealing my breath for a moment. I was not expecting this display of affection from him. He helped me gather my bags from the car and we said our goodbyes. As I stood on the street corner, watching his car disappear into the distance, I couldn't wait to go inside and surprise Gabriela with her new dress.

With my arms full of bags, I made my way straight to Gabriela's apartment, I knocked on her door. When she opened it, her beautiful face lit up with a big smile and she exclaimed, "I missed you, bitch!" Returning her smile, I replied, "I have something for you." As I presented her with the dress, her excitement bubbled over and she jumped up and down, exclaiming, "It's so beautiful!" She then added, "I am so happy for you. It seems like you've won the lottery. I can't help feeling a bit jealous and afraid that he may steal you away from me. But I also know how hard this job is for you and how much you deserve to be happy and have all the best things in life."

I looked at her with a mix of frustration and sadness. "You fool," I said, my voice tinged with anger. "When I get out of here, you're coming with me. We'll find something better than this place - maybe open a saloon or a boutique." Her response was nonchalant. "Let's see what happens," she said, her eyes scanning the room.

"What I have to tell you is quite the gossip, but it's not exactly pleasant," she continued, leaning in closer to me. "Do you remember Fatima?" I racked my brain for a moment before nodding my head. "Yeah, I think so."

"She was the Brazilian girl with dark hair who always hung around with those idiot girls," she explained bitterly. "She got mixed up with some lazy Portuguese men who claimed they were part of the Mafia. They pimped out girls like Fatima and used her as their own personal plaything."

My heart sank as I listened to her words, knowing where this was heading. "And then she went missing for three days. When her mother finally went to the police, she must have talked too much because one day later, Fatima's head was found decapitated on her mother's doorstep."

I couldn't believe what I was hearing - it was like something out of a horror movie. "As a warning to keep her mouth shut," she finished, her voice trembling slightly. "It's just so tragic, don't you think?"

I was in shock at what I was hearing. My mind couldn't process the words that were being spoken to me. "God," I finally managed to say, my voice trembling with disbelief. "One of those guys actually bought me a drink and offered me drugs." The memory of the encounter made my stomach churn. The man had been handsome, in a rugged, dangerous kind of way. I continued "He told me I was sexy and he was very attractive. He suggested we could have a great time together, with wild parties involving sex and drugs. As long as

I paid him a small commission for protection, he promised to look out for me. He also claimed to know many wealthy Portuguese men who would be interested in me. And at this time I did not know that they are such assholes but I told him I do not need protection and I do not take drugs. What a world this is, this really is a dark and dangerous life!"

That night Tomotee kept me on the phone all night, interrogating me about my whereabouts and keeping me under his watchful eye. Every moment feels like a suffocating trap. Despite trying to relax and enjoy my time with Gabriela, I couldn't shake off the feeling of being watched and controlled.

Each day seemed like an eternity as I waited for Timotee to reveal his next move. I was full of anxiety as I realised I was completely at his mercy. When he announced that he would be picking me up Friday morning instead of Saturday evening, I felt a sinking feeling in my stomach. It was clear that he was not only monitoring my movements but also manipulating them. I reluctantly agreed, dreading what awaited me on Friday morning when I would once again be completely under his control. His parting comment to me was "He would be taking me back to the Algarve and on the way we would visit the shopping centre Vasco Da Gama"

My hair is perfectly coiffed and my nails are freshly painted in his favourite shade of red cherry. My outfit is carefully chosen - tight jeans, a white t-shirt, and a sleek suit jacket paired with killer high heels. He calls me from the corner and orders me to come down. Without hesitation, I comply with his every demand. As I reach the bottom of the stairs, I see him waiting for me in his Lamborghini - a yellow one that wasn't there when I last visited his house. My gaze is fixed on the car's stunning contrast to his piercing blue eyes. But as I walk towards him, my focus is shattered by stepping in a massive pile of dog shit - so much so that it seeps into my shoes. Disgust washes over me, triggering my gag reflex as Timotee watches. He finds it amusing, erupting into uncontrollable fits of laughter.

Frustrated and disgusted, I flung the shoe away in a fit of anger and rushed back to my apartment, limping on one foot as I hopped through the building. My skin prickled with revulsion as I washed the filth off my feet in the shower, trying to scrub away the memory of stepping in Kakka. Desperate to rid myself of any trace of that cursed shoe, I called Gabriela and told her what had happened. She laughed at my misfortune but offered to retrieve the shoe and wash it for me, insisting that it was expensive and worth saving. I vehemently refused, wanting nothing to do with that tainted footwear ever again. But Gabriela was determined and declared that she would take it with her to Brazil and give it to a cousin there. Relieved to be rid of it, I agreed without hesitation.

That week, he showed me a side of himself that I had not seen before. A gentleman with impeccable manners and a kind heart, he was incredibly attentive to my every need. Despite his obvious wealth and power, he never let it go to his head. He constantly tried to impress me with lavish displays of his riches, whether it be through extravagant gifts or whisking me away on his helicopter to the picturesque town of Davos in Switzerland. There, he opened a bank account for me and gave me a taste of the luxurious lifestyle in Saint Moritz.

The opulence surrounding us all the time was unbelievable. Helicopters roared overhead, luxury cars glided past, and sleek yachts dotted the crystal blue water. In just one week, we jet-setted to Switzerland in the morning and returned the next day by helicopter. That same evening, we hopped into a private jet and flew to Marbella, Spain, where he had a lavish house and many affluent friends. He explained that he had business there, but I couldn't help but feel like I was living in a glamorous fantasy. As our whirlwind travels continued, he showered me with financial and emotional security, making it clear that I held a special place in his life. Despite the lavishness of my surroundings, his attention and care made me feel truly valued and loved.

As I sat across from him, on the private plane, he made me an offer I couldn't refuse. A partnership in his successful company, all I had to do was make a quick trip to Brazil to legalise myself and obtain the necessary Visa documents. It seemed like a dream come true, especially for someone who had been struggling. He even started buying things for me and my family to take back from Brazil, creating a sense of trust and camaraderie between us. Despite my initial doubts, I began to believe that perhaps we really could work together as partners.

Excited and full of hope, I finally confided in my sister Rebecca about the amazing opportunity that had presented itself to me. She was both stunned and overjoyed, being the only one who knew the truth about my past as a 'Hooker'. For once, I felt like things were finally looking up for me and my future. Little did I know, this was just the beginning of a tumultuous journey filled with unexpected twists and turns.

Our intimacy was built on tender kisses and gentle touches, filled with a longing for more. He explained to me that when we had the time, we would both need to undergo blood exams in England to ensure our health before finally being able to make love like a true couple. And just recently, he had asked for a Visa so that I could visit his home there. He told me about the two houses he owned in England - one surrounded by acres of lush green land and a grand, magnificent house. His eyes lit up as he shared his plans to fill the space with horses, knowing how much I adored them. It was clear that every detail of this fantasy was carefully crafted for our future together.

He whispered to me that his life was rooted in England, with a French father and a gypsy mother from the town of Stoke on Trent. His father was a member of one of the thirteen wealthiest families in the world, a man of great influence and power. But he confided that his fortune did not come from his family's wealth; rather, he had become a self-made multimillionaire over the past ten years through his business ventures. "Money flows like water for me," he boasted with a sly smile, "it comes so easily."

My curiosity becomes insatiable as I learn more about him, especially after the day he left me alone with Nikita in Portugal. He disappeared for two or three hours, only to return in a red Ferrari with a look of fury etched into his face. As he emerged from the car, I noticed blood splattered on the exterior and the beige leather seats - both of his hands and arms were drenched in it. Trembling with fear, I ran to meet him, desperate to comfort him and understand what had happened. But he recoiled from my touch, warning me not to come near him. "What has happened?" I pleaded, but he dismissed me with a cold tone. "It's none of your concern," he spat out, sneering at my innocence. "Just an old woman who crossed in front of my car." My heart sank as I asked the inevitable question: "Is she alive? Did you kill her?" With a twisted smile, he replied, "I hope so." And then without any remorse, he casually washed away the evidence from his hands and arms at an outdoor tap before giving orders at Nikita in Russian, leaving me shocked and horrified.

As I woke up the next day, my mind felt like a clean slate, devoid of any worries or warning signs. I really have a cat memory. It was as if all the red flags and dangers that had been present the day before had been magically erased from my memory. I couldn't help but feel a sense of immaturity in how eagerly I anticipated the events to come, like a child waiting for an action movie to start. The excitement bubbled within me, and I couldn't wait to see what would unfold in the upcoming episode of my life. I am not a morning person, so my Timotee has learned to let me sleep until at least 10 am.

My heart was light and I felt as free as a bird, singing with gusto. Suddenly, a barrage of "Yeah's" and "Boom's" shattered my peace like thunderbolts. The sounds grow louder and more insistent, luring me towards their source. As I approach, I am hit with a sense of foreboding and clarity - Nikita and Timotee are in the gym, practicing martial arts on the Tatami mats. But it's not just for fun - it becomes clear that Nikita is Timotee's deadly bodyguard, a lethal weapon disguised as a stunningly beautiful top model. My initial assumptions are shattered as I realise how clever and dangerous this seemingly harmless Barbie-faced girl truly is.

The decision to stay for more than just a week was driven by my unwavering curiosity. As the days passed, I found myself increasingly drawn to the mysterious allure of this place. One day, Nikita extended an invitation to join her in training. It had been revealed to her by Timotee that I held the esteemed rank of Kung Fu Second Dan Black Belt from a young age, and she was eager to witness my skills firsthand.

Nikita was a professional multi-martial arts fighter, skilled in various forms including Sambo, a versatile and agile version of Jujitsu. As we began our training session, it became clear that Nikita was the superior fighter. Her movements were precise and fluid, every strike calculated and powerful. I, on the other hand, was rusty and out of practice. But watching

Nikita move with such grace and strength, only gave me more determination to learn from her. She was not just a master of Sambo, but also adept in Taekwondo, Aikido, and numerous other disciplines. I watched in awe as she effortlessly switched between techniques, each one executed flawlessly. After our session, Timotee revealed that Nikita had praised my potential and talent. The compliment filled me with excitement and renewed passion for martial arts.

After two weeks, I decided to return to Lisbon. Timotee's watchful eyes followed my every move, I could also sense that one of his team was assigned to tail me. While I enjoyed Nikita's company, there was something special about being with Gabriela. It was as if our time together was limited and precious, even though we were just friends. My heart felt heavy as if a subtle sense of foreboding warned me that our paths were about to diverge. But I couldn't put my finger on why or how. All I knew was that destiny was pulling us apart.

The few days I spent with Gabriela in Lisbon were filled with joy and laughter, but one morning she knocked on my door with tears streaming down her face. Her voice was filled with anguish as she cried out, "My beloved four-year-old son has just passed away." I remembered how he was born with a heart condition, but he always seemed so full of life and energy. The memories flooded back of him calling to talk to his mother, laughing and joking as we chatted together. He had the same playful spirit as his mother. As I watched my friend grapple with her grief, I could feel the raw pain and desperation emanating from her. My heart ached for her, as I too have young children and parents far away from me in Brazil. This loss was devastating and a reminder of the fragility of life and the bonds that connect us all.

The bad news hangs over us like a dark, heavy cloud. Tears fall from my eyes as I hold her close, knowing that time has slipped away and there will be no last chance for her to say goodbye to her son. At this moment, I must be strong for her. "I will do whatever it takes to help you through this," I promise, taking on the role of her rock in this storm. "We will go to the travel agent and buy tickets for you. I will give you the money and you can stay there for three months. If needed, you can change the date - anything to show my gratitude for all that you have done for me."

She looks at the suitcase under my window, she knows it is filled with the toys we have been collecting for six months for her little boy who now will never receive them. "And don't worry about your apartment," I added, trying to ease some of her worries. "I will keep it safe and pay for it while you are away. I have made arrangements to vacate my apartment. I will look after yours for the next four months. Okay" As we leave the house together, our mission for the day is clear: get her ticket, pack her bags, and get her to the airport as soon as possible. She will fly from Lisbon, Portugal to Salvador, Brazil. Leaving behind her life here but with each step we take towards that airport, she also leaves behind a friend who will always be there for her no matter what.

After Gabriela departed for Brazil, I made the decision to move in and stay with Timotee. As a busy businessman, his schedule often took him away. In those times, I would be left in the care of Nikita or one of Timotee's other bodyguards.

My Visa to England was finally approved, granting me the opportunity to explore this famous country. I knew that Timotee's father resided in Paris and though I longed to meet him, it would have to wait. Luckily, I would have the pleasure of meeting his mother, who lived in a charming house in Stoke on Trent and had a love for horse-drawn caravans in the countryside. My heart raced at the thought of staying at Timotee's luxury penthouse apartment, in the bustling heart of Kensington, London.

As the sun rose on a crisp Tuesday morning, we arrived at the City of London airport via private plane. My excitement was obvious as I stepped foot for the first time in England and London, a place I had only seen in movies and read about in books. As we made our way to Trafalgar Square, I couldn't help but be struck by the enormity of it all – the towering advertising screens, with their flashing advertisements in front of me like a mesmerising light show. But amidst the buzz and bustle of the city, one thing stood out to me - the people rushing around with no time for pleasantries or hellos, solely focused on their own agendas. And don't even get me started on the pigeons; those flying rats that flocked around the bustling streets, leaving behind a trail of feathers and filth. This was London, a city alive with energy and chaos, both dazzling and overwhelming at the same time.

During my brief stay in London, I didn't have much opportunity to truly explore the city. Timotee, always seemed to be busy with business meetings and appointments. Whilst he was absent, I was also kept busy, constantly shuttled from one location to another by Nikita and my new security detail. Never able to make my own decisions or enjoy any personal freedom. Despite this, I couldn't help but feel like I had been destined to meet Timotee, just as he had claimed I was his **'fate'** on numerous occasions.

This feeling only grew stronger when he introduced me to a striking Russian woman one evening at his apartment. Standing at an impressive 5'9" with dark hair and piercing green eyes, she exuded a certain magnetism that drew me in immediately.

Her name was Natasha and she possessed incredible clairvoyant abilities, able to unlock past lives and uncover repressed traumas and obsessions in our present ones. Timotee trusted her unquestionably and explained she was also a healer. His unwavering belief in magic, spirituality, and otherworldly powers was further confirmed by his reliance on Natasha's guidance. In fact he also believed I had mystical powers, he often remarked to me with a fond tone, "You are such a strong witch, just like my mother," who was renowned for her gypsy heritage and mystical abilities.

His luxurious apartment was a hidden oasis, complete with a cinema, fully equipped gym, sauna, and indoor swimming pool. But there was also a strange place, he called it his healing Zen room. The room itself resembled a temple, adorned with intricate carvings and inscriptions on the walls. Candles and incense filled the air, casting a soft glow over ancient symbols from various cultures - Sumerian, Egyptian, and more. It was a place unlike any other, a fusion of mystical elements that created a sense of wonder in all who entered. His secretive nature was evident, a mysterious aura surrounding him. I couldn't quite place which clandestine secret society he belonged to, but it was clear that he was part of something elusive and exclusive. However, at this moment, everything felt entirely unfamiliar and foreign.

We had taken a shower before this meeting, it was important to be clean to meet Natasha. He had chosen very specific new white clothes to wear tonight and then both of us laid down on two massage beds in the middle of the temple next to each other. Then Natasha started to guide us with calming music in the background. And she with her soft voice, took us to centuries ago, before Jesus Christ in Rome. The amazing thing was both of us had the view of the same day, in the same situation but from a different viewpoint. I always saw him fascinated with Rome, not Italy but Rome and the Colosseum. We had even watched the movie Gladiator no less than eight times recently. His obsession was always with Greek and Roman decorations, even this house in London was full of images and statues of Caesars.

Then I started to get very relaxed and felt so good, then I was no longer in the cold weather of London and now I was in Rome on a bright sunny day. I was stood in the middle of the Colosseum, I could feel the warmth in the air. As I walked in the middle of the stadium, I reached down to the ground and grabbed some sand and it was warm in my hand. It was completely different to what the Colosseum is today, it was alive and full of people. Noble people and peasants alike.

As I stood in the Colosseum, my eyes fell upon a young man, he was no more than thirty years old, kneeling on one knee with his forehead resting against the handle of his sword. The blade was buried deep in the sand as if it were an accusing finger pointing directly at him. He had olive skin and a head full of wild, black curls that framed his sharp features. His profile was Roman-esque and he sported a well-kept beard and moustache. Dressed in elegant military garb of white, sky blue, and gold, he exuded an air of authority and power.

In the blink of an eye, I was no longer Angelina. Instead, I found myself inhabiting this man's body. Before I could fully comprehend the situation, screams erupted all around me as the middle gate swung open to reveal a horse-drawn carriage approaching at breakneck speed. Everything about it was white and gold - from the majestic steed pulling it to the intricate details adorning the carriage itself.

But as it drew closer, I saw who was riding inside - Timotee, now in his sixties and he wore the Laurel crown of the Caesar. He was filled with unbridled hatred and anger towards me. In one swift motion, he drew his sword and held it high above his head before swinging it down with brutal force. With a sickening thud, my head rolled off my shoulders and landed in the dirt.

I couldn't believe what had just happened. I cried out in pain and confusion as Natasha pulled me away from the gruesome scene. Timotee too appeared shocked by his actions, his face contorted with guilt and remorse.We both now understood - he was my father, and I was his bastard son. I was once the trusted commander of his legion but I had become too powerful, too dangerous although honourable and with the support of the people. He saw me as a threat that had to be removed. He had killed me in front of those who adored me and those who saw me as their protector, just to demonstrate his dominance.

The burden of killing me overwhelmed Timotee, consuming him, he now felt the need to constantly protect me. But this protection soon became stifling, I was now a golden caged bird once again. We were engaged in a precarious and risky dance, one that only destiny could possibly disrupt.

Driven by his guilt, he began to shower me with more luxurious gifts. He treated me like a precious baby girl, bringing diamonds, designer dresses, expensive shoes, and Rolex's as easily as one would purchase water from the corner store. He had eagerly showed off his collection of watches in his lavish penthouse apartment, which included an impressive assortment of forty Rolex timepieces. He had explained that the watch in his collection which was his favourite was a blue

Patek Philippe watch. He claimed it was worth a whopping £300,000 and was the same model David Beckham wore. He took great pride in this prized possession and made sure to highlight its value to me.

Within a week I was now the owner of four Rolex watches, the latest one adorned with sparkling diamonds. I was overwhelmed by its beauty. Despite being fully aware that I was being bought and indulged, I couldn't find it in myself to be bothered by it. The rush of excitement and luxury overtook any concerns about my intentions or expectations. I burst into the bathroom, unable to contain my excitement any longer. I jumped up and down in front of the mirror, waving my hands in the air like a crazy lunatic, and let out an ear-piercing scream of joy.

Suddenly, there was a loud banging on the door. It was Timotee, asking if everything was okay and what had happened. My moment of bliss quickly turned to embarrassment and panic. Without hesitation, I blurted out the first excuse that came to mind: "There's a rat in here! I saw it!" But this was a grave mistake; Timotee had a strong aversion to rats and was extremely particular about cleanliness and organisation. We spent over an hour frantically searching for my imaginary rodent, while I struggled to hold back the laughter, the situation was absurd.

The dawn of a new day brought a sudden and unexpected decision from Timotee. "We're leaving London," he declared, his voice seething with agitation. "Going back to our sanctuary in the Algarve, but this time in a different spot, we are going to Albufeira which I know you love so much." The words "going back" were like a symphony playing in my ears, but my mind couldn't shake the guilt that lingered over my deceitful actions. The urgency of leaving, was actually all because he could not stand the thought of being in an apartment with my fabricated rat.

We arrived at the airport, waiting for us on the tarmac was the Falcon 900EX private plane, its sleek silver exterior gleaming under the soft orange sunlight. Timotee, ever efficient, had already arranged everything and guided me onto the plane without me even realising. As we flew towards Faro, Portugal, I couldn't help but admire the breathtaking views of the coastline below.

Upon landing, we were whisked away in a chauffeured car, heading straight to Albufeira. Timotee always had a car waiting for us at every destination. As we drove through the streets of white houses, I caught glimpses of bright blue ocean waves crashing against the shore.

Finally, we arrived at our destination - a magnificent villa overlooking the marina. The houses around us were a burst of vibrant colours - orange, greens, yellows, and blues - standing out against the serene backdrop of the marina.

Timotee spoiled me that afternoon and as always every detail was meticulously planned to perfection. Among today's surprises, he had arranged for me to have my nails done at a luxurious salon near the centre of town.

The sign above the door read 'Studio 59 Hair Styling' and I was greeted by the owner, a beautiful Brazilian woman who exuded warmth and professionalism. As she pampered me, we engaged in easy conversation, quickly forming a bond. Her skilled hands painted my nails in a luscious Cherry Red while also providing tips on where to find the perfect dress for my scheduled intimate evening. When she finished, I left the salon feeling like a showstopper.

Timotee was occupied with business and this required the attendance of Nikita, I now had the rare opportunity to be on my own the entire afternoon to fulfil my duty - preparing dinner. But before that, I was determined to find that perfect red dress because tonight was to be our intimate night. Braving the busy streets and designer shops, on my own. I searched for the dress that would make me feel confident and alluring. As the sun began to set, I finally found it - a stunning red dress that hugged my curves in all the right places. With my hair styled flawlessly and my nails shining bright, I couldn't wait for Timotee's reaction when he saw me at dinner.

Lost in my thoughts, I had drifted away from the present moment and completely lost track of time. Suddenly, when I glanced at my watch, panic set in as I realised I only had thirty minutes to cook dinner, take a shower, do my makeup, and be ready for Mr. Timotee's arrival. My heart raced and my mind scrambled as I tried to figure out how to make it all work.

I knew I had to find another solution. That's when an idea struck me - I rushed back to the salon where my new friend was and begged her for advice.

After hearing my predicament, she suggested ordering Brazilian-style food from a nearby steakhouse that delivers right to your door. It was like a gift from the heavens - a way to save precious time while still impressing Timotee with gourmet food. Without hesitation, I placed an order and then rushed off to head back to the villa.

Breathless, I sprinted towards the taxi station and hastily jumped inside. I was struggling for breath as I gave the driver directions to my destination. Once I arrived, I practically flew out of the car and into my home. The food arrived from the restaurant shortly after and in a frenzy, I grabbed onions and garlic from the kitchen and began to chop them with reckless speed, trying to create the illusion that I had been cooking for hours. I also dirtied several pans and threw them in the dishwasher, the illusion was complete. The smell of garlic sizzling in hot oil filled the air, adding to the facade of a busy kitchen.

In a rush, I stashed the wine in the fridge and transferred the food to serving dishes, then slid them into the oven to stay warm. After that, I quickly grabbed the bags and containers the food had been delivered in and any other incriminating evidence. I hurried far away from the villa to dispose of them safely and out of sight. I returned to take a brief, two-minute shower. With only five minutes remaining, I applied my makeup in a rush, my hands shaking with nerves. I noticed the savoury aroma of Brazilian cuisine filled my apartment, I slipped into my dress and felt a surge of confidence. This was going to work out just fine. Just as I finished, I heard the key turn in the lock and my heart skipped a beat.

My composure was still shaky as I tried to act nonchalant. "Hi, my love," I said with a forced ease. "I've been waiting for you." He smiled and remarked, "Wow, you look stunning in red. And what a perfect choice of scent - 'Santal 33' on your skin." A blush crept into my cheeks as I responded, "Shall we begin our meal?" His response caught me off guard. "No, my dear. The night is young. I'd like some vodka and orange juice." I inwardly cringed at the thought of the wine sitting in the fridge, getting colder by the minute. Yes, I had put red wine in the fridge. It seemed like a normal thing to do at the time.

After some small talk, I heated up the food and set a lovely table. Then, I hurried to uncork the expensive red wine. I poured his glass first and handed it to him proudly. As I poured myself a glass, he suddenly yelled, "Fuck off woman, what have you done? You have destroyed the wine! I am not going to drink this shit." The words hit me like a nuclear bomb, causing a surge of hot energy to rise from my stomach to my head. I was filled with hatred and wanted nothing more than to smash the bottle over his head. But what separated me from a killer and made me not do what I wanted to do, was only the penal code.

Ultimately, who was the one who lost? It was agreed that I would have sexual intercourse with him tonight. However, I changed my mind and decided to wait until I went to Brazil. Only if I had overlooked his disrespectful behaviour, perhaps he would have been fortunate; after all, he left me without any intimacy for three months, so now it was my turn to deny him.

After only two days, I found myself on a plane bound for Brazil, sitting comfortably in first class and sipping my first glass of champagne upon takeoff...

TO BE CONTINUED

Printed in Great Britain
by Amazon

37251017R00175